Stormy Rescue
Sarah Urquhart

For all my Wild Ones enjoying their time in Firebrook!

Firebrook Bears

Chapter One

May thanked whatever higher power listened that Poppy's tastes ran simple. They translated into comfortable bridesmaids' dresses, making her job as photographer easier. She'd photographed hundreds of weddings. Never as a member of the wedding party. But May wouldn't allow anyone else to do her best friend's wedding.

When Poppy first came home after their hellish vacation in Firebrook, May hadn't understood the romance or her sudden need to return to the guy. No guy was worth uprooting everything in an instant. Especially after their experience.

May never made it on the trip. Poppy, Blair, and Harlyn came to Firebrook with Poppy's ex and his two friends, Scott and Luca. Turned out the entire trip was some front for a job the three guys were on. It ended with Poppy's ex murdered and Poppy and Blair stuffed in the trunk of an old car.

It took Blair coming back on her own to find out what they'd been up to. They'd been looking for someone. No one knew who. Now Scott was in custody and Luca was in the wind, but they expected no more trouble from him.

One would think that the murder and kidnapping would be the most shocking revelations her friends brought home from that trip. But, no.

Poppy's soon to be husband was a bear shifter. An honest to God man who turned into a grizzly bear. Him, his brother, and two cousins. The terrifying idea of letting her friend return to live her life with a bear dwindled as she'd seen how much pain Poppy had been in, how much she needed her mate—because that's what they were—May didn't stand in her way. Nor did she stand in Blair's way when she returned with her new mate in tow to move all of her things to Firebrook.

Things changed fast. Two of her best friends had mates and were either walking down the aisle in a few hours or in a few months. That left herself and Harlyn. Unattached. Unmated. Uneverything. But May wasn't complaining.

She'd just finished with the bride's photo shoot. Poppy's family arrived earlier in the week, shortly before May. It was her busiest season after all, but May moved things around and brought in help in her business to be here. Her little photography company, *MayBe You*, was growing, and she wasn't sure how she felt about that. May even brought an assistant along with her to Firebrook after training another to take over for her in the city.

Her assistant, Skye, helped with the bride's photos, as May was part of the wedding party, but she went to the church to take some empty images of the venue while May went to *Bearbrook Cabins* to photograph the groom and his party.

The top half of the bodice of her dress fit snugly, allowing her to wear her camera and move around freely without fear of a wardrobe malfunction. But the rest of the dress flowed light around her body. And flats were essential.

May gripped her camera as she walked up the front steps to the main lodge. The moment she opened the door, she snapped a picture.

"Candids are important." She dropped her gaze to each man in the room, seeing their reaction to the surprise photo, but they all wore calm smiles. The groom hadn't been easy to ruffle the past few days. May had met almost all the groomsmen. All except one, a cousin. The last one she let her eyes land on.

Tavis.

He still sat on the couch while the others all stood, ready to get started. His eyes were such a vivid green they seemed to pierce her soul. May shivered from the intense connection—a full body reaction to only a look.

This couldn't be what Poppy and Blair had talked about when they'd met their mates. They said they knew something about the other person was important. An undeniable recognition. Despite those same thoughts, May refused to delve deeper. Not on the day of her best friend's wedding.

But she never wanted to forget this moment. Lifting her camera, she looked through the viewfinder and pressed the shutter button. That vivid, piercing gaze would forever exist in her pictures.

"You must be Tavis." She broke the moment, needing to get to work.

He nodded. "And you're May."

"I..." She put her hand to her belly to stop the quiver his voice caused. Damn, his eyes were lethal enough without that baritone to add to the package. Tavis set his drink down and moved from the couch. The closer he got to her, the more her senses filled with him. Oh, he smelled good. With every step, the scent of pine and leather grew.

"Shall we?" He offered her his arm.

May set her hand on his arm and the contact made every nerve in her body spark. She gasped, and looking up at him, she saw his lips part, too.

He led her outside where Wyatt, the groom, and the other groomsmen waited near the trees they'd discussed as their location for pictures. It took her some time to reorient herself, but she moved them through the basic poses she did for every wedding without much concentration. And when it came to the fun ones, she'd calmed her racing heart enough to focus and enjoy her job.

And to enjoy the stolen smiles between her and Tavis.

Her breath still shook as she left the groom and groomsmen. May instructed Skye to take the pictures leading up to the ceremony and during, but once the minister announced Wyatt and Poppy as man and wife in the centre of town, May took over, sinking into her element and creating art through a lens out of the special moments of people's lives.

She gave in, letting her creativity take over and snap pictures of not only the bride and groom and their families, but of everyone in attendance. She understood what Blair meant when she talked about the people here. Their energy and love of life and the people around them were infectious.

But as the night wore on, and people became more inebriated, May slowed, enjoying the night celebrating her friend's happiness. She took a break at the table reserved for the wedding party. The decorations in the park drew the eye. Cream-coloured lights shone over the greenery and bright flowers. If ever May married, she'd do something similar, using the natural beauty around her to create a fairytale.

Pine and leather surrounded her and she inhaled. She turned her head, ready to look up at Tavis, but he'd crouched down in front of her.

"Would you like to dance?"

She didn't have the barrier of a job to push away her thoughts. Tavis was someone important to her and impossible to ignore. May was thankful she'd snapped that picture of him seeing her for the first time. That look said so much more than she'd let herself see.

Nodding, she set her hand in his and let him pull her up and to the dance floor.

Couples filled the floor, pulling each other closer for the string of slow songs that played. He spun her outward, then pulled her close with his hand at the small of her back.

Anything she wanted to say didn't feel like enough. The pressure of the moment grew and saying something like, *beautiful wedding*, sounded lame and unnecessary.

"I want to kiss you, pixie."

"Pixie?" Her head reared back, but she laughed. Those words were anything but lame.

"Yeah. Pixie. I think it's the hair." Her hair was the only thing she ever wore with pink. The dyed stripes made her happy when she looked at herself in the mirror. Like saying, *Look at that badass. You've got this.* When she never really felt like a badass at all.

"Is that a bad thing or a good thing?" She tilted her head and moved a little closer.

"A good thing. A very good thing." Tavis matched her movement.

"So, you want to kiss me?" She'd drunk enough that her natural accent came through. Nothing more than growing up on a farm. Her family owned all the animals and planted all the gardens. They attended and competed in every stampede within a thousand kilometres. But her heart hadn't wanted to stay in that life. She'd always been artistic. Not that she couldn't still barrel race with the best of them.

"Yes, I want to kiss you." He lowered his voice and leaned close enough their breaths mingled. "I want to taste you."

"Then do it." Her own challenge shocked her. Despite that, her lips parted, and she kept her eyes on his.

Tavis lifted her hand to set on his shoulder and ran his fingers over her cheek and down her neck. "I think *pixie* is the right choice for you."

She smiled until his lips touched hers. Her heart beat to a harsh, erratic rhythm. His body moved against hers, and there was no mistaking the bulge pressed against her belly.

May let him control the moment, not worried about the people around them. His fingers splayed on her back, moving lower until her skin pebbled. The hand at the side of her neck grounded her. There was control in his touch.

When he lifted his head, she opened her eyes. Her vision was a little fuzzy.

"I could make some really bad decisions with you, Tavis."

He laughed. "You and me both, pixie."

Those bad decisions were about to start now. Tavis kissed his mate again before letting her go. The celebrations weren't yet over and neither of them could disappear. If he kept her with him any longer, he'd take her somewhere secluded and start something he didn't have time to finish.

He loosened his hold, and May slid from his arms, delicious promises dancing in her eyes. When they came together, they were going to be explosive.

But not during his cousin's wedding.

Fuck.

Wyatt and Poppy made rounds through the guests in be-tween dancing and drinks. The entire event was like a family barbeque at the lodge on steroids now that the formal portion of the celebration was over.

Tavis tracked May, following her steps on the other side of the crowd. She looked over her shoulder as she rejoined Blair and Harlyn at the front table. A smile never stopped playing on her lips, catching the attention of her friends.

Blair's eyes rounded as she snapped her head back and forth. She started to ask something, but May tore her gaze from his and cut off her friend before squeezing her shoulder. Harlyn frowned.

Blair, being mated to Tavis's brother, understood the con-nection between him and May.

Her friends kept her attention, so Tavis tuned into the recep-tion. The bride and groom were becoming increasingly more handsy with each other. Midnight approached. He didn't expect them to last much longer, even though the town would continue to party for at least a few more hours. But once the bride and groom had left their own wedding, his obligation to stay was also over.

He intended to pull May back to his side and see what kind of bad decisions they could make.

"Saw you with May." Noah, his brother, appeared by his shoulder.

"I'm sure many people did."

"Just saying, anytime you need a good punch to the face, I'm your man."

Tavis chuckled. Damn, that had been a fun day. His brother needed to concentrate on work rather than his stubborn mate and had pulled Tavis aside with a request to punch him. Tavis had taken it upon himself to hit his brother a few times that day. Retaliation-free strikes at his brother? What guy wouldn't jump at that offer? "I'm good."

"We'll see. So, I'm not wrong in saying she's your mate? We all noticed it this afternoon when she arrived to take pictures. Fuck, that air was thick."

"Yes. She's my mate."

"Good luck, man." Noah clapped Tavis on the shoulder.

"Think I'm going to need it?"

"We all need it. She's a sweetheart. And Blair and Poppy adore her."

"I'll take that as a warning."

"Good." Noah smiled. He'd been doing that a lot more lately. He may have struggled to settle things with his mate, but the change in his brother was a good one.

Wyatt and Poppy joined them before Noah moved away.

"We're going home." Wyatt spoke to them, but his eyes were all over his mate. The couple had been together for only a few months, and every look and touch seemed like their first. Tavis looked forward to that for himself.

"Good. I want to get my mate home, too." There was the brother Tavis knew best. The grumpy one that wanted things his way.

"Goodnight." Poppy waved at them and started pulling Wyatt toward the front table where the bridesmaids sat with Caiden standing watch.

Tavis moved away from Noah before he questioned him further. No one needed to know he intended on taking his mate home tonight.

But Noah's attention had moved to Blair. The independent journalist settled her roots down in Firebrook easier than any of them predicted. Head strong and curious, she had a way of putting herself in danger. Although since a trip over a cliff, she'd slowed down.

The DJ announced the departure of the newlyweds, and the guests applauded, shouting their congratulations.

Tavis veered to the edge of the park and hovered behind the table, waiting for Caiden to pull Maggie away and for Noah to take Blair. Leaving only May and Harlyn.

"Hello, ladies." Tavis sat down across from May.

"Hi, Tavis." Harlyn's automatic smile appeared.

"Enjoying yourselves? I trust this trip back to Firebrook has been a pleasant one for you, Harlyn."

"Almost anything would be more pleasant than that trip." She scoffed and rolled her eyes, letting them settle on the people who'd resumed dancing after the bride and groom left.

"I can see the appeal now that I've finally made it here." May let her gaze roam over the decorations and the night sky, but when they settled on him, her words had a whole other meaning.

"Firebrook has a lot of appeal." Tavis added to her intention. The last thing he wanted to do was make Harlyn feel unwelcome, but he was eager to be alone with his mate.

"I appreciate Poppy having her wedding before school started. I wouldn't have been able to come if she'd had it next week." Harlyn taught middle school. The beginning of fall brought the beginning of nearly inescapable work for her.

"Poppy had said it was even difficult for you to miss work now." Tavis might have missed the week leading up to the wedding, but he'd been there for most of their planning. Stressful though it was, the result seemed to be worth it.

"Yes." Harlyn pursed her lips. "But I went in a week earlier than everyone else to prepare. I've had to attend a few meetings over the phone and will need someone to fill me in on anything I missed, but I'm more than ready to meet my new students for the year."

May smiled at Harlyn. Love for her friend shone in her eyes. Harlyn was a sweetheart who loved the children in her life. Even Tavis recognized that, and he'd only met her a handful of times.

But as Tavis settled his gaze on his mate, she moved her attention to him. Something between them turned molten. Unbearably hot, his skin crawled with the need to touch her.

Harlyn cleared her throat. Tavis didn't know how long they'd stared at each other.

"I'm going to go dance. It's my last night of partying before school starts."

"You don't need to leave." Tavis tried to stop her.

"Oh, yes, I do." She laughed while she said it and hugged May before walking away.

"She'll be all right." May stared after her friend, who joined Dakota and some of her friends dancing. Dakota was Wyatt and Caiden's sister. The bright light amongst a family of boys. But that never stopped her from trying to be one of them growing up. But as far as Tavis was concerned, it made her one hell of a strong female. Growing up with four bear shifters was a sure way to build endurance.

Tavis nodded and turned his focus solely on his mate. "And what about you, pixie?"

"Me?" She laughed. "Will I be all right?" May leaned on the table and tilted her head. "I think that depends on if you plan to kiss me again."

She admitted to herself the importance of Tavis. Poppy and Blair had described it in enough detail that May had no doubt Tavis was her mate. Or she was his mate.

Watching her friends try to fight it taught her one thing. Don't. At least the physical stuff. And she didn't want to. The nerves in her body sparked like tinder—not quite starting a fire, but trying oh so hard. She wouldn't fight the physical as long as they could develop a normal relationship. Time spent together, dates, taking him home for the holidays. She wanted the growing butterflies and love.

May wanted that kiss.

Wanted to hear him call her pixie again.

He smiled as if he heard her thoughts.

"I'll give you whatever you want, pixie." Tavis stood and moved around the table, taking Harlyn's seat.

"Then you know what to do." This rare confidence in her only appeared in certain situations. On top of a horse, behind a camera, and never with men. Except right now. The challenge fell from her lips with ease.

Those deep green eyes, the colour of the evergreens, dropped to her lips as his hand curved around her neck. That same grounding grip sending shivers over her body. His lips moved as if to say something, but in the end, he shook his head and brought his lips to hers. Having already kissed him once should have doused the shock, but no. This was even more intense than the first. The only thing keeping them apart was their positions sitting at the table.

His teeth nipped at her lips between kisses, pulling her bottom one in to lick before releasing her for more. The texture of his full beard only added to the sensations. She had no idea what attention they drew, and she didn't care. But it was late enough in the night that others had their own desires to attend to. Or she hoped so. Otherwise, they were missing out.

"Come home..."

"May!" a drunken Dakota screeched from somewhere before a hand clasped on May's upper arm. Turning her head, and cutting off her nod to Tavis's question despite him not finishing it, she looked up into the beaming face of his cousin with a tipsy Harlyn close behind.

Tavis growled and it turned into a curse. The vibrations shocked her enough to make her hand resting on his chest twitch.

Dakota pointed a firm finger at Tavis. "Watch her camera with your life. May is dancing with us." Two separate hands gripped her elbows, pulling her backwards off her chair. Laughter ensued, as May had to catch her balance to keep from falling to the ground.

Tavis popped out of his seat with a hand on her back in a blink. The heat from his palm cut off her voice and the giggles Dakota and Harlyn forced from her. He helped her stand, then took her camera bag and threw it over his shoulder.

"I'll put this somewhere safe. Go dance, pixie." He winked. That playful gesture made her grin. The man was lethal. May had been ready to agree to anything before Dakota and Harlyn interrupted them. And when he asked her again, she wouldn't hesitate. There had to be something wrong with her, but May didn't care.

With a smile full of her own mischief, she let the girls pull her away to the dance floor. The next time she looked back, Tavis had disappeared. To put her camera somewhere safe. Of course where she'd have to rely on him to get it back.

Shaking her head, May let the music fill her. The thumping beat vibrated the floor they'd laid out in the park. Every woman wearing heels appreciated it. The bride herself had a solid three inches on her feet.

Comfort mattered more. If her shoes ever stopped her from getting the right shot, she kicked them off, and often spent time without them.

As the country music got louder—or the crowd got louder singing along—Dakota hooked her arm with May's, spinning them in a circle before letting her go and doing the same to Harlyn. Soon, she found herself circling on the arms of strangers. People she'd met over the past week, but not as familiar with as Blair or Poppy, or even Harlyn. But they accepted her into the dance as if she belonged.

It was nice—fun.

Enough to distract her from what she would have been doing if Dakota hadn't interrupted. As if she conjured him from her thoughts, Tavis appeared as the next person to hook her arm. Laughing and hot from dancing his way to her.

Her camera bag was nowhere in sight. When she raised her brow, he leaned in. "It's safe."

Clasping her fingers, he spun her, forcing them both into the dance.

Tavis was well loved. He twirled his cousin, then Harlyn. And it didn't take long before many other locals had their turn with his attention. But he always met her gaze over their heads. And what a heady feeling, boosting her confidence that already made an appearance with him. Only him.

When Dakota and Harlyn broke away for a drink, Tavis closed in on her. "Need something to drink, too?"

"Please."

He steered them off the dance floor, but stopped before reaching the bar. Clasping her hips, he turned her toward him. "I have drinks at my place."

"Subtle, Tavis." Dakota hip-bumped him while sipping on a straw. Tavis didn't budge, still holding her firm. The slow turn of his head toward his cousin was comical, though. May tried to hold in her laugh, but it resulted in a choked chuckle.

Tavis changed direction and gave her the same slow tilt. She lost control and let out her laugh.

"Do I amuse you, pixie?"

"Only a little." May leaned toward him.

A heavy sigh came from Dakota beside them. "There goes another one." She shook her head and hooked arms with Harlyn. "Have fun, you two."

They walked away, but not before Harlyn sent May a worried look.

"What do you say, May? Come home with me tonight?"

Despite the music still being upbeat, it slowed in her ears. The thrum as steady as her heartbeat. She answered him by leaning up on her toes and kissing him. She pressed against him, loving that he stood still for her.

"Let's go." He cupped her jaw and pressed his lips harder against hers before walking backward. Once they cleared the reception area, he let her go.

"Where's my camera?"

"In my truck." He pulled keys out of his pocket and jangled them in front of her. "I wouldn't let you dance without me."

"I think you made the right choice. Thanks for taking care of it for me."

"Of course." Tavis stepped up to a royal blue half ton Dodge and opened the passenger door. His chest rumbled with a growl and he stood, holding out his hand for her.

Bad decisions indeed.

"How much longer are you staying in Firebrook?" Tavis pulled out onto the quiet street, then reached over and intertwined his fingers with hers.

"The day after tomorrow. Although I've had a few people ask about my services. I can see several trips in my future." May heard something unsaid between them. She knew what he was and suspected what she was. But she didn't bring it up. Didn't want to. There was still time for a conversation to ruin the moment and make her turn away from him. She wanted to do this and she let the confident side of her control their night.

"I like the sound of that."

Chapter Two

May didn't want to call the home that appeared up the gravel lane small, since it looked like it had at least two or three bedrooms, but it wasn't a full house. Charm shone from the small home as the lights he had lining a front garden and the porch gave it a fairy-like glow.

They got out of the truck, and the sight made her slow her movements, as if moving too fast would disturb the scene. Somehow, it was exactly what she expected from Tavis, a man she only just met, but felt as if she'd had a sighting of his soul.

He reached for her hand.

"Wait." May couldn't stop herself. She pulled her hand back and swung her camera bag to the front. Taking out her camera, she adjusted for a night picture with lights, then took the picture. And another. Moving to the side, she dropped to her knee, uncaring what her dress landed in, and snapped a couple more.

When she looked back toward Tavis, he'd leaned against a tree with his hands in his pockets. Heat filled his eyes and a sexy grin made the beard on his face twitch.

"Sorry." She felt a blush creep over her cheeks. Sometimes she had to capture what was in front of her before it disappeared. Everything always disappeared some day. Her camera held so many important things.

"Never apologize for that."

Before he pushed off the tree, she lifted her camera one more time and snapped a picture of him. His smile grew at the last second. Tucking her camera away, she waited for him to stalk toward her. And stalking was what he did. Slow, methodical steps held intention—purpose.

The gracefulness of the animal wasn't hard to recognize. His muscles filled out the short-sleeve button-up shirt, bunching with every movement.

"This is a beautiful spot." May gestured toward his home.

"Thank you." Tavis reached for her, setting his hand at the small of her back to guide her toward the door. He opened it and held it inward with an outstretched arm, her shoulder brushing against his chest when she moved past him.

The inside was as charming as the outside. Woodsy cabin atmosphere, but with large plush furniture and a modern kitchen. The appliances were stainless steel and black, but dark wood made up most of the surfaces.

May took her time looking around in the entryway, but froze as she turned. Tavis moved to her back, his heat covering her. Large palms landed on her shoulders, then traced down her arms.

"May." His voice was a whisper behind her ear. His beard tickled her neck and shoulder, and she imagined how it would feel on the rest of her body.

She still had her camera bag over her shoulder. Tilting her head, she pulled it off, but in doing so, gave Tavis instant access. He nibbled his way down the column of her neck. May moaned. A low, throaty sound.

Tavis took her bag from her hands and walked them a few steps in until he could reach the closest chair to set it down.

"I'll offer you something to drink or whatever polite refreshment you prefer after." His hands settled on her waist, steering her past the kitchen.

May covered his hands with hers and let him take her weight while following his lead. "I had all the refreshments I need at the reception."

"And what is it you need now, pixie?" Down the hall, he nudged the last door on his right. It swung open to a bedroom that matched the decor of the rest of the house with a large, fluffy bed and shiny wood furniture.

May turned in his arms. "I need you to finish what you've started."

Tavis counted every beat of her pulse in her neck. Watching the base of the long column thump, luring him in for more. It took effort to keep his sharper teeth from scraping her skin. Tonight was only about getting the physical tension out of their system.

But he needed to say something first. He hoped he was correct in assuming Poppy and Blair had explained everything to May and Harlyn.

"That gives me a lot of options." He continued to back her up into the room. "I could make this quick and dirty." He pulled pins from her hair, letting them drop to the floor. "Long and slow. Gentle."

Her nose scrunched for only a second before she smoothed it out.

Tavis chuckled. "Or hard." She rewarded him with a sigh.

Her fingers worked on the buttons of his shirt. She was such a complicated mix of shy and bold. She challenged him, but her hands shook while she worked on his shirt. Tavis set both hands on her back and took his time with the small loops around the buttons hiding the zipper.

"I need to ask you something, May."

She chewed the inside of her cheek and tilted her head.

"Do you know what Wyatt is? What Noah is? What I am?" Tavis pulled down the zipper, allowing the bodice of her dress to gape open.

"Yes," she whispered, tugging his shirt from the waist of his pants to finish the last of the buttons.

A surge of pride and acceptance filled him. His bear puffed out, standing tall for his mate, and let himself show through Tavis's eyes.

May's lips parted. She set her palms to his bare chest and slid them upward. To his shoulders, his neck, his jaw. A slender finger with a slightly pointed nail brushed over his brow and circled his eye. "They're so... consuming."

"Do you know why we're so attracted to each other?" He pushed her dress down, exposing her torso with the lacy strapless bra and then over her hips to show off the matching panties.

"Yes." May followed his actions with her own, sliding his shirt down his shoulders.

"I won't mate you tonight, pixie. But I'm going to devour every part of you."

"I'm good with that."

With a firm grip on one buttock and his other hand on the centre of her back, Tavis pulled her as close as he could. "I mean every part."

She gasped, soft and breathy, and let her head fall back. "Promises, promises."

Tavis moved his hand to thread his fingers into her hair. He dipped his head and nipped at her lips, holding in a laugh while he did. "I keep my promises, pixie." He moved her to the bed and followed her down, pressing his hips into hers. The bra she wore clasped in the front and went a few inches down her ribs.

Her chest rose and fell with harsh breaths while he wrapped an arm around her to move her higher.

"Arms up."

She obeyed beautifully. He'd never thought he was the type to enjoy such easy submission, but the eagerness they both had to reach the pleasure they felt tickling their senses fed a new need.

With her arms splayed over the pillow, May arched her back, rubbing her body against his. Tavis took it as an offering. Undoing her bra, it fell to the sides, exposing deep rose nipples. They looked as delicious as the sweet cherries she smelled like. Tavis dipped down for a taste, running his tongue in a circle around one already hard peak.

A satisfied husky sound escaped from her throat and she froze. Tavis didn't stop. He circled more before pulling it into his mouth to suckle. First soft, then hard to see the reaction he'd get. The reaction he expected.

She cried out, and she brought her arms down, her hands fisting in his hair. He nipped her harder before releasing her with a pop. "Arms, pixie. Put them back." Tavis hovered over her breast until she put them back, but not without a growl of her own.

He resumed, but only a gentle lick before moving to the other breast, building up to the harsh bite he'd given the first. And May did the same thing, but this time her hips bucked against him for more.

"I could tie them." Tavis slid his hands up her arms to put them back in place.

"Sounds like a genius idea."

He laughed. "Don't move them again, May."

"After a threat like that, I'm not sure why I wouldn't." But she fisted her hands into the pillow.

"Behave, pixie."

"Maybe." Rich brown eyes looked down her body at him. Desire and laughter danced in them, but the moment he moved further down her torso, her gaze melted and her breathing picked up.

Tavis didn't want to take the time to take her panties off. Moving them to the side, he licked up her slit.

"Tavis. Tavis. Tavis." She begged, his name ripping from her with every swipe of his tongue.

"I've got you, May." He pushed two fingers inside her while flattening his tongue over her bud of nerves. Her walls quivered, bringing her to the edge of release. Sensation pumped through his body with force, building an explosion at the base of his spine. And she hadn't even touched him yet.

Banding an arm over her waist, Tavis held her as her hips thrashed when she came. Her walls squeezed, trying to push his fingers out.

He ripped his hand away rather than easing her down from the top. May's wide eyes locked onto him.

"That wasn't enough."

"I know." It wouldn't be the only one he tore from her over the next several hours. Tavis moved away from her, taking her panties with him. Standing at the end of the bed, he unzipped his fly.

"Oh, finally." May groaned and pushed herself up on her elbows to watch.

The female appreciation made his chest swell. Fuck, he felt ten feet tall with the way she devoured him with her eyes alone. When he pushed his pants down, May licked her lips.

"You want it, pixie?" Tavis kicked away his pants and boxers.

"Oh, yes." She sighed and pushed herself up, but paused, looking to him. For permission?

"Come and get it."

What a moment to want her camera. Tavis was a piece of art. Every ridge defined a hard body. She tried to imagine the stories he had in his past.

May crawled to the end of the bed. She'd waited. After he'd ordered her to keep her arms above her head, she wondered what other orders he may issue. And it surprised her she wanted to know. So she'd waited until he'd given her permission to move.

Unsure of herself, she dropped to her knees. Running her hands up his thighs, she looked at him. His bear's eyes still shone in his. They were one. It was easy to speak of the animal as being separate, but it was one being looking down at her now with enough heat to make her combust on the spot.

His shoulders tensed, but his expression held patience. May explored, moving her hands inward to wrap one around the base and the other to cup his balls. His hum of appreciation made her bolder.

Holding him out, she opened her mouth and took in the head, tentatively licking. He tasted so good. The woodsy scent of him translated into a spicy flavour.

"Pixie," he growled.

She pulled off him and looked up, worried she'd done something wrong. He frowned.

"You didn't have to stop."

"Sorry. I thought..."

"Fuck. Give me a history lesson. You done this before?"

"Of course." Heat fused her cheeks, a touch of embarrassment. She'd done it. A few times. May enjoyed exploring the male form. Slowly. But each time the guy cut her off saying, "never mind."

"I'll go fast. Just please don't stop me."

Tavis cupped his palm under her chin. "There's no need to go fast. And I'm not stopping you. You do whatever you want to do to me. And if at any point you want me to take over, just tap my leg. Understand, pixie?"

May blinked, stunned by how he controlled this while seeing what she needed. He wouldn't let her fail him. "Okay."

She leaned forward again and took him back in her mouth. He palmed the back of her head, but didn't bring her closer. Tavis let her take control. And with the promise he wouldn't stop her, she focused on the job.

Letting her tongue slide over him as she bobbed her head. The sounds coming from him were low, creating vibrations through his body. He continued to hold the back of her head. His touch was gentle, as if he looked down at something precious rather than his mate sucking him off.

He thickened in her mouth and his legs tightened. Her own body heated and tingled. Wetness trickled down her thighs.

"Fucking gorgeous, pixie. I can smell you. You're getting wetter, aren't you?"

She nodded with him still in her mouth. Wanting to give them both more, she tapped her hand on his hip twice and looked up at him through her lashes.

"You sure?"

May tapped him again.

Tavis moved his hand back to her jaw and tilted her head back. He pressed down on her chin with his thumb to hold her mouth open further. Then his hips moved. Shallow thrusts took him to the back of her throat. It didn't take him long to pick up the pace, pushing her to sit on her heels. He towered over her in a way that pushed him further down her throat.

May closed her eyes and relaxed under him.

"You take me so beautifully. But I'm not ready to come yet." He pulled out and held her face. She leaned her cheek against his hand.

May stood and her body filled with more need. "Tavis." She didn't want to beg, but she heard the crack in her voice.

"Where's the sassy pixie that challenged me to kiss her while we danced? You're nervous." His hands moved up and down her sides as he tilted his head while examining her. Such patience and kindness reflected at her.

"That girl is rare. That's why I usually have a camera in front of my face." The moment he stripped her and took control, he stripped her confidence.

"You don't need to be nervous with me now."

"I'm not nervous, just shy."

He flashed a grin. "I can help with that." With his hands holding her hips, he pushed her back to the bed again. He gripped her knee, pulling her leg up as he settled at her core.

"You can help my shyness?"

"Oh yes. It won't be long until you're screaming my name again."

His cock prodded at her entrance. Short thrusts let him in and the moment he set his forehead against hers, he pushed.

She gripped his shoulders as if she could catch her breath on him. So full and thick, he moved slowly.

"Tavis."

"That's it, pixie." His voice was strained. A scratchy undertone made her look at his lips. Sharp teeth peeked out.

"Your... Tavis. Your teeth."

"I know. I won't bite you, May. I promise." He kissed her and moved faster, hitting the top of her centre, making her yelp. She pulled away from his mouth, needing the air as much as she needed him.

"You can't bite me without mating, can you?"

"No. I can't."

That was a shame. As she eyed the fangs, she imagined what they'd feel like sinking into her skin. Fuck, there was something seriously wrong with her. Bold and confident, shy and unsure. And to top it off, she wanted things she shouldn't.

"Soon, May. I won't fight this. Will you?"

"That's asking a lot." But she already decided she wouldn't fight this desire. May never would have let him touch her if she hadn't intended to go along with the physical need Fate created.

Tavis slid a hand down her centre, turning his wrist so his finger moved over her clit. He grinned. "I'll catch you if you try to run, pixie." A promise, a threat, and comfort.

May exploded. Sudden and harsh, fire lanced through her veins as her walls squeezed him. She cried out as his cock throbbed inside her. He roared through his release, their sounds mixing in the air.

Her voice wasn't her own. Raspy and hushed, she buried her face against his chest and issued another challenge. He gave her the confidence to let another part of her loose. "Maybe a fight would be fun."

Chapter Three

They laid awake in his bed for an hour before either of them said anything. Tavis couldn't stop touching her. Running his hands and fingers up and down her sides, over her breasts and dipping between her legs—building up the passion again, to ease it back while holding her close.

He saw the thoughts run through her eyes. She was amazing. Challenging and sweet.

"Maybe a fight would be fun."

But she didn't pull away. She smiled through the words. He'd felt her lips lift on his chest before she started kissing her way to his collar.

Tavis hadn't broken the silence because once he did, it would tarnish the fun moments of their first introduction with the truth they both had to face. They could joke and tease, dance around the facts while fucking. But this was important.

He'd witnessed the struggles of his brother and cousins. The result was the same in each. He didn't want that for him and May.

"We should talk."

"Mmm, maybe."

"Maybe?" He leaned in and nibbled on the shell of her ear.

"You're a shifter and I'm your mate."

He paused and slid his hand up to her cheek, turning her head to look at him. "Is it that simple for you?"

"No."

"Good. But I've seen what fighting Fate does. I don't want to."

"I've seen it too." Her lashes closed a fraction, hooding her eyes. "Tavis, I can't just jump."

"I don't want you to jump." Tavis didn't want regrets once it was too late.

"Seems we're on the same page then." Her eyes lifted and she blinked.

"I guess so." Although, he didn't sound as certain as May. Not fighting and not jumping, but shouldn't there be more to that?

"I suppose we should sleep."

But they hadn't fallen asleep yet, and wouldn't until they got more out of their system. "We will. Soon."

Tavis rolled on top of her, settling between her legs. He already smelled her arousal, but that wasn't enough to make him hammer into her without a little fun first. With a hand on the back of her neck, he put his other between them and played. Circling, thrusting, and repeating.

"Want more, pixie?"

"Yes!" She arched beneath him.

"Then you need to take it." Tavis rolled them so she straddled his hips. "Fuck me, pixie. Show off for me."

He clasped his hands behind his head and watched as she came out of her shell. May lowered herself on him, taking her time to adjust.

It was a joy to watch the change in her as she took her time to learn how their bodies fit, how to pleasure not only him, but herself. By the end, she wasn't only moving up and down, but she rolled her hips in full circles with each thrust.

"Fuck, May. You're perfect. Don't stop."

"I'm close," she whined.

"I know." He was close too, and he kept his hands behind his head until the last possible second. Until her body convulsed and her climax interrupted her careful rhythm. Grabbing her hips, he slammed her down on him while thrusting upward.

They came together, and this time, they faded into the bed with exhaustion. Tavis forced the energy to clean them up before tucking her against him to sleep. Fate dealt him someone perfect. And he intended to treasure her.

May woke before Tavis. Lifting her head, she looked around the room. It was a mess. Their clothes sprawled across the floor and they'd twisted the blankets around their waists. She'd love to get up and make some breakfast. Her stomach growled loud enough she worried it would wake Tavis. But her only choice of clothes was something of his. She didn't want to cook in her dress from the wedding. And the walk of shame didn't appeal to her either.

Damn.

It felt odd to make herself at home in his. With his clothes, his kitchen. But at no point last night had he looked at her with disdain or disgust. His eyes heated further with every gaze. Like he adored her before even knowing her.

That was what brought out her confident sass. She shouldn't stop now.

Lifting his arm off her stomach, she slid out from under him. When she checked to see if she'd been successful, his eyes were open and he smiled up at her.

Putting her finger to her lips, she made a shushing gesture while grabbing his dress shirt from the floor and tiptoeing from the bedroom. His low chuckle echoed behind her.

This bit of space was what she needed. May hadn't fought the sensations flooding her last night, but eventually she'd have to evaluate them.

Pulling her phone from her camera case Tavis had left on a chair in the livingroom, she sent a text to Blair.

In two hours, can you bring me some clothes? At Tavis's. Don't ask questions.

Blair would ask a dozen questions and they were going to come through as texts in about two minutes. May put her phone on vibrate and let it buzz away in her bag while she made her way to the kitchen. She needed breakfast. And tea. But she didn't see Tavis having tea in his kitchen. As she searched through the cupboards, she realized she was right.

With a shrug, she opened the fridge and found eggs and bacon. That would do. A loaf of bread sat on the counter.

Her stomach growled again.

"Seems we both worked up an appetite." Hands slid around her waist and pulled her hips back.

May tilted her chin to her shoulder while still holding the carton of eggs with both hands. Tavis dipped down and kissed her. A soft pressure that sealed their night together.

"I'll help." He let her go and pulled out frying pans. They worked in silence, but they touched every chance they had. Even May reached over to run her fingers over his bare chest. Sweatpants hung low on his hips, with his cock constantly hard beneath them, jumping every time she made contact.

His image fit the town perfectly. Rugged and strong. His hair flopped after being messed by sleep. The thick beard on his face wasn't so long it didn't move with his expressions.

He owned *Rockhard Bears* with his brother. A climbing lesson and rental company. And May tried to picture him geared up and climbing a dangerous-looking rock surface. Her hands itched for her camera.

"Not that I mind you staring, but the eggs are done."

Shaking herself, she turned off the burner and pushed the frying pan to the back. "Sorry. I was picturing what you look like when you're climbing."

"I can show you."

"Some day. I'll stay on the ground."

"With your camera."

She pointed her finger at him. "You got it."

"Do you drink coffee?"

"I prefer tea."

"I'll make sure to get some." Meaning he intended her to come back. Often enough to have what she liked in the house. But wouldn't that be what would happen? They were mates. Of course she'd be back.

"And I'll have coffee at my place."

Ice crystallized in the air. All bare skin pebbled with the chill. But when she looked up at him, he still had that same soft patience in his eyes. It was too soon to take this conversation further. They both accepted what they were. And that was enough for now.

Tavis pulled her closer. After a kiss to her temple, he sat her down at the table while he dished up, finishing off the plates with the toast.

"So, do you mostly photograph weddings?"

"Only because they take so much time and pay well. But I'll photograph anything a client requests. I've done more artistic photography of my own on the side. But I'll do family shoots, head shots, sports events. Even boudoir."

"And yet you blushed for most of the night last night."

May felt a fresh rush of blood infuse her face and he chuckled.

"Just like that." He ran the back of his knuckles down her cheek.

"That's different. There's an artistic side to boudoir."

"I can understand that." His eyes heated and dropped down her body.

"What about you? How did you and your brother start rock climbing?"

"Sport of choice growing up. It was easy to turn it into a business and it comes in handy during a search and rescue. Tourists love Firebrook. It wasn't an activity that anyone offered. Despite Noah's grumpy nature, he's a pretty great teacher."

"As I imagine you are."

"I have some charm."

That made her laugh. He was full of charm.

"Is that your phone?" Tavis frowned at the bag sitting nearby. The buzzing had stopped about the time they had food cooking in the pans, but restarted.

"Yes. But I know who it is and I don't need to answer it just yet."

"Blair?" he asked with a quirked brow.

"I need clothes." May shrugged.

"I rather like what you're wearing."

"It's comfortable, but makes the walk of shame even worse than last night's dress."

Tavis pushed his plate away and took her hand, lifting it to his lips to kiss her palm. "There's no shame between us." He had a firm hold on her hand and wouldn't let her look away.

"I know. I don't feel shame."

"Good." He leaned closer.

May moved to meet him halfway, using the hand he still held near his cheek to play with his beard. She hadn't had enough of that last night.

They were a breath away from each other when knocking on the front door interrupted.

"Delivery!" Blair's voice sang out from the other side.

"We both should have seen that coming." Tavis closed the distance, but made the kiss quick before getting up to open the door to her friend. His sister-in-law.

At least it seemed Fate didn't intend to keep the group of friends apart. Most of them.

Tavis didn't bother trying to block Blair from coming in. She was a force no one fought.

Blair grinned up at him and made her way inside. "Good morning." Her eyes moved between him and May. "And a good morning it looks like. Not that I'd know when someone ignores her phone." She passed a bag across the table to May.

"Thanks, Blair." She widened her eyes at her friend before taking the bag. "You're early."

"You're welcome." She took Tavis's seat at the table. "I can wait until you're ready."

May fidgeted in her seat. Rich brown orbs glanced up at him before down at her almost empty plate. She didn't want to go. Not yet.

And Tavis wouldn't have anyone rush her out of here if she didn't want to go. Even one of her well-meaning best friends. He loved Blair, but calling her a force wasn't an exaggeration. Tavis moved in behind May, setting a hand on the back of her neck. "I'm not quite done with her yet. You don't want to wait."

"For fuck's sake, kitten. I was still talking." Noah appeared in the still open front door. His brother scowled down at his mate, then seemed to clue in to the scene around him. Seeing both Tavis and May half dressed. Nodding, he moved over to Blair, pulling her head back with a grip in her hair. "I wasn't even out of the shower, telling you to wait the two hours."

"Sorry." She shrugged. "She wouldn't answer me."

"I remember someone else keeping to herself when going through something similar." May leaned into Tavis's hold.

"You're right. But maybe that's why I'm here."

"Interrupting." Tavis had to clarify that while he allowed her in, he wasn't thrilled with the company.

Twisting her lips, Blair nodded and left. Noah nodded at each of them and followed his mate to the door, but before she made it out the threshold, he spun her and threw her over his shoulder.

Tavis crouched beside his mate after the door shut. "Shower?"

"Yeah." May whispered.

As much as Tavis wanted to fuck her again, he didn't. After leading her to the shower, he spent most of it on his knees, making her come with his tongue and fingers. While she regained her strength, he washed them.

When he turned off the water, he held her against him. "Will you come back tonight? I'll cook dinner."

"Yes, I'll come back."

Tavis hated to see her walk away from his house. He tried to walk with her, but she insisted on leaving alone. She had a point. Neither of them wanted to fight this, but they didn't need to push things too far too fast because of it.

They'd closed *Rockhard* for today, giving themselves time to recover from the wedding festivities. Wyatt and Poppy were leaving on a honeymoon. But he and Noah took the opportunity for a day off where they could.

They rarely closed during the warm seasons, but the night after a family wedding, they'd planned on being too tired.

Tavis ventured back into his bedroom and inhaled, replaying the night. At least he didn't need to tell her what he was. He'd dreaded that ever since considering a mate might be somewhere out there for him. Facing down an extra large grizzly was terrifying. Discovering that being was only half of a person was a shock. They were a species unknown to the world.

May's sweet cherry scent covered his bed and floated in the air. Mixed with sex and passion, Tavis had a hard time not chasing after her.

"Fuck. I need to get out of the house."

Shifting and running through the trees sounded like a good idea, but that felt like avoidance. Tavis went to work. Not to open, but to busy himself with the schedule. It hadn't been long ago he remembered his brother wasting time with the same task. The town was quiet after last night. Wyatt and Poppy's wedding had been a big deal for the residents.

When that didn't work—every time he licked his lips, he tasted her—Tavis caved and stalked into the woods. Spending twenty minutes devouring her in the shower imprinted her flavour harder than any divine meal.

The breeze in the trees was the only sound. And the further into the woods he walked, the quieter everything became. Pulling on magic, Tavis shifted.

As he landed on his four paws, he cursed. The magic only made the scent and taste of his mate stronger.

Their conversation about coffee and tea still bothered him. The implications could be painful. But he couldn't have unrealistic expectations of her. They'd only just met and needed time. Even he felt he needed time to get to know her better.

She was an adorable enigma. But her love for her career, for her art, was the biggest piece of her heart.

Tavis kept his pace at a jog until he reached the river. Splashing in the water helped cool his thrumming blood. Helped wash away the sweet cherries from his tongue.

Until the next time he had his mate in his grasp.

Chapter Four

May flopped onto the bed. Her body tingled. Incessantly potent sensations filled her core. Not for a second did she regret going home with Tavis. They didn't discuss the elephant in the room—or rather the bear in the room, but that hadn't been what she'd needed. What he needed.

She still had another hour before brunch with the bride. The newlyweds were leaving today for some much needed isolation. The best kind of honeymoon.

May pulled out her camera and took out the memory card. Opening her laptop, she got started on sorting the pictures from the wedding, first organized by what she labeled as events. The first was the bridal party. Skye had already gone through her shots and sent them to her, organized perfectly. May added her own to that folder.

She froze before opening the groom and groomsmen pictures, knowing that the first pictures would have Tavis. The single one of Tavis where he saw her for the first time.

"Nope. Not ready for that." May skipped those, scrolling through the thumbnails until she came to the ones after the ceremony. From there, it was easy to drag photos where they belonged.

The groom and groomsmen would have to wait for another day. *Sorry, Poppy. But you'll understand.*

Her cell phone rang from her bag on the bed. She answered without looking.

"Are you coming?" Poppy asked before she could say hello.

May looked at the bottom corner of her laptop. "Shit, sorry Poppy. I got distracted with all of your pretty pictures. I'll be right there."

A quick save and a backup, and May had her crocheted purse settled over her shoulder as she left. She'd had the same bag since high school, refusing to get rid of it. It was one of those things that she never wanted to say goodbye to. It was irrational, but nostalgic—washed and repaired too many times for her to count.

Bella's Bakery had the entire left side sectioned off with a reserved sign hanging from a rope, and they'd pushed three of the tables over to fit them all. Poppy, Blair, Harlyn, Dakota, Maggie, and Bonnie stared after her as she walked in, ducking behind the sign.

"Sorry, guys." Scrunching her nose, she took the only vacant seat in the back corner. As all the eyes turned to her, she realized they blocked her in on purpose. She and Tavis hadn't been subtle about things last night. "Stop looking at me. This is all about Poppy."

"Nice try, but my day is over." Poppy shook her head.

"I'm hungry." May tried to deflect.

"I bet you are," Blair quipped and leaned forward.

"Tea. Just give me tea and maybe I'll give you something. Maybe. Depends on how good it is."

"Oh, now that's a challenge." Bonnie slapped the table and left to stand at the side of the counter. She spoke low to the teenager working the espresso machine. "Six of them, please," she called over her shoulder before sitting back down.

"You know the drinks will be worth every drop of detail we want from you." Blair somehow leaned even closer. "Spill."

"We danced. We kissed. And I went home with him."

"And..." Dakota waved her hand in a circle for more.

"And exactly what all of you think." Licking her lips, she lowered her voice to a whisper. "I'm his mate."

Several sets of eyes landed on her neck, searching for the crescent mark that told other shifters what she was. If he'd bitten her last night, they'd be mated. May shrunk in her seat, hunching her shoulders up.

"No. We didn't."

"But you talked about it." Blair didn't quite make it a question. It was closer to a demand.

"Yes." Sort of. Just clarification they were both on the same page in between touching and kissing. If that was considered *talking about it*, then yes, they talked. "Enough about me. Give me some time to process. Turn your attention back on the bride."

It took them several seconds to stop scrutinizing her, but the discussion turned to the wedding, and how absolutely perfect it was. Everyone seamlessly moved into a discussion about Blair's upcoming wedding.

But May didn't miss the side glances they all sent her way.

As promised, the tea was perfection. Full of sweet, steamy goodness. A London Fog with a twist. She took another sip. Was that almond? And maple syrup?

"What are you doing today? I can be free to hang out?" Blair touched her arm, then extended the same question to Harlyn.

"I'm heading home today. I have almost everything ready for school to start, but the sooner I get back, the better." Harlyn wrapped her arm around Poppy's shoulder and squeezed. "I'm so glad I could be here."

"I'm taking my camera out on a date. This place is too pretty not to capture." And it would give her some peace to process. Or better yet, ignore. May would rather push it all to the side for a little longer and let her inner self work on their issues before she bothered with too much thought. It would only lead to confusion and headache. It was better to let things run their course before wasting energy. They may not be able to control the physical aspect of the relationship, they could allow it to take a natural path. Fate didn't have to control the rest of their relationship.

"I can come with you." Blair grabbed her purse off the back of her chair.

"I can show you some great places for pictures." Dakota's offer was sweet, and maybe even tempting.

"I think I'd like to explore on my own first. But I'd love to check out your astronomy tour sometime, Dakota. Poppy, Blair, and Harlyn told me so much about that night." Their first trip here, they'd joined one of Dakota's tours. May had made them recount every detail of their vacation. The good and the bad.

Part of her wished she'd been here to support them, but at the same time, she'd been happy to be safe at home. That made her feel like an awful friend sometimes, despite the reassurances they gave her.

They all separated on the sidewalk outside *Bella's Bakery*. As the sun grew higher in the sky, it was a lot hotter than it had been when she'd left Tavis.

May sent a text off to Skye to see if she'd left town before going back to change.

Haven't left yet! I'm taking in some sights.

Good for you. I'm about to do the same. Let me know before you leave town. She'd make sure her assistant was hale, whole, and paid before she left.

Now, May needed to get lost in her own art for a little while.

Hikers were close. But no one veered off the path near him. Tavis hadn't gone home yet. He had no need to. Not without work and not without May. The longer he stayed in fur, the calmer he became.

After splashing in and out of the river for an hour, catching fish, he basked in the heat on the bank. His thick fur held the moisture, but the sun was strong enough to penetrate the layers. He listened to the hikers pass throughout the morning, wondering what his mate was doing. Likely the brunch with her friends.

Tilting his head up, he judged the position of the sun. They should have finished a while ago. But if Tavis let himself leave this sanctuary, he'd search for her. Maybe that wasn't a bad thing, but they didn't dig deep last night. Only choosing to get lost in the desire rising and overflowing.

He'd also have to sneak past hikers unless he wanted to take the long way around. When instead he could stay where he was.

Stretching, he lumbered back to the river for a drink.

Hikers were usually in groups of two to four, and full of conversation. Smart practices to avoid wildlife.

The next sound carrying on the breeze was a single set of feet. Lifting his nose, he inhaled a scent that made his knees go weak. Sweet cherries.

His mate was exploring. Alone.

Splashing across the river, he stalked through the trees. After a quick check with his senses to discover no one else was nearby on the trail, he shifted. She was walking toward him and had a corner to go around before she saw him, leaning naked against a tree.

Her eyes watched her feet, and she had a firm grip on both sides of her camera hanging around her neck.

"Find anything pretty enough for a picture?"

May gasped. Wide brown eyes snapped up to meet his. "You're naked." Her gaze dropped, and a blush filled her already heated face. The colour of the blush differed from the redness of exertion. It held a pinker tone that reached places he wanted to kiss.

"I am."

"Why?"

"I didn't hike up here on two feet."

"Oh."

He pushed off the tree and gave himself space. Holding her gaze, he pulled on the magic, on the warmth that enveloped his body.

"What are you doing?"

The air swirled around him and through the fog of it, Tavis winked. Bones popped and cracked. She winced at the sickening sounds, but never dropped eye contact. He wouldn't let her. His own will kept the two of them attached while he shifted.

Landing on four paws, he inched closer to her. It wouldn't be long before more hikers came through.

May didn't move, except for her shallow breaths.

It's okay, pixie. It's just me.

She didn't react. They couldn't yet communicate this way. But they would, some day.

Tavis nuzzled her arm, encouraging her to let go of her camera and touch him. She seemed to do it without thinking.

Laughter came from up the trail. He doubted she heard it, but people were coming. Stepping back, he made a follow-me gesture with his head and left the trail.

"You're really just you? Just Tavis?"

He dropped his head in a single nod. After blowing out a breath through the 'o' of her lips, she followed. Tavis took her back to the river. She stopped while he continued to the water, taking a seat in the grass with her back next to a tree. Seconds later, he heard the click and shutter of her camera.

Tilting his head over his shoulder, he raised his brow. May grinned and shrugged a single shoulder. "You asked if I found anything pretty enough for a picture."

Tavis huffed, then bent his knees, readying himself to jump into the river. *Hope you're ready to take the picture, pixie.*

He lunged. Her camera clicked several times as he flew through the air, mixed with the sound of her joy.

Fucking beautiful.

The splash drenched all his dried and warm fur, and scared away every water creature. Her camera didn't lower from her face until he pulled himself back up on the bank.

"Now, do it again. I don't want to watch it through a lens this time."

For her, he'd do anything.

He shook the heavy water off him before steadying himself near the edge. Launching himself into the water didn't elicit the same squeals and laughter, but he sensed her awe. Warm eyes bore into him with every move he made.

"I can't believe this is something I get to see up close. You're magnificent."

Shaking the water again, he walked toward her. She'd already tucked her camera back in its case. He stuck his nose in her neck and breathed.

"I can't believe I'm this close at all." Her voice turned breathy, shocked and timid.

Tavis smelled her nerves, but her fear didn't grow. Her arousal did. He let the magic in to shift while he still touched her, only putting distance between them toward the end and the worst of the change.

"Tavis?" Her hands reached out for him, but didn't make contact. When he finished, he moved to his knees next to her.

"I'm here, pixie." He smiled down at her, cupping the side of her neck.

"Does that hurt?" Her eyes searched his body. He wondered if she looked for scars.

"Not anymore." Pulling her up, he took her place and settled her on his lap.

"What are you doing?"

"What does it look like?"

"Looks like something we shouldn't be doing out here." She whipped her head around, looking for people that weren't there.

"And why is that?" he asked with a chuckle.

She blinked. "No reason, I guess."

Tavis set a hand at the back of her neck and pulled her down to kiss her. The bark scraped against his back, but he'd endure anything as long as she didn't pull away from him. Her hands settled on his shoulders, moving up his neck and to his hair.

The kiss didn't need to be frantic. They'd pushed through their initial desire last night. What they needed right now was exploration. A chance to get to know each other.

A chance to taste each other. May grew eager, leaning into him. Tavis let his head rest against the tree. He snaked his tongue out whenever she gave him an opening.

His calm mood from basking by the river extended here. The warm air carried a sweet scent of the foliage. He could stay like this all day.

But his mate seemed to have other ideas. Soft hands moved over his shoulders, back and forth, as if she revved herself up with bravery. Each time she moved them down, they went down his chest a little further than before.

Tavis was more than content to wait for her to do what she wanted.

Come on, May. Don't be shy now. May enjoyed the feel of him under her hands and the more she touched, the more aroused she became. But they were in the woods. The trail she'd hiked wasn't far away.

Her hands moved over the ridges of his muscles, through his chest hair and up to the hard columns of his neck. And Tavis sat back as content as a bear in the sun while she tried hard not to writhe on top of him. It was getting increasingly difficult. Her hips developed a mind of their own.

The breeze created a soft hum through the trees, almost like a song calling to her. May listened. The song was a guide. She let it control her. Her hands took on a pattern. Her hips rolled.

Warmth from the air fed her heat and desire. Her clothes felt too heavy.

Breaking the contact of the kiss, May reached for the hem of her shirt. Embarrassment gripped long enough for her to look around them again.

"No one is here, pixie." Tavis set his hands over hers and helped her lift the fabric, but he didn't take it further. He only settled back against the tree.

"Maybe talking is what we should be doing." She wouldn't be able to process without more information. Or at least make sure she knew everything she should. Maybe she did. Blair and Poppy had been more than forthcoming with everything.

"We can talk. But I'm pretty good at multitasking. Are you?" He ran his hands up and down her thighs, and she cursed the fabric muting his touch.

May reached behind her for her bra, letting it drop down her arms. "I am. I should know everything there is to know."

"Why don't we start with you telling me everything you know?" Tavis slid his hand up her back and brought her closer, so her breasts were level with his face. Lazily, he let his tongue circle an erect peak.

She gasped. "Oh... okay."

He chuckled and did it again. "Go ahead, pixie."

"I'm your mate." She had to set a hand against the tree behind him to keep from falling on him.

"Mmhmm." He hummed around her nipple and she moaned. Damn it. She was having difficulty concentrating.

"Fate chooses who."

He let go and spoke while moving to her other breast. "Depends who you ask. Some of us think She chooses." Lick. "Some believe She shows us." Lick.

"Which do you believe?"

"I'll let you know." Tavis pulled her nipple in hard enough to make her back arch and start her hips moving against his erection.

"Once we're mated, there's no going back."

He let go of her and tilted his head up, dark green eyes narrowed. "Correct."

"And you need to bite me."

"Yeah, pixie." His hand steadied her at her waist as he held her gaze.

"It gets painful if we fight it."

Tavis sighed and started kissing along her collarbone and back down to her breasts. "Unfortunately. I'm sorry."

"I don't need you to apologize. It isn't your fault." His mouth wasn't enough. May stood and unbuttoned her pants. Stepping back, she took off the rest of her clothes. "I'm not upset by this turn of events."

"No? I'm happy to hear that."

Both of her friends were happy. Bonnie was happy. Maggie was happy. May wanted that for herself. At least some of that happiness.

"You're beautiful, pixie."

Standing naked in the woods and she still blushed. His grin grew as she felt the heat fill her cheeks.

"Coming back down here with me?"

"Do I know everything?"

"Other than I need you right now. Yes."

May's gaze dropped down his body where his cock twitched for her attention. Licking her lips, she dropped to her knees and straddled his legs, but didn't move all the way up. Setting her hands on his thighs, she moved them upward, watching his face as she moved closer to his cock. He glued his gaze to her hands.

She hadn't expected how powerful she felt. One hand cupped his balls, and the other wrapped around the base of his erection.

"Seems I'm trapped."

Somehow, in a moment of utter seriousness he made her laugh. Sparing him a glance, she bent her body until her mouth hovered over the tip.

"Don't torture me, May. Please."

"I'm not capable of torture." She dropped her head and took him into her mouth, taking the time to taste him with her tongue.

He groaned. "We'll see about that."

May tapped back into the rhythm of the wind again and moved with it. He tasted like the air, like the river. Nature. The more she moved, the more of it she wanted. She quickened her pace, and she was sure the song of the wind did the same to match her.

Tavis stayed utterly still until he pulsed in her mouth. His hand grabbed her hair and pulled hard. She came off him with a pop. Her scalp stung.

"I'm about to come."

"That's the idea." She pulled against his hold, wanting to taste more of him. Wanting to feel him shoot down her throat. Where the hell this girl came from, May didn't know. But she turned into someone wantonly confident with him. And she loved it. "Let go, Tavis."

He growled, his lips lifting. But he didn't release her, only pulled a little harder.

"You trying to tell me you don't have the stamina for more than one?"

"Fuck, pixie." Tavis pushed instead of pulled, bringing her back down. The moment she made contact, he let her go.

May made up for the lost time, working him harder than before. A roar ripped from his chest, but it was low enough it didn't echo.

Seconds was all it took for him to swell in her mouth. She tasted the beginning drops before he exploded. With the first pulse, she sank down so he hit the back of her throat. May swallowed until he had nothing left.

Tavis reached between them and gripped her chin to pull her up. "Your turn. Turn around."

When she frowned, he guided her so she was on all fours in front of him. He wasted no time pinching her clit and setting his mouth against her opening. She dropped to her elbow and set her forehead against her fists.

Their location was vulnerable enough, but this position put it over the top. He had full access to whatever he wanted to do to her. And he feasted, forcing her clit to swell further. His tongue licked from her clit to her entrance and between her buttocks.

May squealed and tried to pull away, but he gripped her hip, chuckling while pulling her back and setting his mouth back at her entrance. Her thighs trembled, and she knew her climax would hit soon.

"Give it to me, pixie, so I can take more."

Whimpering, she fell over the edge.

"Good girl."

But the climax never finished before he straightened and thrust inside her. The position was almost painfully full, but every muscle quivered with relief from being connected with him. Her ears buzzed and the only thing she heard was her heart hammering and Tavis's voice.

"Fucking perfect. Come again, May. Come with me." He reached up the front of her body and circled his hand around her neck. Pulling, he brought her up until her back met his chest. Sharp teeth nipped her ear, and she came.

Not a sudden explosion, but an increasing pleasure that left her weak.

Tavis banded an arm around her hips and tightened his grip on her neck. Hot spurts filled her. They collapsed against the tree, his arms around her, as the calming hum of the wind settled around them.

Chapter Five

Tavis let her go, not walking her back to the trail. The foot traffic of hikers had picked up while they'd lazed against the tree. And since he didn't bring clothes with him on his excursion, they had to leave in different directions.

His body tingled in every place she touched and ached in the ones she didn't. Pins and needles spread over him, trying to grasp onto the sensations she gave him.

Tavis jogged back through the trees toward home, keeping away from the trails. As he got closer to town, he heard the commotion. People gathered, someone shouting orders. Caiden, his cousin. Wyatt was the head of Search And Rescue, but with him having left for his honeymoon, Caiden took his place.

Tavis picked up his pace, finding where he stashed his clothes and getting dressed. He joined the crowd of people around his cousin, but didn't have any of his gear with him.

"What's going on?"

Caiden looked over at him and inhaled. After raising his brow, he filled him in. "Missing child. Six years old. Turned their back for a second and the child veered off. The trail has so many bends, they don't know which direction. The father is still out there. He's on the trail where she disappeared."

If it were Tavis, he wouldn't be staying on the trail and waiting. That meant the shifters had to be careful when searching. They likely wouldn't be able to search in fur.

"We're heading out in five. There's extra gear and clothes in my truck."

"Thanks. I'll gear up." He headed over to Caiden's truck. Never knowing when they'd need the spare, they all kept extras in their vehicles. This wasn't the first time one of them had been caught unprepared because they were out running in fur.

All the Greer men wore approximately the same size. He could search in his jeans, but it wouldn't be comfortable if the search took a long time. Caiden's clothes were a little big on him, but not baggy. Before slipping his phone in his pocket, he started to send a text to May, but realized he didn't have her number yet. He'd planned to get it tonight.

He sent one to Blair instead, telling her he joined the search and to tell May that dinner might be late. Noah stood nearby, geared up and ready to go, so Blair already knew the situation.

Caiden called Tavis over once he shut the tailgate on the truck. "You can come with me. You didn't see or hear anything while you were out?"

"No. Wrong trails. I was on the other side of town and up by the river."

"I hate it when it's kids." His gruff growl was more for himself, but Tavis heard him. And felt it.

"We all do." Tavis slapped Caiden on the shoulder. "Where are we heading?" Tavis had missed all the planning and assignments. Caiden handed him the map and tapped their area.

This wilderness was as much their home as the wild animals that lived here. He and Caiden had one of the most dense parts surrounding that trail.

"Who's meeting with the father?" He refolded the map, but kept it accessible.

"Easton and Max."

"Easton can keep him closer to the trail. Maybe we'll be able to shift." Tavis spoke low.

"I hope so. We'll find her faster."

They searched in silence from there, only checking in when needed and listening over the radio. Easton found her scent leading off the trail. She had gone toward Noah's section. They paired Noah with a human.

Shifters still had an increased sense of smell even in human form, and they all used it to their advantage. Once Tavis and Caiden cleared their area, not finding her scent anywhere, they moved toward the others. They looked for tracks and signs as much as scent.

The tension in the searchers increased the longer they remained out there. Even a short amount of time was stressful when it involved a child.

An hour before dusk, Noah caught onto her scent, a recent one. He found visible footprints and heard whimpering. The human with him hadn't heard her, but Noah sent in the location of the tracks, adding a few keywords they all used to let each other know what they couldn't say in front of others.

Tavis and Caiden relaxed, knowing Noah was close to her. They slowed their pace and waited for the confirmation before heading back into town.

"Got her." Noah's gruff voice was abrupt and clipped. They waited a few minutes more for him to tell them her state and their exact location. "Some scrapes and bruises. She's all good. Heading back now."

"Thank fuck." Caiden sighed.

Tavis let out one of his own. With kids, they moved quick. Because things happened so fast. Everyone was always on board for these searches. This had been a short one with a great outcome. But they didn't always end that way.

Now Tavis had other plans he wanted to get back on course before the night faded away.

May worked while waiting to hear word about the search. It distracted her enough once she sunk into it and added a splash of her own creativity to some photos. Just for fun. But the sparkly effects suited them.

She saved the completed photos in a folder ready to send to Poppy. But she wouldn't send them during their honeymoon. Maybe a few sneak peeks.

Dinner had come and gone, and she ended up ordering a pizza to eat while she worked. Blair had sneaked in to grab a couple slices for herself before heading out.

But now, May had sat hunched over her laptop too long, and work wasn't enough anymore. After the afternoon in the woods with Tavis, she looked forward to the night with him. Especially since she planned to leave in the morning. Those plans hadn't changed. And they wouldn't.

But she'd come back to Firebrook. As often as she could or needed to.

Her phone buzzed on the bed. Blair's name flashed on the screen.

"Hello?"

"They found her." Blair's voice burst through the speaker. "They're on their way back."

"Oh, that's great news." May shut her computer.

"They should all be home in a little over an hour."

"Thanks, Blair."

Silence hung over the line. "Want to talk about it yet?"

"No." May pulled the phone away from her face and hit the end button. She loved her friends, but this wasn't anything they could help with. Fate happened, and it was up to her and Tavis to do with it what they wanted. Just as Poppy and Wyatt had. Just as Blair and Noah.

May had all the information she needed.

An hour. She had an hour to meet Tavis at his place. She'd take the rest of the pizza with her so he'd get something to eat, too. Assuming he hadn't yet.

She took a shower and dressed in denim shorts and a tank top. With her hair blow dried and make up applied lightly, May got in her car. She was early and would beat him there, but she saw that as a benefit.

Dark hadn't covered the town just yet, but the place seemed busy as tourists roamed for evening activities. *Poppy Mack's* had a steady stream of people coming in and out, and the restaurant patios were full.

May was thankful she drove a little slower due to the many crosswalks, but that didn't matter when an older grey sedan zipped around the corner, cutting it too close, so it veered into her lane.

She screamed, instinct forcing the sound from her as they collided. It wasn't enough to set off the airbags, but enough to make her stiffen and jolt her forward.

She took a minute to catch her breath, calm her heart, and mentally check for injuries. Looking through her windshield, she saw the driver of the other car. A man with lanky, square shoulders, short blond hair, and glasses. Anger tightened his face, but he seemed to take a minute for himself too before getting out of the car.

Once her heart's erratic pace eased, May got out and moved to the front to assess the damage. It didn't look too bad, but she knew the possibility of more unseen damage.

"I'm so sorry. Are you all right, miss?" His speech was oddly articulated.

She nodded and tried for a smile, unsure how it looked. "I am. And yourself."

"I'm fine. That was my fault and I'm terribly sorry. I'm new to town and still getting used to the area."

There was no need for her to point out he'd been going a bit too fast and missed his own lane. He'd owned up to the fault of the accident.

He crouched down and looked closer at both vehicles. "It doesn't look too bad. I don't think the service station is still open. Can you meet me there in the morning? I'd be happy to pay directly for the repairs."

The offer was so direct, May stumbled for words for a moment.

"May?" a deeper voice called from the sidewalk. Tavis. She looked over at him, forgetting for a second where she was and what she was supposed to be dealing with. He ran toward her, cutting through the few people that scattered around them, gawking at the accident.

"This says here they open at eight. Should we meet there then?" The man had his phone in his hand and looked back and forth between her and the screen.

"Are you hurt?" Tavis reached her and cupped her chin, forcing her attention on him.

"No, I'm good."

He let her go, and she turned her attention to the other driver, who seemed impatient.

"I'm sorry. I'm leaving town in the morning. As long as my car is okay to drive, that is. I think it's just best if we exchange insurance and contact information."

After a second of recovery, the driver smiled. "Of course." He went back to his car to get his papers, and May did the same while Tavis inspected her car.

When they met back at the front, they each snapped pictures of the other's information and exchanged phone numbers.

"I am leaving town tomorrow, but I'll be back every so often."

"And I've just moved here. I'm the new principal at the school." The man beamed and pushed his metal-framed glasses up his nose.

"Congratulations."

"Thank you. I'm sure I'm going to love it here." He tucked everything in his back pocket. "Well, Miss May Preston, you have my apologies again for the accident. There's no need to rush in a place like this. I hope the damage doesn't affect your travel plans tomorrow."

"Thank you," May glanced at the image she took on her phone, "Duke Greyson."

There was a little creaking of metal as he pulled away, but it eased and stopped as he kept driving.

"Let's get out of the road." Tavis opened the driver's door for her and jogged around to the passenger side. "I don't think it's so bad you can't drive home tomorrow, but I'll call Eric to come over and take a look tonight."

"Thank you." May started the car and cringed as she pressed on the gas. Her car didn't sound as bad as Duke's, but it eased and she made it to the house with no problems.

Before she could get out of the car, Tavis reached for her. "Are you sure you're all right?"

"I'm sure. I was a little shaken when it happened, but I'm fine."

He made a call before leading her inside. He poured them both a drink and they waited on the couch. May didn't misunderstand the way his hands roamed over her body, massaging with light pressure—hiding the fact he searched her for injuries. She didn't stop him or call him out on it. Instead, May reveled in the feeling of being cared for.

Tavis hadn't liked the panic when he saw May standing in the street next to a car accident. But he kept control of himself, kept himself from ripping the guy a new one. It was clear the guy was in the wrong lane.

Eric said he'd be over in half an hour, which gave Tavis just enough time to make sure for himself that May was all right. He sat on the couch with her between his legs and leaning on his chest. They only breathed while he moved his hands over her. Soon, their breathing matched the same rhythm and his touch had more purpose than examining for injuries. But he took nothing further, only satisfying himself with knowing she was okay. It was a small fender bender, and he knew this panic was an overreaction.

But as he'd told Blair when she'd put herself in danger, mates are the most precious thing to shifters.

Eric knocked on the door. Tavis waited for May to stand, then kissed her cheek before answering the door.

"Thanks for coming, Eric."

"No problem. I was free." Tavis took him out to the car, and he felt May following close behind. They waited, his arm wrapped around her middle while Eric looked under the hood, then jacked it up and crawled underneath.

After about five minutes underneath, Eric came out and lowered the jack.

"As far as I can tell from here, you're all good to hit the road in the morning, but I'd get it in to someone right away."

"Thank you for taking the time to come. I appreciate it. What do I owe you?" May stepped out of Tavis's hold and toward Eric.

He chuckled. "Nothing. I owe Tavis there more favours than I care to count."

"Thank you."

"Thanks, Eric." Tavis shook his hand and waited for him to put his stuff back in his truck and drive away. With a hand on

May's back, he turned her back to the house. "You could have stayed another day."

"No. I need to get back. So unless I had to, I couldn't."

"I didn't get the night with you I wanted."

"We had a better afternoon." She looked over her shoulder and up. Even her eyes smiled and a light pink filled her cheeks.

"We did. But call me selfish."

"You and me both. Although, I'm glad you guys found the little girl."

"Me too." Speaking of the search reminded him he needed a shower. But his mate looked pretty and fresh.

He took her into the bedroom and set her at the end of the bed.

"Strip, pixie."

She narrowed her eyes and shook her head.

"We've skipped half the night, and now I'm getting desperate. We'll go out for breakfast in the morning instead. Do we have a deal?"

"Okay." May pulled her shirt over her head and moved to her shorts. Tavis rid himself of his own clothes, finishing before her.

"Lay back on the bed and get started without me. I need a shower."

"Do what?" She froze with her thumbs hooked in her panties.

"Get on the bed."

Her eyes flared before she obeyed.

"On your back, knees spread."

"Tavis?" she whispered, but still did as he said.

"Now start playing, but don't come. I'll be back in a few minutes."

"You're serious?"

Tavis leaned over her, taking hold of her chin to tilt her face toward him. "Very." He held her there until her hand slid down her body and she gasped with the first touch. "Good girl."

It was the quickest fucking shower of his life, but when he finished, he didn't storm back out to the bedroom. He paused in the doorway to watch her.

Her back arched, and she moved her hand slowly between her legs. It was as if she was still testing herself.

The moment he made a noise with the door, she stopped, snatching her hand back.

"Don't stop, pixie."

The determination taking over showed on her face. Narrowed eyes, flared nostrils, and her tongue running over her lips. She set her hand back between her legs, but he saw the glistening of her cream on her lower lips. Her knees spread further and her back arched again.

Sinking to his knees, he grabbed her hips and pulled her to the end of the bed.

"Keep playing." Tavis breathed against her and readied himself to move at her pace. He licked around her finger, playing with her clit, going left when she went right. Her little gasps increased.

There was a sweetness to the moment that existed not only in her taste. Gentle licks and kisses to match her own touch brought her slowly to a strong peak.

Tavis lapped at her entrance before letting his own finger circle her there.

"Tavis?" Her finger faltered, her hand shaking.

"Not until you come." He sank his finger deep, curling and playing before pulling out with an excruciating drag. Her walls fluttered and Tavis latched onto her clit, flattening her finger against it and sucking hard.

Adding a second finger, he pulled the orgasm from her, letting the slow build up explode with ferocity.

Tavis lifted her back up the bed and settled himself on top of her. He held her and waited for her to catch her breath.

"I know you have to go back tomorrow, but don't stay away too long. Please."

May raised her hand and cupped his cheek. "I won't."

"Good." He sank into her and groaned. The only thing more perfect than this moment would be if she promised never to leave at all.

Chapter Six

May felt heavy as she walked back into her apartment after a week away. Home always smelled different after a trip. A little stale. A little cold, despite high temperatures. Without life, it seemed as if the home was lonely.

Well, she could relate. Not even an hour on the road and the loneliness settled without Tavis. She mentally went through her calendar on the drive, ticking off the next time she had a few days to spare. Two weeks away. She could last that long.

May called Nonna, needing the warmth and comfort. Nonna wasn't her real grandmother, but the closest she'd had growing up. She was her parents' neighbor, still living in the small ranch house on the outskirts of the city. While May was close with her parents, she was even closer to Nonna.

"Bee! You must be back in the city." Nonna's excited voice came through the line. Her nickname for her helped May come up with the name for her business, *MayBe You*. It had a meaning of its own with a hat tip to Nonna.

"Hi, Nonna. Yeah, I'm back."

"You'll come over for tea tomorrow, won't you? I want to hear all about the wedding." Dishes clanged over the line as if Nonna was making herself tea.

"I'll be there."

"Good. You get unpacked and settled. We can talk more tomorrow."

"Okay, Nonna. Love you."

"Love you too, Bee."

Nonna had never had children of her own. It was a natural relationship that built between her and May's parents, creating a grandmother for May. She couldn't imagine not seeing Nonna every week.

Tavis was part of her life now, but he wasn't the only part. May needed to find the balance.

Her phone dinged not long after she'd set it down.

Tavis: Talk to me, pixie. She heard his voice through the words.

May: I'm home.

Tavis: Good. When you coming back?

May didn't bother hiding her grin. She liked being wanted. And she'd been thinking the same thing during her drive home.

May: Two weeks. You free?

Tavis: I will be.

May pulled her suitcase and bags into her bedroom. She narrowed her eyes at it. It wasn't late in the day and she should unpack it, making it easier to settle back into her routine tomorrow. It's what she always did after a work trip. But letting the suitcase sit felt like holding onto her time there.

Ridiculous. She inwardly shook her head and hauled the suitcase onto her bed to unzip.

Sitting on top of her pile of clothes was a small stuffed grizzly bear. He had a ribbon around his neck with a tag. Nibbling on her inner lip, she lifted the soft toy to read the tag.

Don't forget to kiss me goodnight.

-Tavis

Setting him on her pillow, she unpacked her suitcase, putting most of it in her laundry basket. With mini Tavis watching her, she didn't feel as lost and distant from where she wanted to be.

May set her laptop up at her desk, putting everything back in order to work more on the wedding pictures tomorrow. She planned to have everything done for Poppy when they got back from their honeymoon.

The first thing to do was to check in with her assistants. Sending off a mass message, she let them all know she was back in town and would like to meet with everyone in the morning to see how they made out without her and to check in with Skye about the Firebrook wedding. She could help with the edits.

May opened the conversation with Tavis without thinking.

May: Thanks for mini Tavis

Tavis: You're welcome, pixie.

She tucked her phone in her pocket, reminding herself she needed to keep her balance. Grabbing her planner, May took it with her to the kitchen to review while making dinner and meal plans for the rest of the week.

All while thoughts of Tavis hovered in the back of her mind.

The first thing Tavis did when he went into work the next day was look at the schedule for two weeks out. Fall was busy, but not as busy as the summer months, making it possible to pass most lessons off to Noah and bring in someone else for the ones he couldn't rearrange. If his time with his mate was limited, he intended to make the most of it.

Tavis smiled when his phone vibrated in his pocket.

May: I miss Bonnie's London Fog.

They'd talked for over an hour before bed last night. He'd laid under the covers, staring at the three dots blinking over and over. She'd told him about her business. *MayBe You Photography.* She worried about needing to expand. In a year, her repeat client list had doubled and the requests for weddings and other events never seemed to stop. Tavis didn't want to admit the amount of worry that caused him. May had told him about her family, her Nonna, and her riding days. All things they should have discussed while she was here, but they'd had more important things to do. This distance gave them a chance to get to know each other more.

Tavis: She'll be happy to hear that. I'll have some waiting for you as soon as you get back.

May: Mmm. I can't wait.

Neither could he.

Tavis: What are you doing now?

May: About to meet with my assistants. Just waiting for one more to arrive.

Tavis: You sound important.

Three dots blinked and disappeared. When they didn't come back, Tavis typed his next message.

Tavis: You're important to me.

Any normal relationship, it would be too soon to say that, but this was different. He saw no reason to hide what she meant to him.

She didn't answer, and he tried not to be disappointed by that. He understood it wasn't the same for her as it was for him.

Noah came back from the first lesson of the day, waving off the small family before coming inside.

"How are you frowning and smiling at the same time?" Noah rolled his neck while moving behind the counter and updating the logs from the lesson. They kept notes on each lesson in the event they had repeat customers. It was a waste of everyone's time to teach the same thing twice if they didn't need to. Many took this up as a new hobby and came back for lessons several times a month.

"I'm just that talented." But Tavis smoothed out his frown.

"Talking with May?"

"Yeah."

His brother didn't offer any unsolicited advice. But they'd seen this a few times, discussed mates at length. They all knew what to expect at this point.

The next customer walking in the door forced Tavis to put his phone away and focus. It was his turn to take the next group out.

Talking with his mate would have to wait until the end of the day.

May: So, Bonnie's drinks might not be the only thing I miss.

May had spent the day editing not only Poppy's wedding photos, but the other wedding her assistants photographed. She'd turned the entire day into an event, setting up work spaces all over her apartment and ordering pizza.

She had one more wedding and three family sessions in the next week. May hadn't turned people away. Yet.

She'd set a goal to have everything edited and sent to clients before she went back to Firebrook. She could do it, but the next two weeks wouldn't have much spare time.

Tavis: What else do you miss, pixie?

May: The smell in the air. The quiet streets. You.

She hadn't answered him this morning after he'd declared she was important to him. Those words stuck with her all day. But jumping in and accepting what he'd said wasn't finding balance. It wouldn't help keep the important things in her life separate by dwelling on Tavis and their attraction.

But she admitted she missed him.

Tavis: Same, pixie.

May hung her housecoat on the back of her bedroom door and climbed into bed.

Tavis: Where's mini Tavis?

May: Beside me.

Tavis: In bed?

May: Yes.

He took longer to answer, the dots on her screen blinking, but never going away.

Tavis: Want to play a game? I have a couple in mind. Simon says or poker?

She stared at the screen. How he intended to make either of those things work, she didn't know. Her body stirred, anticipating whatever he had planned. Not even apart for forty-eight hours, and she wanted whatever he could give her.

May started typing her response, but the phone rang before she finished. Swiping up, she answered.

"What do you say, pixie?" Tavis's voice had a deep crooning lilt. The sound coaxed her body to relax.

"I'll play. But don't we need video for either of those games?" He'd already taken her to her most vulnerable point in the woods.

"No. I believe in the honour system." She heard rustling over the line.

"What are we going to play?" May fingered the soft ear on Mini-Tavis.

"I like Simon says."

Why did that not surprise her? Seeing how jovial he was at the wedding compared to the other Greer men, his domineering side in bed had been a bit of a shock. A good shock. "Do we both get a turn to be Simon?"

"I wouldn't have it any other way."

"All right."

"But I get to go first."

May laughed. "I wouldn't have it any other way."

"Good girl." He pulled in a deep, smooth breath. "Simon says, give Mini-Tavis a kiss."

May lifted the small stuffy and gave him a quiet kiss. She smiled while she did. The cheeky shifter made sure the first thing he asked her to do made a noise.

"Now, tuck him away for the night."

"I think I'll hold on to him." She pressed him to her chest and dropped her chin to rub against his softness.

"Smart girl. Simon says, tuck him away for the night."

"If I must." She put on a heaving sigh, setting Mini-Tavis on the other pillow.

"You must. Simon says so." Playful and demanding. Tavis was a fun mix, and that did things to her. "Ready for the next one, pixie?" His voice changed.

"Maybe." Her cheeks heated. Ridiculous. Even alone in her bedroom, she blushed with embarrassment. Tavis was a fun mix, but she was an odd one. Bold with his attention, but that never stopped her from being shy at the wrong moment.

"Simon says, take off your pajamas."

"And if I'm not wearing any?" Right there! Blushing to teasing. And her cheeks warmed while she purred through the phone line. What the hell was wrong with her?

"I think I'd call your bluff, pixie." Of course he would. "Am I right?"

"Yes."

"Take them off, May."

She pulled the phone away from her ear when he spoke up.

"Put me on speaker."

She froze. Was this a test?

"Sorry about that. Simon says, put me on speaker."

She laughed.

"Oh, that sounds lovely."

May put him on speaker and set the phone down beside her. Standing, she pulled the nightdress off.

"Are you wearing any panties?"

"No," she answered breathlessly. She wore one of three things to bed. Thin, stretchy nightdresses or pajamas and no underwear. Or only panties. It was a mood thing. When dressing for bed, she'd almost reached for underwear, feeling the need to have less. But she'd had Tavis on her mind and quickly made the opposite choice.

He groaned. "Simon says, lay on your back."

"You know? I've never done this before." May spread herself out in the middle of the bed.

"Simon says? Oh, I'm sure you played as a kid." His tone carried surprise.

"I'm not talking about the game."

"Ah, grown-up Simon says."

"That too." She laughed.

"You've never had phone sex before, pixie?" The teasing left his voice, and it dropped. May turned her head toward the phone.

"Have you?" As if she really wanted to know. She didn't like the idea of becoming jealous, yet she waited for his answer.

"No, I haven't. I'm having fun though. Are you?"

"Yeah, I'm good."

"Good. You in position?" The demanding alpha she'd quickly gotten to know appeared in those four words.

"Yes."

"Spread your knees for me."

She almost moved with the same easy obedience she'd given him while in Firebrook. May wondered if he left out the key-words on purpose or forgot in the moment.

His chuckle was her answer. "You didn't do it, did you?"

"No."

"Simon says, spread your knees."

The phone sat on the bed beside her. His voice wasn't the same through the speaker as it was in person. The technology-coated hum covered the best part of his tone. But it was enough to make her core clench as she did as he said and spread her knees, keeping her feet together in front of her.

"You're being a good girl, aren't you?"

Oh, shit. Why did he have to say something like that? Those shivers turned to heat and the flush in her cheeks spread. She couldn't answer him.

"I wish I could see you right now, pixie."

Did she? She tried to imagine him standing at the end of her bed. But that wasn't right. Instead, she put herself in his bed with him standing in front of her.

"Simon says, touch yourself. Wherever you want. Whatever feels good. And while you do, it's your turn."

What the hell? She was supposed to talk now? There was no way to hide what he made her feel if she had to play Simon.

May set her hand on her belly and moved it down. She tried to speak, but her mouth dried.

"Whenever you're ready, pixie."

Ah, hell.

Tavis wanted to strip, but he waited until he handed her the reins, giving her somewhere to start. Her little breaths made his cock already stand at attention. Not that it hadn't been halfway there the moment her first text message came through.

"Simon says," she paused, "take off your clothes."

He set the phone down and stripped. He didn't want her on speaker. Tavis wanted every single sound she made to be directly in his ear, as if she was there with him.

The next two weeks were going to be torture if they kept doing this.

"Done."

"Someone's a little eager." She sounded shy even though her words teased. It made her perfect for him. Her shy side let him take over, but she wasn't afraid to have fun. He wondered how much she opened up around others.

"You have no idea."

"Simon says, to..." A soft breath, and he imagined her tongue licking her lips for courage.

"You can do it."

"To wrap your hand around yourself," she finished.

It wasn't as good as her heat, but with her breathing in his ear, it helped. Tavis wanted to stroke, but again he waited, giving her the opportunity to take charge.

"Tavis, I can't. I can't tell you what to do."

"Need me to do it, pixie?"

"Yes," she pleaded.

"Are we done with the game?" Tavis didn't know if he could keep it up.

"Yes," she whimpered.

"Good. I was getting jealous of Simon."

May laughed, but breathless gasps escaped in between. She was doing exactly as he'd ordered, giving herself the pleasure he couldn't.

"Circle your clit, pixie. Make it feel good."

Tavis started his own rhythm. He didn't need much, keeping it light to last as long as she needed.

"Where are my hands? Where do you need me to touch?"

She wasn't much for talking and he needed her grounded in the moment and not overthinking.

"My... my... Tavis, can't you just..." The whine that came from her made him grin.

"No, May. Tell me." He hardened his voice. His bear coursed with excitement under his skin. The room was more focused, sharper.

"My breasts. Squeezing my nipples." He wouldn't only be using his hands. His mouth would be all over her.

"Do it."

Those soft breaths turned into harsh, sharp gasps. He closed his eyes to imagine everything about her. He'd ingrained the sight of her body in his memory. A thousand days could pass, and he'd never forget an inch.

"Are you wet for me?"

"Yes." Barely any sound came from her lips, but he made it out, anyway.

"Make yourself come, pixie. Don't hold back." Tavis talked her through it, not letting the sound of his voice drop, so she only focused on him and not on the fact she was alone in her apartment. "Don't put your fingers in too far. Save that for me. You're going to show me everything you're doing now the next time I see you. Imagining it isn't enough."

He moved his hand faster to match her panting.

"You're close, May. I wish I could taste you. I never knew I liked cherries so much."

Small moans escaped her, and then silence. She held her breath right before her release. And the sound of her soft cries pushed him over the edge.

"Fuck." He growled, spurting over his hand.

She still whimpered.

"Shh. Good girl, pixie."

"Tavis?"

"I know." He knew the loss and empty feeling she experienced. His room was cold without her body next to his. "Get under the blankets, pixie. Get some sleep."

"Two weeks, huh?" Rustling came over the phone and then her voice sounded clearer. "That's a long time."

"Tortuously long." His bear appeared in his voice.

"Goodnight, Tavis." Tiredness slowed her words. Tavis closed his eyes, wishing he could wrap his arms around her.

"Goodnight, May."

Chapter Seven

Not every night on the phone with Tavis had been that eventful. But the lonely feeling stretched further each night that passed. They talked about their days. He'd tell her about the lessons he taught, the excitement in the kids, or the obvious young love of couples taking their first trip together.

This last week before fall seemed hectic everywhere. She had a couple families contact her for last-minute family sessions. May gave them to Skye, letting her do them solo. Skye had been her shadow for a while now, and May planned to add her to her full-time team. Because she had a difficult time saying no when a customer called. If she said no, she'd still be the only photographer in her little business. Maybe by now, she would have learned balance and boundaries.

And she wouldn't have time to have lunch with Harlyn before her busy life took over her world, too. Although, May was running late.

When she made it to the restaurant and settled in her seat, Harlyn stared at her wide-eyed.

"What is it?" May ran her hands over her hair and clothes, feeling nothing out of place.

"You're pale."

May didn't feel ill, but exhaustion weighed on her. She wondered if it had to do with her distance from Tavis. But there wasn't any pain or sick feelings to make her believe it was the distance. She hadn't considered asking Tavis if he felt anything.

"Are you okay?"

"Yeah." May smiled, although unsure of herself. "I'm a little tired, I guess."

"It's because of the shifter, isn't it?" Harlyn leaned over the table, barely mouthing the words.

"No, of course not." She waved her hand through the air, but paused. "Maybe. But, no."

"That's convincing."

"I don't know. I didn't think there was anything wrong until you said something."

"You've been fine otherwise?"

"Yes." May missed Tavis and felt the separation anytime she slowed down for more than five minutes, but everything was fine. "What about you? School has started."

"I'm good. I was ready to get back to work. I missed the kids." Harlyn's lips twisted up into a smile, shy to her very core. But she made an excellent teacher. She might be shy and quiet, but she naturally commanded the respect from students that some teachers couldn't achieve without years of experience.

"Good. It will be a while before we can get together again like this."

Harlyn let out a snort.

"What?"

"We started out as four. Then," Harlyn waved her hands in front of her face, "shifters, and now there's two of us. It will soon be one. Dig in your heels and say you're staying here and keeping it all separate. Convince yourself you can handle it and because you're not fighting it, you'll be fine. But in the end, I'll be the only one left here."

"Harlyn." May reached across the table.

"I'm not saying that to sound upset. You three aren't rid of me, and I'm not rid of you. But I'm not wrong. You will end up living in Firebrook before the end of the year. Hell, I'd say the end of the month, but I've always expected you're more stubborn than any of us realize."

May blinked at her friend. Arguing was pointless, especially since there was a part of her that thought Harlyn was right. But it seemed wrong to leave her here now. What were the odds Fate chose three out of four friends as mates to shifters, all living in one small town? That Harlyn would be alone and find a normal love?

"Relax, May. I'm happy where I am. And you will be too."

The waitress came over, interrupting any reply. Not that May knew what to say to all of that.

Since May asked him several days ago if he was feeling the effects of their separation, Tavis had been paying more attention to his body. The tiredness he'd been attributing to the late nights talking to her on the phone. The muscle aches must be due to the extra runs in fur and the more advanced climbing lessons and tours. But once she asked, Tavis doubted his theories.

Tavis: Two more days, pixie. His hands itched to hold her. Things had slowed down as soon as school started. Although this was the time of year couples without families travelled. Retirement gave more freedom and destinations were quieter without large families. But everything slowed enough to move at a normal pace for them.

Firebrook always changed in some way each year. Sometimes, it was small. A kid grew up, and the community noticed because they start working with the public. Sometimes, it was big. Like Poppy. And Blair. The community was still on edge from the events of the summer. Meaning the recent additions to town weren't exactly welcome.

A new school principal and his wife. A retired couple looking to build a new home and live here. And a kid fresh out of school from the city, looking for work. Nothing to be afraid of. But everyone wanted to know what work the kid thought he'd find in a small town that he couldn't find in the city.

People were on edge. Not that he could blame them. Blair hadn't let it go, but feeling the unease of the community, she'd stopped actively asking questions and searching. She'd moved her work here, not travelling often yet, and made friends.

Tavis frowned at his phone. May rarely took this long to answer a message. Forcing out a sigh, he stuck his phone in his pocket and continued to work. The sidewalks were full of kids with too-large backpacks hanging on their backs being escorted to school by their parents. Teens pushed and teased each other as they moved around people. School had been in for over a week and still held the newness with excited kids. But that wouldn't last much longer.

He slowed as he approached *Rockhard*. Sweet cherries filled the air. He must miss her more than he thought. Doing a mental check, he searched for aches and pains, nausea. Still nothing more than exhaustion. Most mates experienced pain if they held off mating for too long. But this was still new for their kind. They didn't know everything.

Tavis tried to shake off the smell, but the closer he got to work, the stronger the scent was.

"That was two days too long."

He snapped his head up. May sat next to the locked door of *Rockhard*. Pushing on the wooden deck, she stood. He froze, lapping her up like a dream about to vanish. As if wakefulness hovered at the edges and he was about to lose his greatest desire.

"Tavis? It's okay I came early, right?"

Her uncertainty shook him. He charged toward her, wrapping his arms around her waist and lifting her against him to crash his lips against hers.

She met him with just as much force. If he didn't get them inside soon, this was going to go too far for public eyes. Fishing out his keys, he used one hand to unlock and open the door. He hadn't released her. It was impossible and unrealistic to ask him to do so.

May's hands clung to his shoulders and speared into his hair. She pulled herself up his body as he kicked the door shut, wrapping her legs around his waist. Her thighs squeezed him tight. He took them to the back office.

The need that swept through him shocked his system.

"Tavis. I don't know what's come over me."

"Shh, pixie. It's okay. I feel the same."

"Just don't stop."

"Never." The office door closed with a loud slam, and he pushed her back against it. His weight held her up, and he had more use of his hands to thrust them under her shirt. The first contact of her skin took his breath away. Their breath away. Her chest expanded and froze in place.

Bending his head, he kissed down her neck and into the swell of her breasts. Their collision had pulled the tank top down to expose more of her. The lace of her bra peeked out, covering what he wanted to taste. His mouth watered and heat filled his vision.

The slumbering bear beneath his skin was waking up, interested in what they were doing.

Pushing his hips harder against her to hold her, Tavis pulled her shirt up and kept pulling until it was off her and no longer in the way. Later, he might take the time to appreciate the deep green lace over her breasts, but not right now. He took that off her too and bent his head.

She finally breathed as he latched onto one nipple.

"I'm sorry. I didn't come here for this. Like this."

He nipped, making her whimper. "Don't apologize. Neither of us is in control right now. Just take it, pixie." Lifting his head, he kissed her, running his tongue along hers before moving back down her chest to her other nipple.

He needed to get them off the door. Tavis turned the lock and carried her to the desk. He had enough forethought not to spread her out. There was too much covering the surface, and he didn't feel like replacing a computer. But there were large armchairs on the opposite side.

Using the edge of the desk, Tavis undid her shorts and pulled, taking her panties with them.

"Mmm, just the way I like you, pixie."

She pulled at the waist of his pants. "Not fair." Her fingers fumbled. She had less control than him.

Tavis tore at his own clothes. Round eyes devoured every move he made and his bear lapped up the attention. Appreciative rumbles moved through his chest. May's tongue moved back and forth over her lips. It was tempting to take her mouth, but he needed her heat more.

Setting his hands on her hips, he pulled her against him and sat back in the chair in one motion. She straddled him. Throwing her head back, she moaned as she pushed her hips down, trapping his cock between them.

"Fuck, pixie."

"Please. Please, Tavis."

He took himself in hand, lining himself up to her entrance. She tried to push herself onto him, but he squeezed her hip.

"Look at me."

Soft lashes fluttered open as she dropped her chin.

"I want to see your eyes when I take you." Tavis loosened his grip on her hip and let her sink down on him.

Her cry was both torture and a balm. She moved too slowly for him. With his hands on her hips, he met her thrust for thrust. The slapping of their hips echoed off the walls of the small room.

The main door opened and shut, cutting through the haze enough to make them pause.

"Tavis?" Noah called from the front.

Panic filled May's face, but he only grinned and wrapped his arm around her waist. Standing, he took them to the opposite side of the room and pushed her back against the wall.

The knob on the office door jiggled.

Tavis slid his hand up May's neck and over her mouth. Her body melted, and he put pressure against her before moving his hips. He fucked her against the wall, not worrying about the sounds their bodies made, only keeping their moans silent.

"Ah, fuck." His brother cursed from the other side of the door, then left. The front door shook the building as it closed behind him.

Tavis didn't give May time to be embarrassed that his brother heard them. The moment the door shut, he hammered into her.

This hadn't been her plan. May hadn't expected to feel the sudden rush of heat upon seeing him. Her veins burned and tingled all the way to her fingertips. And the moment he touched her, kissed her, it all exploded.

She felt energized. It was a shock to her system after almost two weeks of feeling exhausted and overwhelmed. Harlyn may have been right.

Tavis nipped along her neck while grinding against her with every push inside. She could have come from the first moment if she'd let herself. But May forced the need away to make it last. She never wanted this to end. If it ended, she'd have to return to the city, away from him, away from this feeling of rightness and home. If it ended, reality would burst through the door to drag her down.

"You're thinking too hard, pixie. Let go."

"I don't want to."

"I know. Let go anyway. It's all right."

How did he know she needed those words? Needed the soothing reassurance in his voice?

"I'm not letting you go, pixie." Did he mean physically or figuratively? Would he try to keep her in Firebrook when she tried to leave?

The panic inside her warred with itself. Both leaving and staying caused the sensation to boil out of control.

"Damn it, May." He thrust inside her and held himself there, pinning her to the wall. "Look at me."

She hadn't realized she'd closed her eyes. His eyes were level with hers, but they weren't his own. They glowed with that of the animal inside him. He moved his hand holding her up under her ass inward so his thumb rested over her clit.

"Just come for me. That's all I want right now. To feel your heat clamp down around me, to feel your wetness gush from your core. I want to hear you cry out in ecstasy. Right now is the only thing that is important. That's it. Just this moment. Give it to me, pixie. Come." He circled the sensitive bundle of nerves and moved his hips just enough for her to feel it, but not enough to drop her. He stayed firmly in control.

The tension ate away at the panic. Sensations thrived through her muscles once again.

"That's it. Come, now."

She did, her thighs shaking at his sides. Once the spasms slowed, Tavis resumed his grip on her ass and moved. Sharp teeth ran along the column of her neck and she stilled. The explosion of her orgasm found new life, and her mind was finally blissfully blank.

And as he roared, exploding inside her, she came again, crying out.

She came to on his lap in the chair where they started.

"Welcome back." Tavis's voice was hoarse near her ear. His hands stroked over her arm and back, bringing life into her body. Warmth covered her skin, and she noticed how sensitive she was. This aftermath was new. Not only the cuddling in the chair after blacking out—that was a little unsettling—but the way her skin had new sparks of life with his touch.

May lifted her head and opened her mouth to speak.

"Don't worry. It's only been a few minutes."

She sighed and settled her head back under his chin. The hair on his chest tickled her nose. Settling her hand there, she played with the coarse strands. The sound of their heartbeats blanketed them, and May didn't know where to go from here.

"As much as I want to whisk you back to my house and spend the day buried inside you, I can't. I crammed a lot in these two days so I'd be free when you got here."

"Sorry."

"No. Never apologize for showing up. I want you here. Always. As long as it doesn't mean your time here ends two days earlier?" Tavis lifted her chin and looked down at her. His expression almost looked like a warning.

"It doesn't."

"Thank fuck." He bent his head and kissed her, supping at her lips until her core throbbed.

A throat cleared on the other side of the door. May pulled away, but Tavis only had a grin as he helped her stand. She hadn't heard Noah come back inside.

Tavis helped find her clothes, passing them to her as she needed them. While she maneuvered her bra, he dressed himself.

But he didn't let her near the door without pulling her against him one last time to devour her mouth. His hands held her waist in a firm grip. He growled when he lifted his head.

"I'll call you when I'm done with work."

"Okay. I'm sure I can keep myself busy until then."

When Tavis opened the door, his brother stood on the other side with his arms crossed over his chest. Tavis only laughed and slapped him on the back as he pulled May past him and out the front door. One more kiss, a chaste one as customers waited, and he let go of her hand.

May breathed deep to pull in the mountain air. She needed it to ground herself after being swept away and left dizzy. If she stood for too long, the panic that tried to seize her while Tavis took her against the wall would resurface. It bubbled behind her ribs. Like a phrase on the tip of the tongue but never connecting to the brain. She didn't want that panic to gain roots in her system. The perfect distraction stood across the street from her. Hands on her hips and an expression May missed.

Chapter Eight

"You're early." Blair pointed a finger at May as she stepped onto the sidewalk after crossing the street. She blinked and lifted her chin. "And you smell like sex."

"Thanks," she said dryly. May forgot that mates gain some of the enhanced abilities of the shifters. She tried not to take the comment personally, knowing that the average person wouldn't be able to determine what she'd just done in the back office of *Rockhard Bears*.

"Couldn't last two more days?" Blair had a hint of smugness in her tone, but there was concern in her eyes as she hooked arms and steered May toward *Bella's Bakery*.

"I finished what I needed early. And then didn't sleep much last night."

"Wait." Blair stopped them and looked at her watch. "You just got here this morning? You must have left at four a.m."

May didn't answer her. She shrugged and urged them forward again.

"I'm meeting Clara for coffee. She won't mind at all that you're joining us."

"Thanks for the invite." May kept her dry tone. Blair had a way of demanding without making it sound like an order.

"Of course."

May held back her grin, but leaned her head on her friend's shoulder. "I may have been crazy busy the past two weeks, but I still had time to miss you."

"We miss you, too. And Harlyn." The 'we' she referred to were her and Poppy. May had no doubt the two of them experienced the same loss as May and Harlyn.

Clara waved from a seat inside the big bay window at the front of the bakery. Clara had been caught in the middle of a couple of villains intent on killing Blair. This town had experienced a summer of murders and mysteries that they were still trying to solve. They had used poor Clara as bait to lure Blair out to a cliff.

May knew how difficult it must be for Blair to let it go without all the answers, but for the sake of the town and for Clara, she had. Oh, her friend still mulled it over in the quiet of her own home and the noise of her own mind. She'd give it a break, but someday, she'd start digging for answers again. The people that knew her well were just watching and waiting.

"Blair. Miss Preston." Officer Henry Coates met them at the entrance to the bakery and held the door open for them. May had met him at the wedding, and recognized how much of an integral part he played in the community. How much he cared. His eyes were deep, with several laugh lines and creases. This man loved with his whole being.

But he was also one of the people waiting for Blair to snap. The glare he sent her was sharp enough to sting. But Blair didn't let it bother her.

"Thank you, Henry." She beamed up at the officer. The two of them seemed to have a love-hate thing going on. May bit her lip to hide her amusement.

"Good morning." She added her own greeting and followed Blair into the bakery.

"Hi, Clara. You remember May, don't you? From the wedding?"

"I do. It's nice to see you again."

"You, too."

May felt a bit like a third wheel for the first half of their conversation. Nothing could replace the friendship the four of them had, but May saw the new life Blair built here. That Poppy built here. As the feeling of being left behind crept up, May considered her business, her clients, her assistants. She had her life shaping into a new form without her friends, too.

"How long are you here for, May?" Her name brought her out of her melancholy thoughts. She blinked at Clara.

"About a week." May hated giving an end date she didn't want to exist. But it had to. There was a way to find a balance between her business and home and her mate.

"Oh, that's great news. You'll be here for the community fall festival. We always gather photos from locals to put together images for marketing and for families to share, but having an actual photographer take over would be amazing. Do you want to do it?"

"Absolutely." May didn't have to think twice about it. This place would put on spectacular events.

"I'm so excited. Can I have your number? I'll talk with the rest of the board and get you all the details. They'll be as excited as I am."

May took Clara's phone and typed in her number. Clara took it back and almost instantly, May's phone buzzed from her purse.

"Sadly, I have to go. I promised my nephew I'd volunteer for his art class today at school."

"Tell Kellan I say hi." Blair smiled as Clara stood, sending them both a little wave.

"You're happy here." May turned in her seat to face Blair once Clara was out the door.

"I am. I didn't think I would be. My work was my life and that meant travelling and being in the heart of it all."

"I've been listening. Your show has changed." Blair's podcast, *Blariable,* was all her own, but she always reported every detail she found, no matter which way it turned the scales. And all with her dashing personality splashed on top.

"In a good way?" Blair's squeak held both hope and fear.

"I think so." May added confidently.

"I've been worried, but my audience has grown. I'm just not sure if they're all waiting for the conclusion about what happened here." Blair reported it all on her show, but in a way that made it sound like authorities weren't looking for more. No one wanted to tip off the big boss of it all that they were still watching and waiting. Scott and Luca hadn't been the mastermind behind it all. They'd worked for someone. And that someone hadn't gotten what he'd been looking for.

Now, Blair's podcast included more direct interviews with people of interest after the fact. And for those that weren't comfortable making themselves public, she turned a show into a silent interview. They were the most interesting to listen to. It was like she had a conversation with herself.

"I'm still travelling some. I don't want to abandon everything I've done."

"Naturally. I'm just glad you're happy."

"You could be too." Blair said, while tilting her head. Her normal powerful impression wasn't there. Those four words were as genuine as Blair could be.

"That isn't my doubt. I've built *MayBe You Photography* from the ground up. And it bloomed into something more than I imagined. Besides, there's Nonna, and I never imagined settling down so soon."

"Settling down?" Blair laughed loud enough to draw the attention of Bonnie behind the counter. "A life mated to a shifter is anything but *settling down*."

"You know what I mean."

"Can't say I do. Do you think Tavis will make you give up your business and become a pretty housewife or something?"

"No..." May stuttered, but no reasonable response surfaced. That sounded ridiculous. She deflated against the seat.

"Nonna is strong for her age. And she wouldn't want you to sacrifice your life for her." She sighed. "Come on." Blair pulled her up. "Let's go bug Poppy. They got back last night and I've heard through the vine that she's already arguing with Mack at the bar." A wicked gleam entered her eyes as she steered them out of the bakery. "Later, Bonnie!"

"See you later, Blair. Nice to have you back, May." Bonnie waved from behind the counter, then turned back to her customer.

May didn't like the feeling of being wrong. She wasn't wrong about the need to balance what was hers. Except she was afraid she might be.

Tavis was in the best mood he'd had in the past two weeks. His mate was here and her taste was on his tongue and her scent covered his body. He hadn't imagined the odd looks people threw his way, knowing there was idiotic joy frozen on his face.

He needed her and counted down the seconds until he could take her home, fuck her again, then take her out to dinner. At lunch, Tavis sent a message to Caiden and asked for a table. His cousin's restaurant wasn't always overcrowded with a long wait, but things could change fast. He was a damn good chef, and he'd created an amazing place.

And Tavis felt the need to take his mate out on a date. He'd also called May after making the reservation and told her the door to his house was unlocked, and that it would be a good idea for her to meet him there.

On his way home, he saw Herb loading the back of his truck with lumber. The man was replacing one of their rental cabins. Tavis crossed the street and ran around the other side of his truck to lift.

Herb blinked. "Oh, thank you, Tavis."

"Not a problem, Herb. Do you have much demolition to do on the old one before kicking off the new?" Tavis bent his knees and took more of the weight as they pushed.

"More than I wanted. And I'm eager to get it done before the snow hits."

"Of course. You call if you need a hand." Tavis pulled up another few pieces, letting Herb take the other side.

"Thank you. Appreciate it. Might even take you up on it."

Tavis doubted that, but he'd be watching and would step in when he needed it. "Have a good night, Herb." He whistled as he walked away, continuing on to his house. Images of May waiting for him assaulted his vision.

She was here for a week. And even now he knew it wasn't long enough, but Tavis refused to let that bring down his mood. He had another busy day tomorrow before he'd scheduled time off with her, so he intended to enjoy tonight.

When he walked into his home, he heard the shower running. The air smelled like an orchard full of cherries after the rain. Damn, she was delicious. And in a perfectly vulnerable position for him to take advantage.

After stripping in his bedroom, he slipped into the bathroom. Steam clouded his vision, and he breathed deep. He let the hum his bear made under his skin rumble through his chest. May's gasp was as satisfying as he'd hoped for.

"Tavis, you..."

"Shh." Stepping into the shower, he crowded her under the water. "Don't talk."

After strumming her clit until she barely breathed, he turned her around and leaned her back against the tile. Dropping to his knees, Tavis licked and nipped the sensitive flesh. Her fingers speared into his hair. He made it his sole mission to worship her from down here, bringing her to the quickest climax he could.

He added two fingers, pushing them deep, and she exploded.

As much as Tavis wanted to bend her forward and bury himself, he couldn't. Since stopping to help Herb, they had little time before their reservation. Standing, he pulled her against him, letting her rest her head against his chest. Her eyes stayed closed while he washed them both. When he turned off the water, she lifted her head.

"Hello to you too."

"Hi, pixie."

They were slow to get out of the shower and dress. But the time passed with no words, only looks, grins, and kisses. It was comfortably perfect.

It had been a good idea to make the reservation. When they got to the restaurant, there was a line waiting inside the front door. The waitress recognized Tavis and gestured for him to follow her. He set his hand on the small of May's back and let her go first. She wore jeans that were snug over her ass and hips, but moved with her. Her top was soft and only reached her waist, covering the button of her jeans.

Tavis held her chair for her.

The waitress left the menus with a smile and quickly brought over water while they looked at their decisions. Not that Tavis didn't have his cousin's menu memorized, but he checked for any changes or new dishes while May looked it over.

"You already know what you're having, don't you?"

"Caiden's fish chowder. He sources sockeye salmon from British Columbia and a few others from their coast to add more flavours. It's damn good."

May set her menu down on the table with her hand on top of it. "Sounds perfect."

"Did you have a good day?"

"I did. The town officially hired me to do the photography for the fall festival this week."

"That's exciting."

"It is. I love those sorts of events. There's so much opportunity for something different, to extend my creativity, and get a sense of the heart of a place. Not that I didn't already get that from Poppy and Wyatt's wedding. This will be different, though."

"It will."

"Do you and Noah do anything special for it?"

"We donate a free lesson to the auction. Depending on turnout and interest, we might add a second one at the last minute. Some years are better than others, but it's always a good time."

"Where does the money go from the auction?"

"Usually the school and the library. Helps kids have better field trips, events, and material for school-wide experiments. And it helps keep as many things available at the library free. However, if there's a family currently in need for whatever reason, a house fire, tragic accident—the money often finds its way to them."

"That's wonderful." May's smile was soft and her eyes darkened. "What an amazing place to live."

"It is." He wished she saw herself here. But Tavis didn't know what she thought about moving. If it was ever a possibility in her mind. He'd wait as long as he knew that someday she'd live here with him. This wasn't the time to bring it up. As much as he burned to ask.

But their conversation wasn't lost on her. Her lips tightened, and she offered an apologetic smile, but no explanation. The waitress arrived.

Tavis gestured to May for her to place her order—fish chowder and a salad. He ordered his chowder, two baked potatoes, a side of onion rings, and a salad. May's eyes bugged out, then she laughed. The waitress left, not thinking anything about the amount of food. There were enough of them that ate like that. No one batted an eye anymore.

Tavis winked. "Takes a lot to feed a bear."

May felt the pull. The moment she stepped into town. The pull to move here, live with Tavis, and rebuild her business base from here. Rebuilding terrified her. But the urge became a vibrant, breathing thing inside her.

Tavis only multiplied it. Seeing him. Feeling him. His touch and his demands. Damn. Harlyn, Blair, and anyone else she'd let speak to her on the topic were right. The feeling of home in the city faded, and she hadn't realized it until she breathed in this air.

May hadn't expected the night to end any other way than it did. Throughout the laughs they shared over funny tales from work and family, the tension grew between them until it pulled tight enough to snap the moment they stepped outside. They didn't even make it back to Tavis's house before he had to park on the side of the road and pull her on top of him.

The need to pay him back for his torture in the shower crawled through her. The moment she pulled back from his grasp, he looked at her with a frown. And so much worry in his eyes. He had to have sensed the sliver of hesitation winding through her.

May had only smiled and undid his fly to bend over and take him into her mouth. She worked him like he'd worked her.

And when they made it back to his bed, they repeated everything they'd done from the moment they met the day of the wedding. Deliciously sinful, heating and throbbing, and comfortable. May still blushed through most of it.

Now, neither of them slept, but they laid together, spent and dazed. With her head on his chest, he traced her hip with the tips of his fingers.

May sensed the words that needed to come out. It was why neither of them had spoken. Emotions were high after everything they just did to each other. But she couldn't comfort him. She had none for herself.

Moving here seemed like giving up on everything she'd built. All from the ground up, starting with a single camera and free editing software. Then it all blew up from there—not in a bad way. She had clients crawling out of the woodwork. Repeat bookings before the first session was over. She had requests for things she'd never done, but without those requests, she wouldn't have grown into a multi-directional business. *MayBe You Photography* took on so many faces.

Would she have to give that all up? Even changing things would change what she was. And that felt like failure. Her business was still so new. A change like that could risk it all.

"I won't like what you're thinking, will I?"

"You don't need to know what I'm thinking right now. And I imagine I could say the same about your thoughts."

Tavis let a heavy sigh out of his lungs, his chest moving beneath her head and his breath blowing the hair on the top of her head. "I guess you're right."

"How about this? We tell each other our thoughts, but not until the end of the week."

"That doesn't sound like a good idea."

"The alternative is to risk that conversation ruining this visit. No matter how that conversation goes, I still have to go back at the end of the week. I have sessions, appointments, and so much more waiting for me."

Tavis's other arm came down from under his head. He set his fingers under her chin and pulled her head up. She loved it when he touched her like that. Worries melted away when he took that control.

"I need this week with you as much as you need it with me." May searched his eyes, his features absent of his always jovial nature.

He nodded. "Okay, pixie. We'll wait." The corners of his lips lifted and his eyes darkened. "Whatever are we going to do in the meantime?"

"Sleep. We should definitely sleep." It wasn't a lie, but her core stirred under his gaze.

"We will. Eventually."

Chapter Nine

T he last thing Tavis scheduled before May's planned arrival was the grades five and six classes from the school. They did this several times a year for different grades, leaving a few days open to devote to the kids. He and Noah worked as a team, rotating kids through stations.

Which meant he'd left May asleep in his bed. He'd kissed her from behind her ear and down her neck until she moaned in her sleep. But she still didn't wake. He'd worn her out. With a smile on his face, he'd left her a note and went to work. Although he wasn't as successful as he'd hoped, pushing aside their *non-conversation* until later in the week.

The new school principal, Duke Greyson, came into the office. He pushed his glasses up his nose and smiled at both of them.

"Good morning." He stuck his hand out to each of them across the counter.

"Morning." Tavis said while shaking. Noah only nodded as they shook hands.

"Kids are all here and eager. Is there anything you need from me before we get started?"

"Nope. We've got it all covered. We already did all the paperwork at the beginning of the school year." Tavis started out from behind the counter. "We do this every year, so we've learned to have it all done early. Saves lots of headaches."

"I can see that. So you've taught these kids before?"

"Some. We start with grade five for lessons. But we do some fun things with the younger ones in the school during the winter months."

"I'm learning things are very different in a small community."

Tavis only smiled, and Noah grunted behind him. His brother saved his mesmerizing personality for the kids.

The teachers stood with their students, already separating them into the groups they knew would work best together. Volunteering parents stood with the groups as chaperones. Duke chose one group that only had one parent to stand with.

"Welcome, everyone." Tavis let his voice boom over all the chatter. They quieted and turned his way.

"You need to teach me how to do that." One teacher pinched her lips and shook her head.

Tavis smiled. His voice wasn't something anyone could learn, only gained through a certain genetic trait that ran in his family. "Some of you have done this before and for some, this is your first time. We're going to go over all the stations and all the rules first. Moan and groan and we'll do it all twice." He raised his brows at some of the kids he suspected would be a bit more difficult. "Safety is important. No safety, no climbing. That simple."

The kids all stood a little straighter. Good. They had their attention.

Tavis clapped his hands. "Let's do it." He winked and started directing groups to the different stations they'd set up. Some things were easy enough to allow the teachers and chaperones to handle, like learning the equipment with games and a quiz. The students that had done this before only had to go through a couple of those stations before moving on to either Tavis or Noah.

It always amazed him the way kids gravitated to his grumpy brother. Noah held their rapt attention with every word.

They'd done this enough, that the stress vanished years ago. Accidents happened and kids were kids. They taught and led by example for the young minds of their home. And they felt they succeeded.

Lunch was a welcome break for everyone. The principal sat with them at one of the many tables they had situated outside. Two kids were about to sit with them, but then curled their noses and changed direction. From what Tavis observed, the kids didn't mind the new guy, but who wanted to sit with the principal at lunch? Tavis hid his grin.

"When you said you had everything handled, you weren't lying."

"Not our first rodeo." Those were the first words Noah spoke to the guy.

He blinked behind his glasses. "Clearly. I'm impressed."

Tavis took a minute to look over the heads, seeing if anyone wasn't enjoying themselves. Some kids didn't take to climbing like others. But they always tried to make sure they enjoyed some part of the day.

"You two seem to know all the children well."

"We grew up with some of their parents. Or their parents' siblings. Everyone knows everyone's business."

"I'd always thought that was an exaggeration about small towns."

"Nope." Noah said before biting into his massive sandwich. Tavis frowned. Something about it was too straight for his brother to have made it. Blair had a little more time on her hands lately without as much travelling for work.

Would that happen to May? Lose half her work and become idle? Was that what scared her? Tavis couldn't say he liked the sound of it either. That wasn't fair to either of them. He made a note to bring it up to Noah later. He'd hate to see a festering rift take over his brother's relationship.

"Why are you staring?" Noah set the sandwich down.

Tavis shook himself from his thoughts. "It's nothing." Nothing he could bring up while sitting with the new guy in town or surrounded by a few dozen kids.

He paused. Something tickled his nose over the scent of food. Looking up, he saw his mate walking toward them, her camera bag hanging on her shoulder.

"Firebrook seems to have some sort of grapevine that can reach anyone it needs to and ask favours. My camera and skills were requested for the climbing lessons, if that's okay."

Tavis reached up and took her hand, pulling her down to sit next to him. "It's more than okay." He leaned down and gave her a soft kiss, aware of the gazes from Noah and the principal.

Even that soft touch ignited embers in her core, but she was here on a job and forced herself to look away just as he did. Her smile faded as she saw the other person sitting at the table. Duke Greyson, the school principal. The one who ran into her car before she'd left town after the wedding. The man whose insurance had been impossible to contact. After a week, she'd paid for the repairs herself and let the hassle die behind her, thankful to be in a position where that sort of expense didn't break her anymore.

"Hello. I'm Duke Greyson, the school principal." He stuck his hand across the table and introduced himself, oblivious to who she was.

"We've met." May gave his memory time to adjust.

His lips twisted in thought. "I'm sorry. I'm new to town and it's taking me some time to recognize everyone."

May pulled in a deep, but slow, breath, ensuring he didn't recognize it as the frustration that it was. "I'm not from here either. We met two weeks ago when you ran into my car going around a corner." She hoped the grin on her face appeared soft and not tight with irritation. *Let it go, May. You didn't want the hassle before. No need to let it get to you now.*

"Oh. Right. Again, I'm so sorry. I hope my insurance took care of everything?"

Don't rock the boat. Just let it go. If I say something, it will stir the pot and it's already over. Nope, not happening. "Actually, my insurance company couldn't get a hold of them. Or you."

"That's so strange." His mouth moved, as if unsure what he should do, clearly not wanting to do anything. Yeah, she shouldn't have said anything.

"Looks like everyone is almost done lunch. I'm going to get my camera ready." She placed a kiss on Tavis's cheek and left.

She started by snapping a few fun pictures of kids at the tables as well as the teachers and parents. So many moms asked for family shoots. The one behind the camera was always the mom. That needed to change. So when May could help in that way, she did.

A few minutes later, she heard Tavis call out. She'd heard that deep rumble before, but only with his bear close to the surface. It worked. Everyone, child and adult, quieted and looked toward him. None of them recognized the command in him. But it sent shivers down her spine. Such inappropriate timing.

Pinching her lips together, she listened to him give the groups directions for the afternoon. Everyone cleaned up and moved into place. May stayed on the sidelines and waited. Her job wasn't to get in the way and put people in places for pictures. It all turned out best when no one paid her any attention. Blending into the background like a fly on the wall, snapping special moments.

The afternoon was warm, and she soon ditched her sweater. Moving from group to group, May quietly circled. Once in a while, she'd tell them to wrap arms around each other or make silly faces. The kids didn't disappoint. And neither did the teachers. Even the principal seemed like a fun guy. But the parents? They were always harder nuts to crack.

She spent most of her time with Tavis and Noah's groups. The action shots would turn out great. And she was selfish enough to take a few of Tavis on his own. Damn, that was a nice ass. While she wouldn't admire Noah's ass in the same way, she did her best friend a favour and took some of her mate too.

The end of the school day happened before anyone was ready. But of course, Tavis and Noah had everything planned perfectly. They'd been winding the groups down for the end of the day without the kids even noticing.

With backpacks and smiles, the kids filed out in pairs to get on the two buses waiting for them.

Duke stopped in front of her before following the last of the teachers onto the bus. "I'm sorry my insurance company didn't respond. I guess I need to shop around. Please let me make this right and reimburse you for the repairs."

While the situation irritated her, she had to hand it to the guy. He tried to do the decent thing. "The apology and the offer are enough. Thank you. It's all taken care of and over." She thought her smile was a little warmer this time.

"As long as you're sure? You're a better person than I." He followed the others onto the bus.

She felt Tavis's heat behind her, and his breath near her ear. "You never told me you had issues with his insurance." His tone almost sounded like a warning, as if there would be retribution later.

"I let it go. I was too busy to dwell on it. My priority had been getting work done to come back here." She sweetened her voice to counter the warning.

"Smooth, pixie." She felt his lips lift into a smile against her neck. "Guess I can't fault that logic."

"You two go. I've got clean up." Noah started stacking chairs.

Tavis sighed. "Not a chance." He turned May to face him. "I won't be long. Meet you at my place?"

She winced.

"What is it?"

"Poppy wants to have dinner and a girls' night."

"Go. But call me when you're done, pixie."

"Guess I'll be without my mate tonight, too," Noah grumbled, but it still reached them. Tavis chuckled and released her.

By the time she got to Poppy's, they already had the wine open and a tray of shots waiting on the counter. May's eyes bugged, and she looked at her watch. "It's not even four!"

"We're making up for a lost summer." Poppy stuck something in the oven. "And I've already been talking to Harlyn. I hate that she's not here too, but she's coming up during Christmas vacation. And so are you." Poppy turned around. "If you aren't already living here." She mumbled the last words behind unmoving lips.

The unspoken conversation from the night before reared its head. Snatching a shot, she dropped it down her throat, then poured herself a glass of wine.

Blair blinked at her. "We were saving those for after dinner."

"Oops." The alcohol burned away the need to open up to her two friends before she was ready. But part of her wondered if she'd cut off her nose to spite her face.

The last-minute plans of their mates drove them all to *Poppy Mack's*. Mack stood behind the bar, glaring at all the new staff Poppy insisted on hiring. It wasn't a secret that he didn't enjoy having extra people around, but Tavis wondered at the real reason behind his frowning and grumbling. Mack might have been a lonely man when Poppy stormed in here, but he wasn't mean.

The four Greer shifters sat at a table near the back, closer to the refinished pool tables. Caiden had shown up last, having gone home from the restaurant to find his mate gone. Checking his phone, he'd discovered he'd missed her messages and calls. He didn't look happy about the change in his plans as he plunked down in the chair.

Wyatt, of course, looked as happy as a man should after coming home from his honeymoon.

"How often do you suppose this is going to happen?" Noah returned from the bar, balancing four glasses in his hands.

"Every time May *visits*." Caiden glared at Tavis.

"Cool your burners, big guy. I have no control over this." Before anyone said he did, he pointed at both Wyatt and Noah. "Don't you dare say I do. You let your mate leave and didn't chase her, and yours basically gave you the finger when you told her she was moving in with you." He didn't drag Caiden's relationship into this. His had been a little more complicated. Maggie didn't have an easy past to deal with.

"Have you talked?" Wyatt, the calm one of the family, spoke low.

"No, but we've made a deal to talk about it before she leaves. Just not until the week is over."

Caiden kept his mouth shut and took a drink. Noah spat his back into his glass, and Wyatt breathed in a whistle.

"I don't need the lectures. It's a bad idea, and I told her that. I know what I want and what I'm willing to give up for it."

Three sets of eyes bore into him while he studied the ale fizzing in his glass. The idea had been circling in the back of his mind all day, never quite reaching the surface, but he recognized what it meant. He wasn't willing to leave Firebrook permanently, but if May wouldn't move here, he'd try to compromise, offering seasonal living. Live in the city half the year and Firebrook the other, or some other similar arrangement.

His bear hated the idea, but he hated the idea of losing his mate altogether even more. Visits like this wouldn't be enough.

"I'm only talking a compromise, guys. Relax. Besides, it's a last resort and I haven't done anything more than consider it." He'd done barely that. What Tavis needed most was May.

He'd known where she was all afternoon while taking pictures of the kids. And him. He loved watching her work. Something in her brightened. The light in her broke free behind the camera. They'd use the pictures she took on the school website and in the yearbook. With permission from the parents, they'd also use some pictures for *Rockhard Bears* and tourism.

The heart behind the camera made the pictures that good. He'd seen that same passion during the wedding, the first time he took her home, and in the woods at the river. Yet again, Fate wasn't wrong. And he didn't think May believed Fate was wrong, either.

Tavis downed his beer. Sometimes it sucked that the alcohol didn't work on shifters, but then again, he'd hate to see a drunk shifter.

"I don't need to discuss my relationship with my mate. Instead, let's all ask the idiot who can't stop smiling how his honeymoon went."

"A lot of time alone."

"You mean fucking," Caiden interrupted.

Wyatt ignored his brother. "A lot of time alone, in the cottage, on the beach, rooftop dinners."

"Romantic fucking." Caiden cracked a smile over his glass before taking a drink.

Wyatt sighed. "Fine. A lot of fucking. Romantic fucking. But without nosy, well-meaning neighbors, brothers, or cousins."

They teased each other for another ten minutes and another round of beer before claiming one of the pool tables.

Years ago, when Mack's bar was still booming with only him managing the place, the four of them often played pool here. It was nice to come back to this. Mack's had been looking sad before Poppy came. The man refused to close, but also refused to do anything to bring the place back to life. The locals made sure he had enough business to stay afloat, but much longer and that wouldn't have been enough. Somehow, Poppy got through to him, and now this place thrived once again.

Henry and some of his officers filled one booth. Newly turned eighteen-year-olds sat at the bar. Coworkers and friends formed groups all over. Couples enjoyed a night out without the kids, using the dart boards Poppy convinced Mack to set up to the left of the pool tables.

A group of teachers played at the other pool table, celebrating getting through the first few weeks of school. Duke was with them, his arm around a woman Tavis had seen but not met. The matching rings on their left hands suggested his wife. Tavis kept his glare to himself, turning around to take a drink, so he didn't draw attention to his dislike of the other man. It was childish, which was why Tavis needed to tamp it down.

"Your bear's growling," Noah murmured next to him.

"Don't mind him." Tavis bent to the table and lined up his next shot. The balls made the cracking sound as they collided and Tavis sunk the eight ball before he should have. "Fuck."

"I think we're needed at the lodge." Noah grinned at his phone. Wyatt and Poppy lived above the main lodge of *Bearbrook Cabins*. Where they all went for their girls' night.

Noah turned his phone around to show them the pictures he'd received from Blair. Five drunk faces filled the small screen and they had taken the last few images as they fell over, laughter shooting to the ceiling. The text in the messages read like complete nonsense.

They all put down their cue sticks where they stood and moved to the door. Tavis felt his nerves fire. He wasn't sure what he'd find when he got there. But knowing he'd see his mate was enough to heat his veins.

Chapter Ten

Her head buzzed. It felt fuzzy and furry which was comfortable rather than acting like a proper filter for her mouth.

"You aren't the only who has fucked in the woods." Poppy pointed her glass at May.

"Nah." Blair waved her hand, her eyes fluttering closed for a moment.

"Nope." Maggie said with a pop over the rim of her glass.

"Hell, I don't even have to be with a shifter to have fucked someone in the woods." Dakota, Wyatt and Caiden's sister, laughed.

Everything May hadn't wanted to discuss came out. She told them her worries about leaving Nonna, her fears over her business and needing to find the balance rather than uprooting everything. She received raised brows from Poppy and Blair for that comment, but she knew they understood. They'd both struggled with the same thing.

Dakota needed a moment to prepare herself before the deeper, dirtier discussion took place. Humming to herself, shaking her head, and muttering "I am not a Greer. I am not a Greer," had been enough for her to listen to the things no one should about their relatives. Only a few times had she visibly cringed.

"You don't want to go home, do you?" Blair leaned over, holding herself up with one hand.

"That's the thing, I do." May's voice pelted out with urgency, but none of the other drunk women around her blinked.

Poppy stood and moved closer to May. "The logical part of you. Not your heart." She plopped down on the other side of her, a few drops of wine escaping the glass.

"No. My heart too." But they weren't wrong either. Her heart also wanted to stay here, as did the logical side of her. Why couldn't balance be easy? She had good balance. She could stand on one foot.

As if the analogy controlled her movements, May stood. Concentrating, she lifted one foot and set it up against her thigh as high as she could get it.

"See? Balance is easy." As long as she didn't allow her gaze to drift away from the lamp on the other side of the room.

The door opened, sending heads swinging, including her own. May wobbled, one arm flailing, the other trying to steady her glass. She ended with her foot behind her and in some sort of surfer's pose.

"I'm a pro." She sent a pointed look at the other women, but when she turned it on the amused faces of the shifters walking in the room, it lost its power.

And she lost her breath as she caught sight of Tavis coming in last and shutting the door. Though he had a smile on his face, his eyes had a haunted glow. He'd heard her. Capturing his gaze, she knew. He heard her say her heart wanted to leave.

"Wow. The atmosphere in here just changed drastically." Dakota whistled and stood to take her glass to the kitchen. "I'm out. I can't look any of you in the face until I've been sober for three days and then drunk one more time."

The men frowned, but the women giggled. Evil giggles. Not May. She couldn't stop looking at Tavis. And he hadn't looked away from her.

Stopping in front of her, he hooked his hand on her elbow as she straightened.

"I'll drive you home." May thought that was Caiden that spoke.

"I. Can't. Look. At. You. I'll walk." Dakota marched to the door.

From the corner of her eye, she saw Maggie and Caiden leave behind her. Overall conversation had seized the moment they'd entered, but more private ones were happening between mates. The giggles and murmurs carried a new feel. Their attention was only on each other.

"I'm taking you home, pixie." His voice was rough, and it scraped over her skin. Not in a bad way. No. Her body heated with a promise. Despite the hurt lingering in his eyes.

"Tavis," she started, but he shook his head.

"Not yet. The end of the week, remember?"

The alcohol reared a shield like a warrior. "Right." She set her shoulders back and pressed her chest against his.

"What are you doing?"

"Kissing you." Sliding one hand up, she curled it around his neck and pulled him down. He met her with amusement on his lips. May tried hard to keep control of the kiss, but it wasn't long before she relaxed.

He chuckled, the sound low and quiet in his chest, and he took over. Tavis wrapped his arm around her and her feet left the ground. He carried her from the apartment and down the stairs, not letting her up for air until he set her in the passenger seat of his truck.

The night passed in her vision out the window. A heated hand settled on her thigh, a comforting weight. Closing her eyes, she wondered what to say. There was so much desire between them, despite what he'd heard. That was why May didn't want to talk about any of this until the end of the week.

Her breathing evened and the next thing she was aware of was his arms looping under her knees and behind her back. Warm lips rested against her head. The moment was sweet, and she wished she was sober to take it in.

An apology hovered on her tongue, but the alcohol wasn't strong enough anymore to overcome her common sense. An apology would cause more harm at this moment.

Tavis carried her inside and straight to the bedroom. He let his hands run up the sides of her body, pulling her dress up as he sat her on the edge.

"Arms up." There was an edge in his voice. She lifted her arms, and he took the dress off her. His eyes heated, but they were a different shape. It was the animal in him that had that control. The tension in his shoulders said something different. The passion from the kiss on the way out of Poppy and Wyatt's apartment was dwindling away.

Tavis crouched down and reached behind her to unclasp her bra. His gaze wouldn't leave hers and she felt at a disadvantage despite being above him.

He was being gentle with her. Not that he'd been rough before, but there had always been a firm demand in every touch.

As he stood, he laid her out on the bed and pulled her panties down her legs.

"Tavis?"

"Shh. Not now, May."

May. Not pixie. She didn't want to admit how much that hurt. But it meant she'd hurt him. He'd heard her admit her heart wanted to be back in the city, but he hadn't heard her thoughts. Her heart wanted to be here too.

Tavis wouldn't know that if he didn't let her talk. She'd set the parameters. He was only sticking to them.

Pushing her knees up, he settled between them on his stomach.

"I want to hear every sound you make," he growled against her, then set his tongue against her clit. May gasped, a small squeak escaping through the breath. "Not enough."

He circled two fingers at her entrance and sucked hard on the nerves. That drew out a mixture of a moan and a cry of frustration. He wasn't giving her enough.

Her heart didn't want to be here. Tavis expected the logical side of her to buck against Fate and want to keep her life, but he'd expected her heart to be torn. What he wanted was to tuck her into bed and sleep the night away, hoping for clarity in the morning. But he couldn't be that cruel. And he couldn't deny the heat pulsing through him.

It didn't matter that her heart wasn't here. His was. And it was all hers.

Enough alcohol coursed through her system that topping it off with a forced orgasm would put her to sleep.

Her taste was as intoxicating to him as the wine and shots had been to her. His bear was angry. And he was hurt.

Tavis worked her, drawing out every touch that caused her to make a sound. Once she'd coated the fingers playing at her entrance, he thrust them inside and curled. His cock twitched against the bed, eager to bury itself in her heat. But not tonight.

Tonight was the start of a new plan. He needed to capture her heart.

May came with a cry, her head thrown back and her body arched. Easing off her, he moved so as not to disturb her as her eyes closed and her head rested to the side. Her lungs worked to catch her breath.

Moving to the bathroom, he got a wet cloth to clean her up. She groaned and tried to close her knees, but he wouldn't let her. She sighed when he finished and pulled the blankets over her.

This visit wasn't turning out like he'd hoped. And it barely started. It had been a mistake to agree to her restrictions about not discussing anything until the end of the week.

He didn't crawl into bed with her right away. He'd sat on the end, driving himself crazy with what to do. And when he made it to bed, he curled himself around her, accepting the warmth as comfort, and slept like shit.

Waking before May, he showered and started breakfast. He called in some favours to get out of the last crammed day of work he'd scheduled so he'd have time to spend with her. Tavis needed to make the most of this week.

Breakfast was almost finished, and she still hadn't stirred. He walked into the bedroom and sat beside her. The pink strands of her hair fell forward over her face. Pushing them back, he leaned down to kiss her temple.

Her heart might not want this, but his did. And he wouldn't hold back. It wasn't in his nature to hold back anything.

"Wake up, pixie."

She stirred. Hazy brown eyes blinked up at him.

"Good morning."

May squinted her nose and turned her head into the pillow.

Nuzzling her exposed neck, he kissed her soft skin before standing from the bed. If he lingered in her scent much longer, they wouldn't get out of the house. And that wasn't what they needed. "Breakfast is almost ready. Have a shower, then come out to eat."

One eye peeked up at him. He smiled and left.

Tavis kept the food warm while listening to the shower. Ten minutes after the water turned off, he set it out on the table.

"Wow. You've been up for a while, haven't you?" Her voice filled with a groggy sound from sleep and her night of fun.

"I have." Tavis set his hand at her waist and pulled her in for a kiss. She braided her hair back, showing off the pink stripes in the crisscross. Her make-up was nonexistent, and she wore soft, high-waisted jeans and a T-shirt. She looked adorable, and he wanted to take a bite.

His teeth grew and sharpened. Tavis pulled away before she noticed.

"I made you tea." He guided her to the table and held her chair for her.

"Thank you." The soft smile on her face was a little sad. Remnants of the night before lingered. She hadn't been inebriated enough to forget what she'd said. "What time do you need to be at work?"

"I'm not. I've called in some extra favours."

"Oh?" Was that excitement he saw flash over her eyes? Or nerves? She hid her face by looking down at her plate of French toast—something he indulged in often.

"You'll need your camera."

Definitely excitement.

Tavis kissed her while they cleaned the kitchen, as they passed each other, and while they made their way out the door. He couldn't get enough of her, but he never let his hands take control. They'd had enough sex to get to know that side of each other. Tavis wanted more. He needed more.

He needed her heart.

There were tours of the town and the sights that tourists took. Then there were the tours that locals only knew about. And they weren't all about sight-seeing. Especially not whenever Tavis walked through town.

He'd intended to take her through the woods behind Wyatt and Caiden's cabins, but getting there took longer than he thought.

He spotted Herb working on the cabin renovations alone. Cursing, he stopped to help him with the section of siding around the window. May patiently waited, her camera often up and ready.

After half an hour of that and a wish he could stay longer, they continued through town and spotted Mack unloading a delivery through the front door.

"Hey there, Mack," Tavis called and picked up the next box.

"Hi," the man grumbled back, but nodded a thanks when he saw Tavis help.

"How come you're bringing this in through the front?" Deliveries happened through the back now that Poppy partnered with him.

"There's already a truck parked there. Deliveries over-lapped." Mack disappeared inside, and Tavis followed.

It would be noon before they made it to their destination.

Tavis had sent her more than one apologetic look, but she ignored every single one. The way he interacted with the people they passed was meaningful. He helped them before they realized what he was doing. Simply by starting up a conversation then getting his hands in there alongside them.

No one asked. He just did it.

And May didn't waste those moments. She captured the core of him, the thing that drove him to be this man. She tried to be subtle about the pictures she took, not wanting to disturb anyone. Most of Tavis and whoever he helped along the way. Others of the town itself. The businesses they stopped next to. Their aged signs and bright charm.

She even snapped a picture of the cars stopping while a squir-rel ran across the crosswalk.

They made it across town, which seemed to be his goal, but he paused and turned to her. "We need lunch. I'm sorry this took so long."

"Don't be sorry. I had a great walk this morning with you."

"Really? You weren't bored?" He ran his fingers down her cheek and kept his hand going until it rested on her hip.

"Not a bit." This was the first moment of closeness that morning that didn't feel strained.

"Did you get some pictures?" Amusement lifted his lips.

Tilting her head back, she stared up at him. "Lots. Most of your fine ass." May set her hands on his arms. "Where is it we're supposed to be going today?"

He cocked his head behind him. "Places that the regular hiking trails don't take you."

"Sounds interesting."

"But I'll need to feed you before we head out. We'll be gone most of the afternoon now."

"I'm okay with that." Her stomach growled, and he raised a brow. "Very okay with that."

Tavis chuckled and turned back the way they came. They chose a smaller restaurant with a patio extending out onto the sidewalk.

And just as it had been walking through town, people stopped to say hi to Tavis. He took the time to introduce her, then the people would move on. They'd have a few more minutes to talk before the next person needed to say hello. Tavis met every single one with a genuine smile.

This man was loved.

But the moment they finished eating, he rushed them back toward *Bearbrook Cabins* and past them to the woods. Behind the trees, he let out a heavy sigh.

May had to laugh. "It's a wonder you get anything of your own done."

"I know my weaknesses. As long as I don't see someone in need of help, I can refrain." But his answer still held some humour. "Come on." He held out his hand and waited for her to take it. "You go in front. This way." Tavis pointed ahead and helped her over the fallen tree that lay along the path leading east.

Pausing, she stared at the tree. "You guys put that there on purpose, didn't you?"

"Maybe." He shrugged.

They met with a few other obstacles that May wondered if a shifter or two strategically placed in the way.

The dense trees made decent pictures difficult, but a few times along the way, she forced them to stop. Tavis never complained. He stood next to a tree or sat on a stump, waiting patiently.

About an hour had passed before he took her hand and set her behind him to take the lead.

"Are we almost there?"

"Yes."

Another ten paces and the trees broke, opening to... an oasis. She couldn't describe it any other way. A small cliff rose on the other side of a fast running brook. A small waterfall fed the stream and filled the air with its sound.

"This is beautiful." The sight stunned May enough she didn't immediately reach for her camera. There'd be enough time to do that after she took it in.

"We used to come up as kids. Before we shifted."

"Before you shifted? You weren't born with your abilities?"

"No. It happens at different times for everyone. Some shift for the first time younger. Others, it might take until puberty. But once we all shifted, we spent even more time up here. We felt safe."

"I can see why." It was secluded on all sides in some way or another. Remnants of an old treehouse clung to one tree next to the bottom of the waterfall. The brush was thick everywhere except where they'd come in. "You made it safer, too." She looked up at him and saw him nod.

As she looked around, May decided she wanted to stay here until the sun lowered in the sky, to watch how the lighting changed throughout the day. Setting her gaze on him, she saw the difference in him this place made.

"Thank you for showing me this."

His attention shifted to her. It was a heady thing to have that much focus. "You're welcome." But the tightness to his lips implied that hadn't been what he'd wanted to say. May didn't like what was unsaid, but she had to remind herself that it was her doing. Talking would ruin their time together, and they still had all week.

Chapter Eleven

He showed her this place because it was important to him. The others joined him on occasion, but Tavis was more likely to run into the wolf shifters in this little hollow than the other bears.

This was a piece of his heart. A place that fueled his peace.

While she'd been distracted with her camera, snapping pictures at odd angles all over the place, Tavis had stripped and shifted. The gasp that escaped from her lips when she looked at him was worth it.

Hours of lazing by the water and playing with his mate, teasing her and splashing her, left him satisfied and full of hope for their future. Her laughter was more than enough, but her eyes had changed while they were there. A softness entered the brown colour as she ran her fingers through his fur. She didn't speak to him and he didn't shift back to speak to her.

Until he glanced at the sky and saw they'd be cutting it close to get back during daylight.

Reluctantly, he stood. May followed suit. She stared at him as the wind swirled around him. The magic of the change didn't ache with her eyes on him. He rolled his spine with the last of the change until he stood tall on two feet.

"We've stayed too late."

"I know. I wanted to see what it looked like in here in the moonlight."

"Next time." He had to have something for her to look forward to for her next visit.

She scrunched her nose, but nodded.

"It's going to get dark before we get back. Want to ride on my back?"

"Seriously? I can do that?"

"Yes." Tavis closed the distance between them and pulled her against his naked body. Leaning his head down, he kissed her with the same relaxing feel that had filled their afternoon. Lazy, but no less passionate.

May sighed when he released her. "I've had a great day." He'd been waiting for that tilt to her smile and the softness in her eyes. Her heart showed. The distance and her so-called balance seemed to have no effect on her. He didn't want this decision to be easy for her. Guilt spread. He considered moving to the city to be with her. Even part time. But until they talked, he couldn't know if she was amenable to compromise. Tavis wanted her heart involved as much as his.

"Pack up your stuff. Do you mind holding my clothes for me?"

"Sure." She turned away from him and packed her camera away while he folded his clothes, shoving them inside his hiking boots. When she slung her bag over her shoulders, he handed her his boots. Frowning, she glanced inside the shoes. "Efficient."

After placing a quick kiss on the end of her nose, he stepped back and shifted again.

"I'll never tire of seeing that."

That's the idea, pixie. I want you to crave it. To crave me. He was free to think the words, knowing she couldn't yet hear him that way.

He lumbered toward her. Her breath caught as he held her gaze. Lining himself up in front of her, he crouched to the ground and waited. With his boots tucked under one arm, she used her free hand to grip the fur on his shoulders.

Patiently, he waited while she adjusted herself a few times. He looked at her over his shoulder and she gave the go ahead.

Blowing out a long breath from rounded lips, she nodded. "I'm ready."

He huffed and stood. Tavis started slow, lumbering in a way to make sure she had a tight grip for when he sped up and climbed over stumps and downed trees.

Darkness filled the woods, the trees blocking out the last remnants of the sun low in the sky. He didn't need to rush. His night vision in this state was excellent. And he liked taking his time while May stroked the fur on the back of his neck.

As he approached the cabins, voices to the west drew his attention. They weren't calm voices. Anger and hysteria filled the tones. Glancing back, he realized May still didn't hear them.

Unable to resist, Tavis turned them toward the voices and away from *Bearbrook Cabins*.

"What's wrong?" May tensed.

He tilted his head, moving his ear forward.

"You hear something?"

He nodded.

The voices came from the schoolyard. A large fence separated the school property and the woods. A precaution for dangerous wildlife that wandered into town.

"I hear them."

Tavis stopped before they reached the fence and crouched down to let May off his back. As soon as he shifted, she handed him his boots. Now that they drew closer, he recognized some voices. Clara. And Blair, her calm but forceful professional voice cutting in to demolish her opponent.

"That's Blair." May's eyes widened, and she started hiking toward the voices.

"Not that way. There's a fence. We have to go around."

"What could be going on?"

"I don't know."

They picked up their pace and found themselves at the edge of a small crowd. Two school teachers, the new principal, and several parents argued out front of the school.

"Everyone, calm down, please." Duke raised his hands and made a motion like patting down the air. "If you all come inside, we'll discuss this."

"We aren't going inside, because our son isn't involved." Davina, Clara's sister and Kellan's mother, wrapped her arm around her son's shoulders.

"We can sort everything out inside."

"My wife said no. Kellan wasn't at the school from the moment the bell rang to let them out until you called us back here." Heath stepped in front of his wife and son, but didn't block them off.

Tavis took May's hand and sidled up next to Blair, who stood with Clara.

"I'm sorry, Mr. Wright. Other students implicated Kellan. We just wanted to bring everyone in and get this cleared up." One teacher, Ava Barlow, in her forties and with her hair pulled back tight, stepped up next to the principal. Her voice was calm and concerned. Sympathy filled her eyes as she glanced at Kellan and a few of the other kids hovering nearby with their parents.

But there were some that held defiance in their crossed arms.

"What's going on?" May leaned over Blair's shoulder and whispered. Blair blinked, only just realizing they were there.

"Someone trashed the principal's office. But those *someones* pointed fingers in all different directions. The new guy thought it was a good idea to call everyone in at once outside of school hours to discuss it as a group. Concerns about bullying is his excuse. Seems like he's trying to turn this into some sort of company retreat for kids." Blair shook her head, making it clear she didn't like his ideas. "He's been trying to get everyone inside for the last ten minutes, but some parents are refusing, knowing their kid wasn't even at the school when it happened. Clara's nephew being one of them. I was with her and her sister when the principal called."

"We're not going inside either. This doesn't involve our daughter." Another father spoke loud and turned his family away.

"You know which students were at the school and which weren't. Take them inside and deal with it." Kellan's father did the same.

The teachers didn't look surprised and stepped in to gather the kids and families that had been involved to take them inside. The principal frowned at each of the families leaving, then sighed before turning to who was left.

A lesson for the man to learn—just because this was a small town, didn't mean there weren't some things that worked the same as anywhere else.

Tavis still held his mate's hand. He pulled her away and back toward the street to walk home. His home, but he wanted it to be hers, too.

That was how most of the week went. Heat filled nights and days spent with Tavis showing her everything he loved. Or everything he thought she'd love. May found it endearing the way he wanted her to see his world—like a child showing off his art creations.

A few times, he reluctantly let her free of him to spend time with her friends. Her friends now included Poppy, Blair, Maggie, Dakota, Bonnie, and Clara. But when Clara was present, they were more restricted in their conversations, which was fine with May. After her feelings slipped at their drunken girls' night, May didn't want anymore accidental misunderstandings. Or worse, a truth that would hurt more.

The Fall Festival had arrived. That also meant the end of her time there was soon. And time for her and Tavis to talk. Really talk.

The centre of town was frantic with preparations. Because of the weather the previous day, most of it couldn't get set up until this morning, with events starting at noon. May stayed out of everyone's way. Most seemed to have a system and more than enough hands. She didn't waste this time for pictures either. She couldn't wait to sort through the candids and heartfelt moments waiting on her camera.

Soon, music stirred from the stage sitting at the centre of the event, signaling the beginning of the festival. May intended to take part in everything, but she needed to get the initial shots in while everyone still smiled excitedly. As the afternoon wore on, people would begin to wane and tire. The city wanted these pictures for tourism and the locals wanted the memories. It was May's job to deliver both.

Tavis and Noah had a station of their own—a small climbing wall and obstacle courses for kids. Catching his gaze over the crowd, May waved and lifted her camera to let him know she was exploring. He nodded, but there were words in his eyes he hadn't yet said to her. She felt them.

She felt them every night and every morning. Each time they came together, the tension thickened. It was difficult for him not to mate her. And May found it hard not to allow it. They'd had to change their positions to find the right one that didn't give him easy access. All without a conversation. She hadn't needed to hear the words to see his struggle. To feel the same struggle.

But May intended to leave Firebrook unmated. No matter how much they both wanted it or needed it, she refused to tilt her balance so soon.

The more people she met, the more distracted from her own thoughts she became. Until she reached Tavis and Noah, and her thoughts on their future came swirling back.

Her second time around had fewer pictures, but she found a few moments she had to capture. She caught up to Blair and Poppy and joined them in some games.

The afternoon was mostly for the kids, and the evening would be for the adults.

"How many embarrassing moments have you captured so far tonight?" Blair wrapped an arm around May's shoulders. Her lips quirked up and her prominent brows expected the number to be high above zero.

"At least a dozen." Some wouldn't see the light of day, but others she expected the people in them would get a good laugh and she would give them a story to tell—with evidence.

"You keep your mischievous side hidden." Poppy bumped her with an elbow.

Not hidden. May only let that side of her out when she was comfortable. She was almost always comfortable with her camera. And until she met Tavis, that had been the only time. Now, with Tavis, bold mischievousness reared forth at odd times.

With her camera safely tucked in her bag for now, May walked around the festival a third time with Blair and Poppy. The other two fit in here, already knowing everyone, but this was their first festival. It wouldn't be their last. Or hers. May would always return to Firebrook. That she knew deep inside. Tavis did, too. Right? He had to.

Her friends dragged her to the ring toss, beanbag toss, the water guns—all the small festival type games that attracted families. And they even swung the hammer to ring the bell, laughing hysterically when none of them reached halfway.

They met up with Clara, who explored with her sister and nephew. Kellen gave them all a shy smile, and a mumbled hello. May saw the little boy lighting his eyes, but he was tall and reaching an age where hugs with adults in public were embarrassing. Not that it stopped Blair.

What Blair and Clara had gone through together had created a special friendship, one that made Blair important to the other people in Clara's life and made Clara and her family important to Blair and Noah.

"We're on our way to the Ferris wheel." Kellen announced with veiled excitement.

"That sounds like fun." May hadn't ever been on one before. But they'd featured in several of her pictures. To her, they were something magical. The thought almost made her laugh, considering what magical things she'd recently discovered.

When they reached the Ferris wheel, Tavis, Noah, and Wyatt waited to the side of the line-up.

"How did you guys know we were coming here?" Poppy stopped with a hip cocked and her arms crossed, pausing their entire group of people. Kellen's wide eyes looked to his mom, aunt, and the three men waiting.

Wyatt only chuckled, not phased by his mate. "We may have had some help to track your progress." Not that the massive shifter gave any hint as to the identity of their helper

But did it matter? May loved the idea of going for a ride with Tavis on something she found magical.

Clara and her sister ushered Kellen to the line, pursed lips keeping their smiles from bursting out.

May felt the strain between her and Tavis. They needed to mate. They needed to talk. That tension was like their bodies coiling around each other like snakes, then having someone pulling their heads back so they couldn't kiss. Instead of look but don't touch, it's touch but don't bite.

She was the last to go to her mate, to take his hand and let him lead her to the line. A few minutes later, Caiden and Maggie came up behind them. His arm wrapped around her waist, holding her against him. Their faces turned toward each other and their lips moved with soft conversation.

"How has your station and climbing wall gone?" May filled the silence. She hated how awkward things seemed.

"A hit, as usual." His low voice curled over her shoulders.

"I'm surprised you guys got away."

"We closed it for a little while. Everyone knows we'll be back. We needed a break."

The weight of his stare forced her to look up at him. The moment thickened. Her lungs struggled. It was almost too hard to go another day with him, but without belonging to him.

"Tavis." His brother called his name from next to the Ferris wheel. Tavis snapped his head up. He shook himself free of the weight, leading her forward to their seat.

His teeth were constantly sharp around her now, just waiting for permission to strike. His cock hadn't been slack in days. If they didn't talk soon, the choice would be taken from them. He wasn't the only one struggling. Tavis saw the way she stretched her neck and tilted her head while he buried himself inside her.

Her blood pumped harder, calling to him. Soon, the pain and heat would force them to mate when they came together.

The attendant, a teenager in grade twelve at the school, put the bar in place across the front of their seat. With a curt nod, he stepped back, and the seat rocked as they moved forward to allow for Caiden and Maggie to get in behind them.

Tavis leaned back to keep the seat steady, and they lurched. May jumped beside him. A nervous chuckle escaped before she clamped her lips shut.

"Come here, pixie." Tavis pulled her close. "Ever been on one of these before?"

"No." She let her weight lean against him while she looked around. They rose above the festival. They could count every single booth and game, the fields with the races, the stage where the live band had played in the afternoon and would be back for the evening.

May's eyes weren't on the festival below them. She looked off in the distance, toward the mountains, with the sun dipping below their peaks.

"It's as magical as I imagined. This whole place is. And not because a family of supernatural shifters live here."

"I feel that every day about this place."

"It's home."

"It is. For me." Tavis agreed to wait until the end of her week here. But what better time than this when he had her trapped above the ground?

Glassy brown eyes searched his. Her lips moved.

"It's time, May."

"Tavis. Not now. Not up here."

"Right now. Right here. You're mine and I want to keep you. I want you…"

"Tavis," she snapped low enough that most wouldn't hear her. Maybe his brother or cousins.

"May," he growled back, putting the same command he used on her in the bedroom into his tone. She closed her eyes and pulled away from his hold, setting her hands on the bar in front of them.

"Tavis, I can't…" she gasped. Jolting, she sent the seat rocking as she scrambled back toward him. He tensed, unsure what was wrong. Her eyes widened and her knuckles white gripped his thigh.

"What's wrong, pixie?" He turned his body toward her, rocking the seat again. She whimpered.

"We're at the top." The words escaped as a harsh whisper, as if she couldn't make her voice work. He smelled the panic on her.

"You're afraid of heights." But it hadn't bothered her until she looked down. "Why would you get on a Ferris wheel if you're afraid of heights?"

"I didn't know I was."

Tavis held back his grin. "I've got you, pixie." He adjusted to hold her again.

"Don't move!" Her nails dug into his leg through his jeans.

"It's okay. I'll go slower."

"You don't need to go anywhere. Didn't you ever play the statue game as a kid? You should practice that now. You never know when some kid will challenge you to a game. In fact, I'm challenging you right now. Statue!"

He'd never heard her ramble quite like this. Her tone oscillated, erratic in volume and fear. "Okay. Let's play. But we're going to play like this." Tavis moved as slowly as he could, so they both leaned back and had their bodies tilted toward each other.

He tightened his arm around her shoulders and set his other hand along her jaw.

"Look at me, May." When he had her attention, he pulled in a deep breath, animating the motion so she'd copy him. At the end of the exhale, he bent his head toward hers and set his lips gently on hers. "Statue," he whispered before sealing the kiss.

Neither moved, but his cock throbbed and his blood heated. Her heart calmed from her fear and then started a new rhythm he recognized.

While their bodies didn't move, he couldn't stop his lips or tongue. Their turn at the top ended. The moment they moved, Tavis slid his tongue along her lips and dipped it inside. Staying true to their game, she stayed utterly still. As much as he wanted to stroke his thumb over her cheek, he didn't. Her lips softened enough to let him in and he moved his just enough to make the touch a true kiss.

The ride continued, circling them around one more time without stopping. May gasped, filling her lungs. Tavis felt the thrill fill her. The same sensation filled him. The thrill of the ride and the thrill of holding such control over a kiss.

Travis tracked their way around the circle, knowing when they reached the bottom. The attendant lifted the bar. He cleared his throat and Tavis smiled against May's lips. She still hadn't moved. Lifting his head, he tilted her chin up. "You won, pixie."

She blinked. Her face was flush, and she looked as if she was slowly waking from a deep sleep.

He led her away from the crowd as the riders dispersed and Caiden and Maggie got off after them. They sent concerned looks their way, but left them alone.

"You okay?" He set his hands on her shoulders and waited.

"Yeah. Thank you. I had no idea." She twisted her fingers in front of her.

"It didn't scare you until you looked over the edge." Tucking an imaginary piece of hair behind her ear was only an excuse to touch her more, to bring her closer.

"You're right. The view before that was beautiful. Too bad I didn't see it for the rest of the ride."

"May, we need to finish talking."

Her spine snapped straight. "No, we don't."

Tavis wished he'd had her back up against a wall, because as soon as the words escaped, she stepped away from him and kept moving.

"May." Her name was a warning. What the hell he intended to do, he wasn't sure. His feet dug into the ground and the bear inside him roared, ready for a chase. But they were in the middle of town and surrounded by people. And Tavis needed to get back to their station.

"No. Don't. We still have more time." May turned and walked away, her head spinning around the crowd, looking for someone to attach herself to. Blair waited not far away. Noah had already gone back to their station.

Blair sent him a sympathetic look and hooked her arm with May's.

Tavis wouldn't let his mate run from this anymore. They were going to talk, or they were going to mate.

Chapter Twelve

May was still shaking as she walked around with Blair who was observant enough to steer them away from Noah and Tavis. She wanted to leave. She wanted to get out of the crowd, give herself some time to cry, to think, but her camera bag burned at her side, reminding her she still had a job to do. A picture from the top of the Ferris wheel would have been a great image. Maybe next time.

Tavis would not let this go. He'd kept it all to himself for days. But May heard it in his voice. It was the same demanding tone he used in the bedroom. The one that she found undeniable. The one that covered his jovial demeanor and turned him into a serious alpha. A grizzly in charge. His bear lingered not only in his eyes, but in his voice. May recognized when the animal was ready to make an appearance.

She'd pushed her mate's limits. When they went home tonight, she wouldn't be able to escape.

Unless she didn't go home with him.

"I have more pictures I need to take. Can you stick with me until the festival is over?" May felt like a coward, but she had to concentrate on the job and not on her mate and what she would do at the end of the night.

"Sure." Blair's answer was short, and she held her shoulders high. She had more she wanted to say.

"What?"

"You need to at least talk to him. It will blow up in your face if you don't. And I think you already know that. There's no way you don't feel it."

"I feel it."

"Then why are you avoiding talking to him."

"I'm not avoiding it. I just want to wait. That discussion is going to ruin this week. Nothing's changing right now. I'm going back and he's staying here. Unmated. And I'll come back again in two weeks. If we leave it until the last minute, we can't get too deep and hurt each other. As long as he understands my heart belongs in both places."

Blair frowned.

"He overheard me the night at Poppy's when I said my heart wants to be back in the city."

"Shit."

"Yeah. It's been tense since."

"May, you can't wait until the last minute. You're both hurting. Neither of you deserve that. And I think you're wrong. Your heart wants to be in your business. Not the city. Your business just happens to be in the city."

"You're talking about yourself, Blair. I like the city."

That was the first time May had ever seen Blair quiet. Not a forced quiet where she held back her real thoughts. Disappointment silenced her.

May sighed and pulled out her camera. Poppy and Mack had opened their town-centre bar a few minutes ago, and the line had formed fast. It was time for her to get back to work.

For the next hour, Blair never said a word, but she didn't leave May's side. The support was there even if her friend didn't agree.

Once the last family left, many of the booths closed down. Including the climbing wall. Tavis's presence crowded in on her. The heat covered her back before he even reached her.

"May, did this start out as avoiding pain?" Blair spoke low before their mates reached them.

"No." May cleared her throat.

"But that's what you're doing now. And it's only created more pain." Her friend forced the truth out for her.

"Yes." May had to swallow down tears. Knowing she was going to leave in two days hurt. And telling him she wanted to leave was going to hurt more.

"Pixie." The endearment didn't hold the same softness it usually did. It held frustration.

She turned a soft smile up at him. "How did the rest of your day go with the climbing wall?"

"It went great." It was Noah that answered her. Tavis only stared down, glancing a few times to her camera.

She'd taken more than enough pictures. But that wasn't how she worked. At least this wasn't her making up an excuse to avoid a conversation.

"Time to dance, kitten." Noah pulled Blair away. She sent May a quick look, but didn't insist on staying as her shield. May's protection was gone.

Before Tavis demanded they leave, she held her camera up. "I want to take more pictures of the adult only events."

"Okay." He gripped her chin and held her face up. "May," he paused, and in those seconds his eyes changed. "May, I love you."

Just as she'd done the first time she met him, she lifted her camera. The angle wasn't the best with his unyielding grip on her chin, and she didn't look through the lens or at the screen. She snapped the picture and hoped she captured everything she saw. It was an instinct she couldn't let go. But what to do with his words was something else entirely.

"Finish working. And then we're going home, pixie." He let her go.

May couldn't concentrate after that. But she stayed ahead of him and took her pictures. She didn't know what she looked like to those around her, but they all smiled and waved at the right times. Stalking around the dance floor, May snapped pictures from all different angles. The couples swung around each other, their feet moving faster than was possible to track. But it was when the women's heads fell back in laughter and the men held the love and admiration in their eyes for their beauty that May loved the most.

Poppy and Mack didn't see her as she approached to capture the way the two of them meshed and worked so well together. But the moment Mack spotted her, she backed away with one hand up and one still on her camera. As soon as Poppy looked her way with a grin, she snapped the picture. Their perfect personalities saved forever on her camera.

May hoped it turned out. She wanted to frame it and give it to them for Christmas. To hang in the bar of course.

Her mate's presence wasn't possible to ignore. He added an extra weight on her shoulder, but he let her do her job.

"I'm done." She got what she wanted, and anything more would be procrastinating. "But I don't want to talk about this tonight. Or tomorrow."

His jaw tensed and he crowded her, setting his hands at her waist, stopping her from backing away. "Do you know what the consequences are, May? You must. I see the same struggle in you."

"Talking won't change that struggle. It will only cause us..." She stopped. If she said it would cause them pain, then he'd know what she was going to say. He'd know she intended to leave here unmated.

"Cause us what, May? Pain? We're already in pain." He pounded on his chest then splayed his hand over hers between her breasts. "Right here."

"Words won't fix it."

"Words can help. But if you want it fixed, I know what can fix it." His fangs peeked out as he growled.

"What words do you want, Tavis? Because what I have to say won't make this better." Her throat closed off. The band was loud enough that the people around them weren't paying them any attention, but the situation was about to become volatile.

"I want everything you have to give me, no matter what it is you have to say."

"I don't want to hurt like this." The pain that had been simmering all week exploded.

"Ah, pixie." Sympathy finally filled his eyes. For that moment, his frustration disappeared. "This is going to hurt."

He had to get her out of here. The pain of not mating suddenly bled from May's face. The scent of their agony grew stronger. And what he intended to do wasn't appropriate for public eyes.

Tavis reached for her camera bag, surprised when she relinquished it. "We're going to draw attention soon. Come on." He slid his hand to the small of her back and pressed his fingers against her. The touch seared. She gasped and arched, but he followed her. He wanted it to burn. That sensation filled his chest, and he knew it filled hers. They needed to let it out. He'd do almost anything for her. The *almost* part was killing him now. Tavis couldn't permanently leave Firebrook. The guilt of that swarmed around his heart.

May walked stiffly toward his truck. She didn't struggle, and Tavis wasn't against throwing her over his shoulder to get her out of there. But when he reached for the door to open it for her, she stopped.

Parked vehicles lined the streets, but not a soul out among them. They were tucked in their homes for the night or at the festival that would still last for hours. No one stumbled home or came back out to join the fun.

"May." The warning snapped from him. He didn't have control over his tone anymore. His emotions scraped as raw as hers.

"If we get in that truck, if we go home and close the door behind us, what's going to happen?" She stood with her head down, staring at the pavement between her and his truck.

His breathing grew harsh as the bear inside him wanted to answer her. Closing in behind her, he pressed his chest to her back. "We're going to fuck. I'm going to tell you I love you again. And you're going to tell me every single thing you're thinking."

"Why can't we just enjoy the last two days?" Tears filled her soft whisper.

"Why are you fighting it?" he countered. "Because you don't want to be here?" His biggest fear. He needed to push her now. If he didn't, they'd mate, giving her no choice.

"Stop trying to force the conversation." She whirled on him, and the tears weren't only in her voice, but running down her cheeks now. "I don't want to say it. I don't want to hurt you!"

Tavis moved without thought. He set both hands on her waist, lifting her and pushing her back against his truck. Slipping her camera bag from his shoulder, he set it on the hood.

"Tavis." His name was a plea.

"Hurt me, May. I'm already in pain, but don't tell me you aren't trying to avoid your own pain. It's not me you don't want to hurt."

Her jaw tensed. "How dare you? You think I'm being selfish? That I don't care about what I do to you?"

His lips lifted and not in a pleasant way. "I know you care, pixie. That's why this hurts so fucking much for both of us." He pressed her harder against the truck, lifting her a little higher so his cock lined up with her core. "But I'm not letting you escape your own pain."

"Why can't you just let this go for now?"

"We've started this. There's no stopping this course now."

"*You* started this. You did. Not me."

"Too late." He lifted her chin, forcing her eyes to meet his. "Are you going to get in the truck now, or do I have to put you in it?"

She shook her head, closing her eyes and shutting him out. "If we go home and you touch me, we're going to mate. That's what you meant earlier by consequences, isn't it?"

Tavis stayed silent. If she opened up to him, he might calm enough to stop himself—if that's what she wanted. But if he fucked her in this state, they'd mate within the hour. He didn't answer, not even when she opened her eyes.

"Then you can't touch me."

"Then you need to talk. Now." His fangs lengthened and cut into his inner lip. He didn't like being told he couldn't touch her.

More tears leaked from the corners of her eyes. Her lower lip quivered. Seeing her like this was killing him, knowing he was doing it, was forcing it. But he didn't know how else to get her to open up to him.

He moved his hips against hers in a slow rhythm meant to coax. Using the back of one hand, he wiped away the tears. "I'm right here, May. I want you. I want to listen. Talk to me."

"I love you, too." Tears choked her confession.

"Don't you dare say 'but,' pixie."

"I love where I live. I love my business. And I love Firebrook. I love Nonna and my family, and I love the people here. My heart wants both."

She'd been right. It pinched. It hurt to hear she was torn, that he could lose her entirely. But knowing she loved him and felt that same pull toward him and Firebrook helped ease him. It didn't ease the need to mate her, though.

"I can't stay here."

"We can work with that, May."

"I need time you can't give me. I'm not ready."

"You think Fate fucked up?"

"No." Her hand flattened on his chest. "She didn't get this wrong, but she just had bad timing."

Tavis released her, letting her slide back to the ground and pulled her away from this truck. Opening the door, he helped her get in. He grabbed her camera bag from the hood on his way around to the driver's side. After storing it in the back seat, he pulled out of the street.

What May really wanted was for Tavis to hold her and tell her everything would be all right. But that wouldn't happen if she let him take her inside and touch her. They'd mate. She felt the pulse in her chest, the warmth of magic ready to be set free. He wouldn't hold her and tell her everything would be all right. He'd hold her and tell her he loves her right before he bites her. And she'd let him.

He parked the truck beside her car. After turning off the engine, he reached for her. May backed away.

"No. Tavis, we can't do it like this."

He frowned. She surprised him enough to give her time to reach into the back and grab her camera bag.

"I'll come back. I can't stay away. I love you too, Tavis."

"Don't do it, May." His hands folded into fists. Before he could talk her out of it, she opened the truck door and went straight to her car. The driver's door slammed as she opened hers. "May!" A deep growl roared through her name.

She shivered. Standing inside her open car door, she looked over her shoulder. He became a blurry figure through her tears. This was a stupid mistake. She knew it, but was it so much to ask for time? Fate was a bitch. May wasn't rejecting Tavis, she wanted him but wanted things to stay the way they were for a while. She wanted a normal relationship. It hadn't been her intention to turn him away when it came time to mate. But her stupid heart wanted both lives. And Tavis didn't deserve only half her heart.

"I will come after you, pixie." If she didn't know him, she'd be terrified of the way he sounded.

"This isn't fair, Tavis. To either of us. To force this when we aren't ready."

"I'm ready." He pounded his chest. "Two days. Then I'm coming to get you."

May got in her car, her hands shaking as she started it and put it in drive. With both hands on the wheel, she pulled away.

She made it halfway back to the city before the tears were too thick for her to see the road. May put her foot on the brakes and turned her blinker on to pull off to the side of the road, but it wasn't her brakes that stopped her.

Chapter Thirteen

She wasn't answering her phone. Tavis didn't believe she'd pick up for him, so he hadn't tried, but he asked Blair to try. And then Poppy. May should have made it back to the city by now.

Tavis had blacked out the moment her car went out of sight. He wasn't unconscious, but he couldn't remember what he did. He may have let out a blood-curdling roar for all he knew. If he hadn't still been dressed, he'd think he might have shifted. His next memory was checking the time and pacing outside his house.

After giving her an extra hour to make it home, he'd gone in search of Blair, giving her a shortened version of the story. It was between him and May and only him and May. Tavis needed her back.

It was the middle of the night, but that didn't stop them from calling several times.

"Something isn't right." Tavis felt his chest ripping in two.

"I agree." Poppy sighed and gripped Blair's hand.

"I'm going. Someone needs to come with me. She may not want me, even if she's hurt." *You can't touch me.* Those words hurt as much as hearing her heart belonged somewhere else.

"That's ridiculous, but of course we're coming with you." Blair shook her head. Pulling away from Poppy, she started shoving Noah's chest.

Tomorrow he could express the gratitude in him.

Noah wouldn't let him drive. Blair sat in the back seat of her mate's truck. Poppy and Wyatt followed behind them. Tavis kept his gaze glued to the sides of the road. The route back to the city had two main sections. A two-lane highway that was mainly used by Firebrook residents before it merged into a divided highway that led back to the city. If something happened before she reached the divided highway, it could be hours before someone drove past her.

His heart pounded the more he thought about her alone on the side of the road. He shouldn't have let her go. She was his. And he was hers. He should have forced the conversation, not let her go off on her own, upset and at night. This was worse than any pain words could cause.

A few hundred metres before the turn onto the divided highway sat her car in the middle of the road, askew with the nose of her car toward the centre of the road.

"May." If his voice had worked, he would have roared. Her name tore at his throat. He had the truck door open and his feet on the pavement before Noah had it in park.

All his logic about bringing others with him, because she may not want him blasted away. May was going to get him whether she liked it or not. Noah was beside him before he could tear her car door open to pull her from the car.

"Don't move her yet." His brother's heavy hand settled on his shoulder.

His nose twitched against the metallic scent of blood. Animal.

"She hit a deer." Noah filled in the blanks, while Tavis looked in the driver's window. May's head was leaning against the headrest, and the airbag had deflated in front of her.

"May!" Tavis hollered her name through the glass. Her eyes fluttered and her head rolled. "May. Pixie. I'm going to open the door." He looked at his brother, ensuring he hadn't missed anything before opening the door.

Noah nodded, giving him the go ahead. "It was a big one." He whistled under his breath as he assessed the damage to the front and to the hood. Tavis gave it a quick look, noting the crack in the windshield and the dent at the top of the hood. How the hell had the deer walked away from this?

Tavis pulled on the door, using the extra strength to get it unstuck. He crouched down. "Pixie? Do you know where you are?"

"In my car," she groaned dryly. It was a relief to hear that small amount of sarcasm. "I hit something. I couldn't see it."

"You hit a deer." Because he couldn't help himself, he reached out and touched her. Running his fingers over her face before drifting them over her body to check for injuries. "Are you hurt anywhere?"

"The airbag packed a punch, but I think that's it."

"Can you feel your legs, your arms, toes?"

"It's all there."

"Good. Do you know how long you've been unconscious?" His biggest concern now was a concussion.

"Not long. I fell asleep. I didn't dare move. And I left my phone in my camera bag. In your truck."

Tavis blinked. If he'd known it was there, he may not have come looking for her and waited until she contacted him.

Her bottom lip quivered as she looked at him.

"It's okay, pixie. Let's get you out of here." He looked closer at the interior of the car. It dented inward, but not so much she didn't have room to get out now that the door was open. "Are you dizzy, nauseous?"

"No."

Tavis put himself in the role he used when on a search and rescue. He breathed deep to calm himself and assess her. His brother and cousins were hovering behind him, ready to step in. But he didn't need them.

While she looked tired, her eyes were clear, her breathing and heart rate were both steady.

"Okay. Slowly." Tavis inched back and put his hand under her arm. She moved her legs out first, planting both feet. Her grip on his forearms tightened while she stood. Tavis didn't grab her. He waited to see if she could stand on her own.

After a second, she nodded. "I'm good."

"I called for the tow truck, and Fish and Wildlife. I don't think the deer got far after that hit."

May closed her eyes and bowed her head. Her guilt carried a potent scent. Letting his fingers trace her cheek to the back of her neck, Tavis pulled her in against his chest. She relaxed against him, but it only took seconds for her to stiffen, as if she remembered their parting words. *You can't touch me.*

Four words that would forever haunt him.

Peeling herself away, she added a soft smile before turning to Blair and Noah behind him. "Would you guys drive me home?"

"Uh, no," Blair said plainly, and gave her a pointed look. "We'll drive you back to Firebrook, though."

Tavis let his hands drop from her sides, releasing any influence. He'd had a moment of respite when he discovered she wasn't hurt and he could touch her, to help her up. But the pain came flaring back as she tried to regain her distance.

And the stupid part of him let her.

May found herself in the back of Noah's truck with Tavis. It was a tight fit for him, but Blair jumped in front of him and stole the front seat with a wink.

His weighted stare carried the pain from earlier and an additional worry that pushed against her. She'd been lucky. The accident could have ended in circumstances much worse than this. But she'd needed that distance that going home to the city would give her. Blair, being the well meaning best friend, took that from her. May wouldn't get that from the shifters.

When they made it back to Firebrook, they stopped at Tavis's house first. He turned to her.

"Stay with Blair. I'll check on you in the morning."

No one argued, but May should have as she watched him slam the door and start taking off his clothes. Tavis stalked towards the trees and shifted.

The thick silence in the cab of the truck seemed to freeze time, and it took Noah a few minutes before he sighed and drove off. May was a mess inside.

Blair helped her inside and settled her in their spare room, and the entire time didn't say a word beyond asking if she needed anything. Her thoughts roared in her gaze. May shouldn't be here. She should be with her mate. She shouldn't have been on the road at all, especially in the state she'd been in. At least she'd been driving much slower than the speed limit, but the car hadn't been slowing when she hit.

Sleep claimed her, although she'd expected to toss and turn with her thoughts focused on Tavis. But her body needed the rest.

Her vivid dreams centred around a grizzly bear stalking her and pinning her against a tree. Familiar green eyes pleaded with her as he ran his head up her torso and along her jaw, the soft fur making her gasp and relax against the tree.

But then he growled, opening his large jaw wide to sink his sharp teeth into her neck.

May woke trying to catch her breath, her hand on her chest and eyes searching around her for Tavis.

"Must have been some dream." Blair sat across from her, sipping on her morning coffee. "Tea is ready to put on for you. I wasn't sure how long you'd sleep."

"Thank you." She rubbed her hands over her face, wincing when she reached her forehead.

"Yeah, there's a pretty bruise there. You okay?"

May took stock before answering. "Yeah. Mostly tired, a little headache, but nothing major."

"Good."

"You have shit you want to say. But let me work it out first. Please?"

"Okay." Tension released from Blair and she had a look of sympathy in her eyes.

"Thank you."

"I just hate to see both of you hurting."

Before last night, she'd been certain they'd work it out, but they hit a point she couldn't guarantee they'd come back from.

Blair hovered while she got out of bed and helped her move to the living room with extra pillows and a blanket.

A firm knock had them both turning to the door. Her heart pounded. It was Tavis. She felt him. His palpable presence impossible to ignore. A thick energy filled the air. It buzzed and hummed, reaching for her through the door.

Blair got up to let him in.

"She awake?" His voice was low and cracked, like he hadn't slept.

Blair nodded and opened the door wider, making space. Her friend had agreed to not say anything to her, but she wouldn't be a shield. "I'll leave you two alone." Blair slipped outside, her coffee still in her hands.

Tavis stood there, staring at her. Her body heated under his gaze, not only with desire, but with humiliation. The way she stormed off last night had been unnecessary and stupid.

"How are you feeling?" He assessed her as he asked.

"I'm okay. Tired." She attempted a smile.

"Did you sleep?" Tavis still examined everything about her and around her. He looked at the coffee table in front of her and to the kitchen.

"Did you?"

"No." He started toward the kitchen.

"I did some." She'd slept hard, but her body hadn't rested well with the dreams she'd been having.

The way he acted confused her. Although she wasn't sure what she'd expected. Dishes clanged, and he set pots or pans on the stove. May frowned and turned around see what he was doing.

He made himself at home, making her tea and breakfast. She'd been so focused on his face, his voice, she hadn't noticed until now that he wore the same clothes as last night.

Staying silent, she watched him work in the kitchen. His shoulders were square and stiff. May screwed this up. She fucked up one of the most important things in her life. Not once had she asked herself what she would give up to keep Tavis. What would she have to give up? What was she giving up by giving up on him?

And that was the question that had the most shocking answer. Him.

Tavis carried a plate with eggs and toast in one hand and her cup of tea in the other. "Here. You need to eat."

"How did you know I hadn't?"

"No scent of food in the house. And Noah went into work early."

"Right." She settled the food on her lap while he set her tea down on the coffee table. "Thank you."

He nodded, looking between her and the food.

They didn't talk while she ate. When she finished, he took her plate out. Lifting her feet, he sat on the couch under them and laid her legs over his lap. She sipped her tea while they sat in silence. If either of them spoke, they'd explode.

They still hadn't said anything when Blair came back. Tavis sighed and stood, setting her feet back down to the couch. Bending over her, he lifted her chin.

His lips moved to say something, but instead, he kissed her. The touch seared hot enough to blister. The explosion hadn't happened in words, but it came out in that kiss. She was transported to another plane, one where only the two of them existed.

He pulled away, panting as he set his forehead to hers. Then he left. His sudden absence made her shiver. Pulling the blanket up over her shoulders, May held back the tears that threatened to spill. And her tears had already gotten her in enough trouble.

That became his routine for the next few days while May recovered. Seeing her, making her breakfast and then kissing her senseless was the only thing that kept Tavis sane. She'd been lucky and if he gave himself any time to think about how bad that accident could have been, he would tear himself apart with guilt for letting her go. May escaped the accident only feeling sore from the impact and needing rest.

He hadn't pushed the conversation again. The last time he did that, he pushed her away. But they needed to talk. Tavis was losing hope that she'd be the one to start the conversation.

"Are you sure you don't need me to punch you in the face?" Noah asked for the tenth time from behind the desk of their main office.

Tavis sent him the glare that question deserved. His brother had been waiting for the opportunity to return the favour. Tavis had taken on the responsibility of distracting his brother with glee. That same eagerness shone in Noah's eyes now.

"So unfair," he grumbled.

"I'm fine. I will be."

"You've lasted longer than I would have. I'm surprised you haven't dragged her out of my place and back into yours."

You can't touch me. But he had been. He'd kissed her like it was the only thing sustaining his life for the next twenty-four hours until he could kiss her again. And she kissed him back. "I'm rebuilding."

Right. Rebuilding.

"Has she gotten out of the house?"

"Not yet. But," Noah trailed off.

"What?"

"Clara was by the other day. She's asked May to take family photos. It's a gift for her sister's birthday."

The way Noah's brows stayed high made him believe there was more. "And?"

"And she's had a few other similar requests since the town council published her pictures of the festival."

"And?" His brother's expression hadn't changed.

"And I asked her to come with us on the school camping trip next week." It was a tradition for the middle school aged kids to go on a fall camping trip toward the beginning of the school year, weather permitting. Noah and Tavis often volunteered to help with activities.

"I'd forgotten about that." His only focus had been May.

"I know."

"Thank you." Excitement beat through him. His brother just handed him an opportunity to continue his so-called rebuilding. It was, in truth, a change of scenery to help break the ice they've frozen themselves in.

Noah mumbled his next words under his breath. "You're welcome, but it would have been more fun to punch you."

Chapter Fourteen

B lair worked as her assistant. Not because May needed one, but because her friend decided she needed to hover. Maybe she thought May planned to run again.

She spent several days working with Skye and her other employees over the phone to get them organized to become her while she stayed in Firebrook. Seeing Tavis every morning became the highlight of her day, but also reminded her of everything wrong between them right now. May lived in limbo and it wasn't the worst place.

Clara bounced behind Blair and May, ecstatic over her gift for her sister. There'd been no way May could have said no to her. Her sister beamed as bright with her arms around her son and her husband's arms around her. It was an easy shoot for May. Family sessions were always about being relaxed and having fun.

May had already taken so many of them individually and together. Shots with her looking down at her son and her husband looking down at both of them. Those were usually posed, but May didn't have to ask them for it. Genuine love and adoration put the look in their eyes.

An hour and a thousand pictures later, May tucked her camera back in her bag. "All done. Trust me, there are some amazing shots. I'll get everything to you as soon as I can." She mentally gave herself a week.

She'd still be in Firebrook for almost that anyway, as Noah convinced her to go on the school camping trip as the photographer. May saw through him. It was a way to put her closer to Tavis that wasn't on his living room couch like awkward, silent teenagers.

"Thank you. I can't wait." Davina turned to Clara. "And thank you. I couldn't have asked for a better birthday gift." The sisters hugged and waved as they all left.

Blair waited for May to grab her bag. "How are you feeling?" She asked at least twice a day, and May had been fine since three days after the accident. Lethargy lingered, but the aches and stiffness were gone. And the accident hadn't caused the lethargy. Not when it seemed to get worse each day.

"I'm good."

Blair glared at May, but never called her on the lie.

"Let's go."

"Sure. We can grab coffee and tea from *Bella's Bakery* and take it home. I have some digging to do."

"Digging?"

Blair pinched her lips tight and raised her brows. She never let go of what happened that summer. First with their vacation and Poppy's ex getting killed, and then again when Blair came back and found Scott and Luca still searching for something. Everyone still remembered, but Blair was the only one still searching for an answer. She convinced herself it wasn't over. But out of respect for everyone involved, mainly Clara, who Scott and Luca used as bait for Blair, she'd been keeping her search quiet.

"You can work on their pictures while I search through some of my own." She shrugged and fell in step with May back to Blair's car. May's was still getting repaired, and she still waited to hear from the insurance company. Staying in Firebrook hadn't made it an urgent need.

They stopped and got their drinks from Bonnie, then took them back to Blair's. They sat on the couch next to each other with their feet up and computers on their laps. May showed Blair all the good shots as she came across them. There weren't a thousand pictures, but it was a lot more than the average family session. Kellan was such a sweet kid who was obviously adored by his parents.

"So what are you looking through, anyway?"

"Sam finally found me pictures from the bar." Sam was Blair's long time hacker friend. She'd kept him a secret for years, but eventually his name started to slip. Although, they still hadn't met the guy.

"Where Poppy worked?"

"Yes. There's a connection there in some form. It might be small, but it has to be there. A decade or more of employees is a lot to go through, and now I have pictures of the employees and even ones taken by customers at the bar."

"That's a lot of work for a hunch."

"It's what I do." Blair didn't look up from the screen. She shrugged and kept up her slow scrolling.

"Do you think Luca or someone else will come back?"

"Not Luca. I saw it in his eyes when he ran. He's bowed out for good. But as far as someone else? That depends on what they were searching for." She paused. "This guy didn't work there for long, but he shows up in a lot of pictures. People liked him." Blair pointed at the screen. "*She* really liked him."

May huffed a laugh and leaned over. The series of images showed a man behind the same bar Poppy had stood behind for years and a young woman sitting on the bar. In some pictures she was singing and others she was looking at the bartender.

May frowned. There was familiarity in the woman's gaze. Not only her features, but something in her eyes—the way she loved.

"What is it?" Blair moved her head around May.

"She looks familiar."

"You sure?"

"No. I don't know her. It's just something about her. Sorry. Must be my photographer's eye twitching."

Blair deflated, but she duplicated and saved that picture in a separate file before continuing her scrolling. May went back to editing, but her shoulders ached and she knew she needed a break.

"I think I'm going to take a walk."

"Seriously?" Shock straightened her friend. May had done little on her own since the accident.

May rolled her eyes. "Yes."

Outside, May pulled out her phone. She needed to hear Nonna's voice. It was time she asked her thoughts.

"Bee?"

"Hi, Nonna."

"Oh, Bee. How are you feeling?" Her parents had told Nonna about the accident. May had checked in with her a few times while recovering.

"I'm good." May paused. Despite being unsure how to say this, she forged ahead. "I've met someone, Nonna."

"Oh, I've been waiting for this. Is he handsome? He must be handsome."

"Nonna." May laughed.

"You bring him back here to meet me as soon as you're better."

"I will. But," she trailed off.

"What is it, Bee?"

"I need to move. Here to Firebrook. But I'm not sure that's a good idea."

"Nonsense. You live wherever you want. And if that is in Firebrook, then that is where you'll be. It's only four hours away, Bee. There's no need to fret as if it's such a big move."

Nonna hadn't batted an eye at May's concerns. She was more excited about May meeting someone than anything else.

Nonna begged May to tell her all about Tavis and about the town. She asked about Poppy and Blair. It felt good to talk about all of this as if it were a normal relationship and not tied up in Fate, magic, and high emotions.

Tavis stopped when he saw May come out the door. Sat on the steps with her phone to her ear. He waited, not letting himself get close enough to listen. This was space she needed.

When she finished, she wrapped her arms around herself and lifted her face to the breeze. Walking down the few steps, she turned toward the trail leading in the opposite direction. She hadn't seen him.

He hadn't been able to visit that morning, as she'd been busy with the family photo shoot. The wind swirled leaves around her feet, but she didn't seem to notice the sign telling her he was near. Tavis followed her, but didn't approach.

Her hair was down with the pink streak braided and tucked behind her ear. She walked slowly, as if each step conjured a new thought. Tavis felt the wind move from her to him and smelled her sweet cherry scent. As hard as it was, he had to trust that he was doing the right thing by not pushing her again.

May stopped. After several heartbeats, she turned. Tavis hadn't hidden himself in the trees. He stood directly in her path behind her about fifty metres away. Her breath caught, and so did his.

Time froze except for the magic pulling them together. It was warm, filling his chest. The looks they gave each other across the distance was like a replay of their time together to this point. The dancing, the teasing, the demands and submissions. The bold confidence that peeked out of her shy exterior from time to time. And then the pain.

He saw the moment that memory hit her. She took three quick steps back. He wouldn't corner her too soon. Not when she'd been out here looking for a moment of peace to herself.

Tavis nodded and sighed. Turning, he walked away.

"Tavis," she called. After barely saying a word to each other, her voice sounded better than he'd conjured in his dreams.

He'd never deny her. He turned back.

"I love you." The words were almost too quiet, but there was no mistaking the way they formed on her lips. If she had punctuated her declaration with anything other than another two steps back, Tavis would have run to her and threw her up in the air and trapped her in his arms.

He closed his eyes to hold her words tight instead. Then he left her.

Back at work, he gave his brother his wish and let him punch him. With too much glee, Noah hit him with enough force to knock him back. But the glee didn't last. Noah clapped him on the back with an assurance that everything would work out.

She wouldn't be able to back away from him in two days. In two days, they had the camping trip with the middle school kids.

They have to function with no one else around them being the wiser of what was between them.

"I'm going to the school to finalize everything for camping. The new guy still seems a bit lost." The new principal tried too hard to make things perfect or right, resulting in daily messages for him and Noah with either a change in plans or more questions. They'd seen the same reaction from him with the way he handled problem kids, the way he spoke to kids and families at the festival, and out in public. No one could fault him for his eagerness to please the community he now belonged to, but it made for unnecessary arrangements for a trip they'd done a dozen times before. But whatever made the man feel better.

Duke took Tavis into his office and went over yet another new plan he'd created for the trip. Tavis brought him back on track to what the teachers had told him. The trip never changed and had quickly become a tradition. After several minutes of back and forth, Tavis had the guy back on track. But before he'd let him leave, he asked Tavis to speak to the class that would be going.

Now, he stood in front of bored eleven- and twelve-year-olds. None of them had been on this trip before, but they knew what to expect as the previous classes talked so much about it. Tavis went through the motions, anyway.

Kellan sat at the back of the classroom, his head down on his desk. The principal stopped Tavis from speaking with his hand in the air. The bear in him thought it might be a good idea to bite it off, but Tavis waited.

The kids sitting around Kellan started elbowing him until he sat up.

"I know we can get tired from time to time, but what Mr. Greer is saying is important for safety during the camping trip this weekend. Do your best to pay close attention." While his words could be for anyone in the class, his gaze was on Kellan.

The kid looked sheepish, but nodded. Tavis frowned. Poor little guy looked a little pale. He'd just had his pictures done that morning with his family. Tavis wondered how he'd been feeling during that. He still wore his button-up shirt with his hair styled on the top. He might not make it on the trip anyway if he was getting sick.

Tavis continued without waiting for the principal's nod. Another ten minutes later and he was on his way out, having felt like it was a waste of an afternoon. But another day was almost over. Another day until he could get closer to May again.

May hadn't put all the pieces together with what it meant to go camping. Noah had lent her a backpack to use, telling her to bring her things out to the living room, and he'd help her pack with everything else she'd need. She kept herself from asking what. Camping with a group of kids couldn't be that bad. Right?

But when she waited on the couch with her things, Noah came in with armloads of more and an empty backpack. He showed her how to pack it, putting everything in it in a logical order.

"Seems there's a science to this." May put the last of her things in the top of the backpack and cinched in tight. Her camera stayed in its own bag.

"Things learned from years of experience. This is something we'll teach the kids this weekend too. The school started this trip for fun, but since we started volunteering we've been putting in our own survival lessons. It's an important skill set for anyone."

Tavis showed up an hour later and the three of them set out to the school together. He looked at her, even touched her. The light set of his hand on her back to help her in the truck heated her to the bone.

Noah got out of the truck at the school and walked over to the group, waiting for them outside. Tavis stopped her on the other side of the truck, blocking them from view.

"Are you okay?"

May tilted her head. "Why are you asking? Are you asking how I'm feeling from the accident? You've seen me every day and have never said a word, let alone ask how I am."

"That, yes, but since I saw you walking the other day. And because I see exhaustion in your eyes."

"I'm tired, but I'm fine."

"I feel it, too," he whispered and set his knuckle under her chin. Setting his lips to hers, he kissed her. Not quite gently, but he didn't let their bodies touch. Now wasn't the time. "Stay close to the group, pixie."

He passed her the backpack, holding it out to put it on her back. "Thanks." May grabbed her camera bag from inside the truck. She needed work to distract her from being so close to Tavis. Taking out her camera, she snapped pictures as she walked toward the group of excited kids and teachers.

Tavis and Noah went around to each kid and adult, checking their bags and making sure they had everything they needed while the principal talked at the front of the group. May's judgment was still out on the man. He seemed flighty, although well-meaning.

Parents could volunteer as chaperones, but none had. With Tavis, Noah, and May, they had enough adults, including the four teachers and the principal.

May spotted Tavis talking with Kellan. He had his hand on the kid's shoulder, looking down at him with concern. Kellan nodded, then looked over at May. She waved and lifted her camera. The kid gave her a smile, giving Tavis a reason to look over his shoulder. May pressed the button one more time.

"Everyone pair up. Time to head out." Noah's deep grumble echoed over the top of all the small conversations. People quieted and did as he said quickly. The effect of a certain voice was powerful.

It wasn't the type of camping trip where they bussed the kids to a fun campground. They all hiked several kilometres into the woods and set up their own camp, giving the kids a different camping experience.

Whenever they stopped on the hike, May took out her camera. It would take her a long time to sort through the images from this trip. Many of the pictures she took didn't have any thought behind them. She was trying to capture everything she could without knowing what the weekend would hold.

But May had to concentrate on the hike as much as any of the others. Tavis and Noah often moved along the group, checking in with all the kids. And the adults. Noah would stop and give her a nod, but it was Tavis that took his time walking next to her.

He didn't have to say anything to ask how she was doing. Those green eyes of his roamed over her from head to toe, not moving on until he was satisfied she was fine.

And she was. The exhaustion she'd been feeling wasn't dragging her down today.

She wondered how much that had to do with her mate being so close.

Chapter Fifteen

Tavis enjoyed this trip each year, but this one hit the top of his list. He intended to bring May out, just the two of them sometime. She'd looked a little lost at the beginning, but now that they'd finished hiking and they had camp set up, she settled in well. Looking comfortable as she photographed not only the kids, but the nature around them. The area looked similar to the waterfall he'd shown her. She'd sent him a quizzical eye toward the north, but he shook his head. They took no one near that little sanctuary. Not that someone couldn't discover it on their own, but as far as they knew, no one had.

They had a couple of campfires going, giving everyone a spot to keep warm. The first night out wasn't more than setting up and settling in. They'd all packed their food for the day, but tomorrow would be different. They used it as an opportunity to teach them what was edible in the wilderness and what wasn't. And teach them all how to fish. Of course, the brothers always packed extra for those that wouldn't sample the goods from the trip, hiking the extra supplies out to the campsite that morning.

Tavis sat with his back against a tree, eating his sandwich while listening to the kids. The first night filled with ghost stories. No adult planned it that way. Kids came up with this part on their own. But Tavis had heard most of the stories by now. Occasionally, a kid would come up with one of their own.

Kellan was that kid this year. It surprised Tavis to see him. The other day at the school, he looked as if he was coming down with something, but after checking in with him before the hike, Tavis was confident he felt fine.

"There are always eyes in the trees." He mumbled it, but all the kids around his circle paused, sensing another story.

Even May made her way over, moving around with her camera. She never tired of her job. Sheer joy radiated from her.

"They watch. They judge. And they wait. They pull him into the woods." There began his story. "Trapping him by moving in behind. The beings those eyes belonged to chased him through the woods, far enough that no one could hear what was about to happen. He was alone as far as he could see. Only the eyes and the feeling of being watched. Until he heard a growl. Deep and dangerous."

Tavis saw that Kellan's shoulders shook and frowned.

"Sudden heat wraps around him before the pain starts. His bones crush, pop, and change, forcing his body to twist and contort. He can hear the growling get louder and realizes it isn't only coming from those eyes. The sound is coming from him."

His vague story enraptured everyone around him. The kid has a way of painting a picture. He doesn't stop staring at the fire while he murmurs. The story is vague to those around him, but Tavis shared a look with his brother over the crowd. Noah turns his frown on Kellan as he finishes.

"His chest is ripped open."

Some kids flinched. It wasn't only Kellan's words, but the way he said it, the haunted look in his own eyes that affected the listeners.

"His heart beating to a new rhythm, not that of a human." Kellan looks up. "Beware of those eyes, or you'll roam these woods as something unnatural, helping to draw in the next victim." The kid's lips twitched as his audience remained silent. That small smile shook off the uneasiness that shrouded Kellan as he spoke. His description was a familiar one for Tavis and Noah, although he added a creepy flair for entertainment.

But the only shifters here were him and his brother. Scent told them a lot about a person. Human or not being one of them.

Tavis shook it off. It wasn't impossible for someone to come up with a werewolf story that resembled a reality the general population knew nothing about.

Not much later, the teachers started sending kids to bed. Group by group, they settled inside the tents. They spread the adult tents out around the perimeter, each adult getting their own space. Except his and May's tents. They were on the same side of the entire group and beside each other.

"If it had been appropriate to share, we would be." He tucked a strand of hair that had fallen from her ponytail behind her ear. "I miss lying next to you, pixie."

"I know. Me too."

Tavis had to stop himself from moving closer. The power that pulsed between them grew stronger. Now wasn't the time with kids still awake in their sleeping bags, but soon. "Soon." He spoke his thoughts, hoping she understood everything that one word meant.

"I..."

"Shh." Tavis swiped his thumb over her lips before taking a deep breath. Gripping her shoulder, he turned her toward her tent.

May looked over her shoulder as she ducked down. Her tongue traced where he'd touched. Tavis groaned. She bit her lip instead and ducked into the tent.

Tavis darted into his, lying on his back. He threw an arm over his eyes and imagined his mate was with him.

She slept surprisingly well. Someone started singing. It took her a few moments to realize it was Tavis. His voice a melodic timbre.

The camp quieted as he lulled everyone to sleep. Including her. Nothing about his baritone was soft, but it was soothing.

May only had herself to blame for this distance. Being so stubborn and running away. Had she been wrong? She wanted to be in both places. And asking for time to figure that out hadn't been wrong. But Tavis hadn't been wrong in pushing her, either.

The past week sleeping in Blair's spare room gave her the time to work through her thoughts. May loved Tavis as much as he loved her. They needed to work this out, which meant May needed to talk.

After this trip. When they hiked back, she wouldn't return with Noah. She'd go with her mate.

Tavis and Noah had been up first, making lots of noise to help wake everyone. May took her time getting herself ready inside her tent. She was here for a purpose and refused to be the one holding anyone back. It surprised her to feel as excited as if she were participating and not just taking pictures.

They separated them into small groups and assigned a teacher to each of them. Each group had a survival mission to complete over two hours. Tavis and Noah made this fun and turned it into a game. The kids turned it into a competition.

May followed Noah and Tavis as they each moved between the groups to help explain the missions and then to help with different tasks. Foraging, building a shelter, fishing, making a fire, knot tying, and trap setting. They rotated every two hours throughout the day, giving each group a chance to complete each mission. It made for a long day, but the kids rose to the challenge with more enthusiasm than May expected.

At the end of the day, they all compared shelters, fires, knots, traps, and they ate the fish and food they foraged.

The stories around the fires weren't ghost stories anymore. They were retelling tales from the day.

May sat on a log near a fire and scrolled through the images she'd taken, deleting the blatantly terrible ones to help make her job easier later.

The ones with laughter or frantic panic were her favourite. The teacher's faces provided just as much entertainment, despite most of them having done this trip before. But in each set of pictures from each group, May deleted a dozen.

But never any with Tavis in them. She tried not to look too far into that, ignoring how long she lingered on those images.

The principal had tried hard to take control of his group, steering them in the direction he thought they should go, but Tavis or Noah always made it back to him before he stole the fun from the kids, setting them all back on track. The man was flustered most of the day.

While May scrolled the images of his group, she paused when she saw something other than panic and frustration. She'd caught a moment of anger. It was her job to see the emotions in expressions. Duke had a fierce glare firing in his eyes.

May looked closer at the image, trying to remember at what point she took it and who he directed the anger toward. Scrolling through a few more pictures, she found one of his entire group, but none of them gave her any clue who he'd been glaring at. She didn't delete the picture as she had others with odd expressions. Something about this one didn't sit right with her.

Sighing, she turned her camera off and looked up, meeting eyes with Duke. His bland face stared, and she couldn't stop her flinch.

Throwing her bag over her shoulder, she stood and started walking around, trying to shake off the eyes she felt on her back.

Tavis didn't like the unease he sensed from May. He tracked her progress. She stayed close to as many people as possible, but after a few minutes, she turned away from camp to walk on her own. Nodding to his brother to tell him he'd be unavailable for the next little bit, Tavis followed his mate.

She went further on her own than he would have liked, but the distance from the camp worked in his favour.

He didn't hide his steps behind her. At one point, she paused, tilting her head over her shoulder, but she hugged herself and kept walking. The cool night air didn't ease the need to be close to her. It carried the magic of Fate. He breathed in the pull full of her sweet scent.

Tavis closed the distance, having decided they travelled far enough from camp no one would interrupt them, but not so far to find trouble.

The second his hand slid around her waist, May stopped. Curling his fingers, he spun her around. His other hand cupped her face.

"I thought I told you to stay close."

"Sorry." She shrugged and couldn't sound any less sorry. "I knew you were behind me. I didn't mean to go so far."

"You waited for me to stop you." Tavis read between the lines. "Something is bothering you."

"It's nothing. I was just scrolling through my pictures."

"May." Tavis urged her backward, pleased she didn't fight him. Once her back hit the tree, he set the weight of his body against hers. "We can't keep our distance anymore. We can't keep silent. Please tell me you're ready to talk."

"I'm ready to talk."

Tavis lifted his head, his gaze boring into hers. He searched for any uncertainty, for any of the fear and pain that had caused this distance between them. Tavis understood the need for her balance and her need to hold on so tight.

"Really, Tavis. I never intended to fight this, and I wasn't trying to. I..."

"You hoped this relationship would take a natural course." And he let her believe it might.

"I guess so."

"There's nothing natural about mates." He traced her lips and her cheek with his thumb. "This isn't the place to discuss everything. I just want to know you're mine, pixie. I want to know you're willing to work together. That in the most passionate moments, you'll be under me, calling my name. That when you're lonely, you'll call me first. That when you have exciting news, it's your mate you crave to celebrate with."

Throughout his speech, he set his forehead against hers. They exchanged air like it was the only thing that would keep each of them alive. He fucking loved this woman.

"This was how we should have started. I was stubborn. And stupid. I've caused us so much pain."

"Just answer me, May. Don't rehash what we should have done. Answer me."

"I'm yours. It's only your name that will ever leave my lips in those moments. I've been lonely all week and only wanted your voice."

Tavis growled. The deep sound vibrated almost to the point of pain. He kissed her. Not gently. Their lips came together in raw emotions. Supping, moving, licking, nipping. Tavis had no control of his hands sliding beneath her shirt, but the strap of her camera bag kept one hand lower than the other. He squeezed her hip and ran the fingers of his other hand over her ribs.

Pulling his head back an inch, he breathed deep. "When we get back from this trip, I'm going to bite you while I bury my cock so deep inside your heat you won't know where I stop and you begin. We're going to mate."

Her lips quivered with her next intake of air. The skin beneath his hands pebbled.

"Do you like the sound of that, pixie? Your heat wrapped around my cock so tight we both explode and I sink my fangs into your skin? Where should I bite you? Right here?" Tavis kissed down the column of her neck until he reached the base where he nipped. Not with his fangs, despite that they appeared the moment he claimed her mouth. He needed to rein himself in. It was too easy to get carried away with his words when he got this reaction from her. Her body was pliant against the tree, letting him hold her up. She'd tilted her head back against the rough bark.

"Tavis," she gasped.

"Answer," he growled.

"Yes. I want that."

"You want it right here?" He nipped again.

"Maybe." Despite her pliant state, he heard the teasing tilt in her voice.

"Oh, pixie. There are so many places I can bite you." As much as he wanted to give her a taste, give her some relief from this state, he couldn't. Not here. He moved his mouth back to hers and continued to kiss her, keeping the heat high for a little longer. But he needed to bring them back to Earth.

Panting carried through the trees. And it wasn't theirs. The sound made him pause, but when several branches snapped with others following it, Tavis lifted his head and turned toward the sound heading their way.

"What is it?"

He didn't answer her, but her breath hitched when she heard the sounds for herself. May pushed herself off the tree and straightened her shirt.

Tavis caught more than a sound. He caught a scent. Breathing deep, he recognized the distinct wild scent of a shifter. There was something strange about the scent. It wasn't matured—it was fresh.

Chapter Sixteen

The scent of an adult human followed it.

"May, I need you to stop the principal." They'd spent enough time with the people on this camping trip that Tavis could determine the distinct identities. But the wild scent overpowered the natural scent of the shifter. The young, scared shifter. What a hell of a time to go through this.

May didn't question him on how he knew who was coming.

The young shifter came into view, heading directly for them. Kellan's wide eyes were glowing, and he dug in his feet to skid to a stop.

"No. Keep running, Kellan. I'm with you." Tavis swung his arm wide and stepped to the side to let Kellan run ahead of him. He pinned May with a hand on her elbow. "He's about thirty metres behind him. You need to stop him. He can't find Kellan. You didn't see either of us." Tavis took off after Kellan as May took off toward the principal to stop him sooner rather than waiting.

"Oh. Duke. Is everything okay?" Her concern was thick. It was enough to stop the rushing footsteps coming after Kellan.

Tavis turned his focus on the kid. "You're going to be okay, Kellan."

The boy ran, his blood pumping fast with panic. Wild eyes looked up at him as they ran side by side.

Tavis let his bear show through his own eyes and softened it with a smile. "It's okay. Let's get as far away as we can. I can help."

"What's happening, Tavis?"

"Keep running. I'll explain when it's safe to stop. I don't want Mr. Greyson to find us."

Kellan nodded with complete trust and some of his fear faded.

Tavis steered them closer to the other side of town, past the limits they'd set for the camping trip and near *Bearbrook Cabins*, and north as close to the clearing he'd shown May. The adrenaline running through Kellan's blood gave him the energy to run farther than he would have made it even the day before.

"We're close. Right past those trees." Tavis pointed ahead of them. Kellan pushed himself harder. The scent of a shifter was getting stronger. He had little time.

Tavis wasn't sure what to expect. This wasn't how it happened to him and his brother and cousins. They found bear cubs in the woods. Gentle wind filled with magic circled them, changing them the first time to identical cubs to the ones they'd found. Those cubs grew with each of them and still lived in these woods.

He couldn't smell any other bears nearby. None of them had experienced the adrenaline and panic coursing through Kellan.

They broke through the trees into the clearing. Kellan stopped and whirled on Tavis. "What's happening?" He rolled his shoulders and neck as if his body ached.

"That story you told around the fire last night? Wasn't just a story was it?"

"I've been having that dream for weeks."

"Okay." Tavis crouched down, so he didn't tower over him. "Kellan, you're changing. But I promise it isn't like your dream or like your story. I promise."

"But it's going to hurt, isn't it?" A small whimper cracked in his voice.

"Some. I'm so sorry for that. It gets better." Not that knowing time would made it better helped at all in this moment.

"You can change?"

"Yeah. Me and my brother. And my cousins. Except for Dakota."

"No one knows that, do they?" The conversation seemed to help distract him, but he was still restless.

"Not many."

"What do I do?"

"Do you feel warm?"

"Yeah. Kinda like a buzzing."

"Good. Take a deep breath."

The kid took the instructions to heart and filled his lungs. As he did, the wind swirled around him. "Do you see that?"

"Yeah. That's a good sign. That happens for me too. Watch." Tavis controlled his breathing and pulled on the magic. Visible wind pulled toward him from the air, making circles around his feet. He'd never tried to slow the process of shifting before. Tavis intended to match Kellan's shift. He had no one else to help him through this. If his parents were shifters, Tavis and the rest of the family would have known. Besides, no one else was here, and this was happening now.

"Okay. Now what?"

"Take your clothes off so they don't get ruined. You'll need them when you shift back."

"I'll be able to change back?" Hope pitched his voice high.

"Yeah, buddy. You will." Tavis waited for him to get rid of his clothes. And Tavis did the same while keeping his distance. "Now, take another breath and let it happen. I'm right here with you, Kellan. I promise you're going to be okay."

"I'm scared." He sounded much younger.

"I know. I was too my first time. And many times after that. Sometimes it still scares me." Like when raging after almost losing his mate and unsure if he'd be able to control the animal in him.

Kellan nodded and took another deep breath. The cries that ripped from him almost killed Tavis. No kid should have to feel that kind of pain. He didn't remember it feeling that way, but he'd also been much younger. Maybe Fate was kinder. Or he'd blocked out the experience.

"I'm right here. You're doing great." Kellan wasn't in control, but whatever assurance Tavis could give, he would.

His cries eased into groans. Tavis thanked Fate for her small reprieve of his pain. He pulled harder on the magic and let himself begin the shift.

Kellan's body morphed into the shape of a young bear. Brown fur sprouted over his body and a low hump formed on his back. He was a grizzly bear.

Tavis held off the last of his shift until Kellan had finished, landing on the ground with four gangly paws. Once he looked up at Tavis, Tavis finished shifting. He was larger than a full-sized grizzly while Kellan was only a little bigger than a juvenile.

Must be something in the air to create all us grizzlies.

Kellan shook his head and blinked. It was strange to hear someone speaking inside your head.

You're safe, Kellan. It's all over.

Until I have to change back.

Tavis chuckled, but the sound came out through their thoughts. *Until then, yes.*

What do I do now?

Rest. Explore. Take your time to learn how to move. I won't go anywhere. I promise.

"Oh. Duke. Is everything okay?" May hiked back toward camp, keeping her pace as casual and close to the rushing footsteps. Duke ran into her. He grabbed onto her arms to stop the collision and keep moving, but May dug her fingers into his forearms to stop him from moving on.

"Yes. I believe one of the students is ill. Didn't you see him run past you?" He tried to pull away from her, but she gripped him tighter.

"No." She dropped a healthy dose of shock into her tone. "I haven't seen anyone out here until you came along. I just needed some quiet and went for a walk. I was on my way back."

His brows dropped and the same frown she'd captured on her camera covered his face. May didn't like how she hadn't fooled him. A shiver raced down her spine.

"There's no one else out here. How about I come back to camp with you? I'll help you do a head count."

"No. Someone came out here. I'm sure he was sick. The health and safety of these kids is my responsibility."

"And I'm telling you I haven't seen or heard anyone. They aren't out here. If they're sick, they've probably gone back to camp to tell a teacher or go to their tent. It's best to check in with the other adults and then set up a search if needed. Noah and Tavis are part of search and rescue. They'll know the proper procedure." May firmed her grip on one arm and turned him around.

He followed, but the stare in his eyes made May nervous. Anxiety filled her from whatever vibe this man threw off. Of course the man responsible for these kids would go after someone he thought was sick. May had no reason to look past that. But it was the expression in his eyes she found on her camera that had her taking her walk into the woods to begin with.

"Do you know who it was you saw?" May raised her voice. If the other adults and kids couldn't hear her, at least Noah should.

"No."

May picked out the lie, shocked at her own intuition. She hadn't expected to catch that twinge in his tone.

"Let's fill in the other adults first and start a head count."

"This is a waste of time. I saw someone run off. I should go after them instead."

"I understand your concern. But I'm sure it's hard to know what the right decision to do is when you're still so new to a place like this." The backhanded compliment felt good to say. May had tried to give the guy the benefit of the doubt, but she decided it was easier to just let herself dislike him. Trusting her instincts and all that.

They made it to the edge of the camp, and Noah started toward them. Slowly as if he understood they needed to waste time. He had to have sensed the same thing Tavis had as Kellan ran toward them. May wasn't sure what it was but she could guess. Kellan's eyes had a wild glow she recognized.

Duke tried to urge her forward.

"Wait. We don't want to cause any unnecessary panic. He's coming. Be patient."

His arm tensed under her hand, but she ignored it.

"Is something wrong?" Noah spoke low, looking to her first and then settling his gaze on the principal.

"A kid ran off. I was going after them, but couldn't find them. We need to do a head count and find out who's missing."

"Did you see who it was?" Noah made a show of looking over the heads of the kids at the camp.

"No, I didn't." Duke put on a better act this time with the lie, but she still caught the same undertone of frustration.

"I was out there and didn't see anyone. Hopefully, they circled back here."

"They did," Noah stated flatly.

"What?" Duke's head shook as he stared back at Noah.

"Kellan is in my tent. He wasn't feeling well. Thought he was going to be sick, but when he wasn't, he came back to find me."

"Well, thank you for looking after him. I'll go check on him."

"He's asleep. But in case it wasn't him you saw, we still need to do a head count. If someone's missing, I'll start searching while everyone else remains at camp." Even the principal, with his frustration, couldn't argue with Noah when he spoke like that.

He gave a stiff nod and stalked off to the closest teacher.

Noah gave her a knowing look before he started counting heads on his way back toward his tent. May needed to make the same show, but as she went around, she spoke to the teachers to tell them Kellan was in Noah's tent, so to make sure they counted him too. None of them questioned her, their trust in Noah unshakable.

May breathed a little easier now that others surrounded her and they all believed the lie. Once she had her head count, she reported it back to the principal and the other teachers who'd gathered closer to Noah's tent, as the last kid to count was supposedly asleep inside.

"Everyone is accounted for. That's a relief." May let out a sigh and settled herself on the log Noah had sitting in front of his tent.

But this lie would only last as long as it took for someone to insist on seeing Kellan. May had to force her attention on the small fire in front of her and on the others around them, not allowing it to wander to the woods.

Soon, the teachers spread back out among the kids, but Duke stayed close by.

"Where's your brother?" Duke had pulled up a seat on the other side of Noah's fire.

"I have no idea. He's a big boy." Noah's lips quirked, and he spoke with the general annoying affection of brothers.

After half an hour, Noah went inside his tent. He spent a few minutes in there, letting his low voice carry, as if he was talking to someone.

He came out with a can and a pot. Sitting down, he started prepping the soup. "No fever. Something he ate isn't sitting well. I'll take this soup in for him. It should help." Noah spoke to no one and anyone, his gaze never meeting hers or Duke's.

But he carried on with enough detail that it would be difficult for someone to call him on the lie.

May didn't know how long Tavis and Kellan would be, or if they'd be back at all. She tried not to let her worry show.

At one point, Noah set his hand on her shaking knee when no one was paying attention. "He'll be fine." His low murmur and deeper tone made it difficult to make out his words, but May understood.

Tavis would take care of him. And he and Noah would figure out what to do about the teachers and other kids. She doubted this was the first time they had to come up with a story to cover the existence of shifters.

Tavis was patient, but he knew they needed to get back to camp soon. He trusted May and his brother to cover Kellan's tracks.

The young bear took a while to get his legs under him. Co-ordination was one of the hardest things to start with. Four legs were easier, but not until he understood how his new body worked.

Kellan had rested for the first ten minutes, taking large deep breaths. The kid's nose and eyes had run wild with all the new senses. Tavis stayed quiet and let him process everything.

He'd started with walking, working his way up to a run. He'd stumbled a few times, but soon stayed on all four paws.

Are you ready to go back? Tavis stood from where he'd been laying under a tree.

Do I have to go back?

Yes. He walked toward the young bear, pleased that he'd been enjoying himself. The panic and fear had vanished as he'd moved around. *The thing about being a shifter is we have to keep it a secret. People don't trust things they don't understand.*

Meaning they'd want to hurt us, or something else.

Yeah. It sucks sometimes, but we have to cover our tracks. If we don't go back, there would be too many questions.

What if I can't change back?

You will, but we'll cross that bridge when we come to it. If you have too much trouble, we'll have to cover our tracks another way.

How do I do it?

Close your eyes and take a deep breath. Search for the same warmth you felt when you shifted into a bear. That warmth is the magic that makes this possible. Let it fill you.

He closed his eyes when Tavis told him to, but now he cracked one open and looked up at him. *All of that sounds stu...* *silly.* He corrected himself.

Tavis chuckled, but it came out as a huff through his nose. *Maybe it does, but that doesn't make it any less true. Now, try it.*

The hike back would be easier and shorter if they both had four paws rather than two feet, but Tavis didn't want to chance anyone finding them while Kellan learned to shift back for the first time.

Kellan closed his eyes again and started breathing. Each one he took went a little deeper into his lungs. *I feel it.* Wonder filled his voice.

Good. Pull it in and let the change happen, just like you did before.

This time, Tavis didn't shift with him. He waited until Kellan had finished. The pain had already receded to more of an ache rather than the same agony. His calm state helped.

Small eyes clear of any wild animal looked at his hands and arms, lifting his feet and legs to inspect his skin. Then they looked at Tavis. "I'm okay."

Tavis nodded his big head, then stepped back and pulled on the magic. Kellan watched him shift.

"That looks so cool."

"It is pretty cool. Get dressed. I'll shift and you can ride back to camp on my back. It will be quicker."

"Really?"

"Yup. We'll bring you back up here once this trip is over to help you practice and answer any more questions."

Kellan started dressing. "But tonight we have to go back. I get it." He understood, but he wasn't happy about it.

Tavis gathered his clothes while Kellen finished getting ready. "Mind holding these for me for the ride?"

"Sure." The boy took the boots with his clothes tucked inside.

Tavis shifted, inwardly smiling at the soft "Wow" that escaped from Kellan. Crouching on the ground, he nodded for Kellan to climb on his back.

"Can I still hear you if you talk to me like this?"

Tavis shook his head.

"That would be cool." Kellan adjusted himself, setting the boots in front of him between his outstretched arms that were gripping onto his fur.

Tavis lifted, letting Kellan get a feel for his movement. They didn't need to run back, but they shouldn't take their time. He set himself up for a jogging pace.

Kellan laughed for the first half. Tavis had to stop and look back at him, holding a paw over the front of his snout to tell him to be quiet. They were getting closer to the camp and, without knowing how Noah covered for them, they needed to go in silently.

Tavis stopped several metres away from Noah's side of camp and crouched to let Kellan off. He shifted and took his clothes.

"Stay here and stay quiet. I need to talk to Noah first to find out where they all think you are."

Kellan nodded rather than answering with words.

Tavis approached the camp on silent feet and waited. Noah would catch his scent soon. His brother made his way past the thick brush and trees to where Tavis waited.

"The kid is supposed to be in my tent. I said he wasn't feeling well. I've checked on him several times and even made him soup. It isn't clear yet to get him inside."

"What did you say was wrong with him?"

"Upset stomach. Ate something that didn't agree with him, but he's fine. Get him as close to my tent as possible and I'll give a signal when it's clear."

"Got it." Tavis paused. "You scented the shifter before he ran off, didn't you?"

"Yeah. I couldn't chase him, but I knew he was heading directly for you."

He clapped his brother on the shoulder and returned to Kellan. "Okay, bud. Here's the plan." Tavis relayed everything Noah said, so if someone asked him in the morning, there wouldn't be any confusion over what happened to him.

They made it as close to Noah's tent as they could. He helped Kellan keep his steps silent. It would be a learning process for the kid, but they'd all happily help him. What to say to his parents would be something they'd have to discuss. Not everyone told their parents when they shifted, keeping it a secret from all family members. They hadn't, but Tavis understood the reason behind it. But every shifter he knew had other animals as mentors, a cub and their mother.

Tavis listened to the small conversations and waited. A loud noise came from the opposite side of the camp and rushing footsteps grew distant. The next thing he heard was the high whistle of his brother that mimicked a bird. No one would ever expect a man with such a deep voice capable of making such a high-pitched sound.

He led Kellan back into camp, where Noah rushed him inside his tent. "Get in the sleeping bag and go to sleep. Really go to sleep."

"You need the rest," Tavis added.

"Okay." Kellan crawled in as silently as he could. They caught the yawn before Noah zipped the tent back up.

Tavis would make himself scarce, hanging around the edges of the camp as if that's where he'd been all evening, but first he had to know his mate was safe.

"Where's May?"

"Helping with the distraction. She's fine." Noah understood.

"Thanks for watching out for her."

"She did good."

Tavis moved back into the trees and circled the limits of their campsite, following May's scent. As whatever distraction they'd created dissolved, he moved himself closer to camp, but continued to patrol. It wasn't until everyone started going to bed that he let himself be seen.

"Good job, pixie." Tavis sidled up behind her and murmured in her ear.

Spinning around, she looked up at him. "Is..."

"Shh." Tavis nodded. No one was nearby, but he didn't want anyone to overhear. "Get some sleep. It's a long hike back to town tomorrow."

"You're not going to bed?"

"I doubt it." Not in case Kellan needed him or Noah.

Tavis kissed her. The gentle touch would have to be enough to sustain them.

May let her hand graze over his chest as she walked past him toward her tent. Tavis sat outside of them and built a small fire of his own. He wouldn't need the warmth for a while, but it kept him busy as the hours passed.

Chapter Seventeen

May flopped onto the couch in the living room. The rest of the trip had been quiet. No more disturbances in the night and everyone had been exhausted as they packed up camp and hiked back to meet their parents at the school.

Tavis and Noah had written down their phone numbers and slipped them in Kellan's backpack, also telling him he could call Blair to contact them as well. They hadn't talked to his parents more than to spin the same story of him not feeling well. It was the most they could do for now.

Tavis sat down beside her, throwing his arm over her shoulder and pulling her close.

"We got back just in time." He pressed a kiss to her head.

"What do you mean?"

"There's a storm coming in."

"I hadn't noticed." The skies were clear, and the air was warm.

"It isn't close yet, but I think it's going to move in fast."

"What kind of storm?"

"Just rain and wind. Nothing we'd want to be caught camping in. If it had been any closer, we would have packed everyone

up last night and got everyone home. We have a couple of days."
Tavis adjusted them to see her face.

"What are you going to do about Kellan?"

"Nothing to do except help him. It will ultimately be up to
him if he wants to tell his parents. We'll help him through that
too if he decides to. It can be a scary time, but also a lot of fun."

"He was okay last night?"

"Terrified. But once he got through the shift and calmed
down, he practiced with four legs and played around a bit. He's
going to be just fine." A hint of pride filled his voice. Kellan was
in good hands.

"I'm happy you were there and able to go with him."

Tavis tucked a strand of hair behind her ear and kissed her
forehead. "Me too." Leaning back, he pulled her with him until
he laid down on the couch and her on his chest. "Kiss me, pixie.
I'm not wasting another minute without you."

Butterflies grew and fluttered in her stomach. This wasn't
anything new between them, but after so much distance and
pain, it felt like something brand new. A fresh start where she
would not be stubborn and stupid.

Dropping her head, May kissed him as he'd demanded. Tavis
laid still, relaxed against the cushion while she controlled the
kiss. She expected him to take over at any moment, but he
didn't. His hands crept up and down her sides and his lips
moved with hers, but nothing more.

Warmth spread through her, slow like the kiss. The longer
he left her to take charge, the more she found she needed. The

temperature inside her increased, and the throbbing started between her legs. Before she knew what she was doing, she took what she wanted from the kiss. Using her tongue and teeth, May did her best to make them one.

"That's it, pixie," he growled with the next small breath she allowed him. His hands gripped tighter at her waist. "Take what you want. Because you're starting this with the full knowledge of what is going to happen next. I'll finish it."

He'd promised to mate her, and they'd work out the rest later. And she promised to let him. The only thing she felt right now was love for him. No more hesitation lived inside her for any reason. The war of balance was over.

Setting her knees on either side of his hips, she sat up. His hands dropped to her jean-clad hips. "I know what's going to happen. And I'm ready. I wonder how long you can let me lead, though."

"Careful, pixie." But his warning didn't hit through his grin.

May hooked her fingers under the hem of her shirt. As slowly as possible, she lifted it. Tavis ran his fingers back and forth over her skin with each inch she exposed. It tickled. She laughed, but didn't break her position or her pace.

She tossed her shirt to the floor and lifted her hands to her hair.

"Do you think it's wise to tempt a bear?"

"I think the benefits will outweigh the risks."

"Maybe."

Reaching behind her, she unclasped her bra. She intended to drop it on the floor with her shirt, but something playful in her made her throw it over his eyes.

Tavis growled. Before she thought better of running from a bear, May jumped off his lap and raced down the hall to his bedroom. Tavis was right on her heels. He could reach her, but he was playing as much as she was.

She squealed as she ran into the bathroom. And that was when he caught her, spinning her around so her back rested against the counter.

"Guess I didn't last too long." Tavis trapped her with an arm on either side.

"No, you didn't. I bet I can take control again."

"Really? So bold." Tavis pointed at her to make her stay as he stepped toward the shower. His gaze only left her long enough to turn on the shower. When he came back to her, he stripped. "Better get those jeans off, pixie."

May resumed her slow pace.

"Faster, May." The growl in his voice snapped her into action. She hadn't meant to obey like that, but she knew with him she'd always submit. Her jeans and underwear were around her knees when he finished. He wrapped his hand around her waist and lifted her. The cool counter against her ass shocked her.

Tavis ripped her clothes the rest of the way off her legs. "It doesn't look like you have the control right now, does it, pixie?"

"There's still time."

T avis pulled her to the edge of the counter, groaning as his cock settled against her heat. As much as he'd wanted to take her on the couch, they'd been in the woods for two days without showers. While he didn't mind—she smelled and tasted delicious to his senses, no matter what—they could have some fun in the shower and make this last. The heat of the water would relax them both.

He'd planned to let her play to her heart's content, but when she threw her bra at him, he snapped. And so had she. This was a much better plan.

Lifting her, Tavis held her against him and carried her into the shower. May hissed when the heat hit her back, then sighed.

"Oh, that feels good. I almost forgot I needed that. You're very distracting." She grinned as she tilted her head back so the water ran over her hair. Tavis shifted his hands to set one at her back, allowing her to dip herself into the water further.

His gaze landed on her breasts. Drops of water sprayed over her shoulder to land on the full mounds. Desire peaked her dusky nipples, begging for touch. But he couldn't get to them without dropping her.

He wasn't about to disturb her bliss. He could wait now that he had her in his arms again. Something in his chest clicked into place. It clicked the night before, but everything happening with Kellan distracted him from his mate.

May lifted her head enough to peek up at him. "You don't seem to be in a rush tonight."

"I'm not."

She hummed and pulled herself up until her arms wrapped around his neck. Before he reclaimed his grip under her ass, she dropped her legs from around his waist. Sliding down his body, May let her hands run over his shoulders and down his chest.

Her touch was euphoric.

She'd moved so slowly, Tavis hadn't seen her next move coming. May dropped to her knees, using one hand to catch her fall.

"Pixie." Her name was a warning, a concern, and a prayer on his lips.

Her only answer was a sly grin that was rare to see on her face. This boldness showed in her before she gave in and submitted all of herself to him. Tavis loved every part of her.

"Give it your best shot."

She laughed and wrapped her hand around the base of his cock. He tried not to react. But he couldn't hide that from his mate. As much as she was all his, he was all hers.

Oh so slowly, May squeezed and moved her hand to the tip and back down. He forced his eyes to stay open as his groan turned into a growl.

"I think I just took control."

"Enjoy it while you have it." His voice wasn't his own, and he saw the reaction it had in her. She shivered, and her eyes melted with desire. May needed the darker side of him as much as the light.

May angled his cock and opened her mouth. She kept her tortuous pace, driving him insane. And playing with fire.

He could explode from the sight of her wrapping her lips around him with the water cascading around her.

Again, he had the urge to close his eyes, but if he did that, he'd miss watching her taking him. She held his gaze, and she moved her head back and forth. Teeth grazed against him, but worked hard to keep her mouth wide and her tongue flat.

The heat of her was more than he remembered. Tavis flexed his hands at his sides to keep from plunging his fingers through her hair.

She was right. She had control of him, but it was only because he let her. He wanted to give her this time. Once he wrestled back the control, he'd sink his cock into her cunt and his teeth into her neck. Tavis would prefer they be clean, dry, and on the bed for that to happen.

May took things to the next level, and he had to slap his hands against the tile. The movement leaned him over her, forcing her to take more. But she didn't let that slow her down. Swallowing, the muscles in her throat worked him as she sucked. Taking things further, May lifted a hand and cupped his balls.

"Fuck. May." He almost roared. She ignored him.

In his next breath, he came. An unexpected explosion ripped from his body. May swallowed every drop.

He still had shivers wracking his body when she pulled off him with a pop. It took him a minute to open his eyes. May was pouting as she looked up at him.

"I hope you have more in you than that." Her teasing was a shock to the system, revving him further.

"You're being a brat, pixie. It's a new side to you." And he loved her.

"I'm just making up for lost time." They deserved to make up for that time.

"Stand up." His tone hardened, letting loose the voice he knew she'd obey. He'd let her play and have control. Now it was his turn.

Tavis pinned her under the spray of the shower until he had her washed and rinsed. Then he set her on the other side of the shower while he washed himself. Only then did he touch her again with any sort of intent.

He pinned May to the wall with one leg over his shoulder as he plundered her centre, fingers thrusting hard, forcing her to orgasm in minutes.

She was only half cognizant as he carried her out of the shower and dried her off.

Laying her out on the bed, he settled his weight over top of her. Rough fingers gripped her chin. "You're mine, May. I fucking love you with all I have. No matter what this relationship looks like between us, we are meant to be together. I have to trust that this will work. I can't and I won't live without you. I'm mating you. Now. Tonight. There is nothing that will make me let you run away again. No turning away from this."

May saw the pain that caused him to claim her like that. But she didn't mind. They already discussed this in the woods. May knew what was going to happen and welcomed it. Her body quaked with need. The need to have his mark was as palpable as the air filling her lungs as she panted.

"Tell me you understand, pixie. I need to hear you say you understand."

"I don't understand why you're still talking."

He jerked her chin. "May." His bear's voice snapped at her. She was safe, so the only response she had was easing her fingers down his cheek and through his beard.

"I more than understand. I want it. Mark me, Tavis. I love you, too."

"Fuck." But he muttered, more to himself than to her.

He claimed her mouth, and she suddenly felt everything at once. Her entire body came alive, sensitized to the feel of every part of his body touching hers.

His callused hand slid down her side, over her hip, and down to her knee. Hooking behind it, Tavis lifted it, opening her up to him. His cock bobbed at her entrance.

"Look at me, pixie."

She hadn't known she still had her eyes closed when he stopped kissing her.

He waited until she met his gaze. "There's my beautiful girl."

Her heart fluttered.

"Who has you right now?"

"You do." It would always be him.

Tavis moved his hips, thrusting forward. He adopted the same slow pace she'd used against him. May tried to lift her hips, but he wouldn't let her bury him further.

She whimpered.

Tavis chuckled. "Maybe you shouldn't take control if you can't handle the consequences."

"Tavis." The whine escaping her throat surprised her.

"You'll take what I give, pixie. I told you, I'm not wasting time. I'm going to enjoy it."

When she tried to move again, Tavis slid his hands up her arms until he had both wrists trapped under one had. As she squirmed, he set his other hand on her hip and gripped.

"Move again and I'll pull out. You can't make me rush this. Not when I've been waiting so long to claim you like this. I want to remember every second."

She whimpered, but obeyed. It was harder than she imagined keeping herself still. But she understood the need running through him. When he explained it that way, she felt it too. Her stupidity had denied them what they should already have and caused them pain. That hadn't been her plan. She'd never intended to fight it. But her own confusion and desire to have it all made her do exactly that.

He waited until she lay still for what felt like forever. "Good girl." Tavis pushed in, gaining depth now that she stopped trying to force him inside her. He let go of her wrists. "Touch yourself, pixie. You thought I couldn't come again so soon. It won't take long and I want you there with me. If you can't get there, I'm going to have to stop to do it myself."

This newly discovered submissive side of her wanted to keep her wrists where they were. And she did for several thrusts. She felt so full. So ready to let him take all of her.

But the growl that came from him made her hand move on its own. At least she had enough control to slow it down. Over her chest, her breast, her belly.

She touched her clit and gasped. Oh, it was so sensitive her first instinct was to pull away. Self-preservation from the sensations.

"I can't," she gasped.

"Try again, pixie."

She did, touching her clit, sliding her finger over the hood that covered the swollen bundle of nerves. "It's too much. I need you, Tavis."

"You've got me, May." The words meant so much more than this moment. They extended past this moment of pleasure.

Tavis reared up and pulled out of her. She cried out at the loss. His hands gripped her hip and flipped her. Pulling her up, he lifted her up on her knees and plunged himself back into her. One hand moved up her centre, pulling on her chest between her breasts.

Before she took another breath, her back hit his chest.

"Ready for this?" He dragged sharp teeth down her neck. She froze. His question didn't need any answer. They both knew what he was about to do. And she felt more secure, more protected, with his arm wrapped around her waist and his hand steady on her chest.

Her heart beat harder and her core clenched around him.

His hips pistoned in and out of her. The hand around her waist shifted. The only thing she could hold on to was his forearms. When his fingers touched her clit, she tried to get away from the sensation, but he held her firm against him.

"No, pixie. Take it. You're going to come."

"Tavis, please." She begged. For relief of some sort. Anything.

His teeth grazed along her neck and her shoulder, ready to bite her—waiting for just the right moment. "Now, May. Come."

Her body obeyed before she intended it to. Explosions of sinful sensations flooded her veins. Just as Tavis flooded her. His heat fed hers and extended the climax for both of them. At the peak of it all, Tavis sank his teeth into her skin. She could say it didn't hurt, but that pain felt good compared to everything else they'd experienced.

He pierced the muscle, digging deep as their bodies continued to spasm with their release.

What felt like hours later, he pulled his teeth from her flesh. He soothed his tongue over the wound, then let them fall to the mattress and pulled free from her body.

"I love you, pixie."

She didn't have the energy to say the words. But she thought them. The way he hugged her tighter, May thought he'd heard them, but before she asked, her eyes closed and sleep claimed her.

Chapter Eighteen

avis wanted to laze in bed with his mate—fuck, that made him happy—but he and Noah needed to fill in their cousins about Kellan. They all needed to talk to Kellan. The kid needed to know he had support.

May stirred with a soft moan when he kissed her neck. Stretching, she gave him access to the crescent mark on her skin. He couldn't resist. Tavis kissed it, licked it, then nipped it. May whimpered as bumps formed down her skin. His cock stirred.

"I have to go, pixie."

"No." She wrapped her arms around his neck, attempting to pull him down, but all she did was lift herself off the bed.

"It's early. I need to catch Wyatt and Caiden before they head off for work."

May sighed and let go. "Okay."

"Go back to sleep."

"Sure. So simple when what I'd rather do is pin you to the bed and have my way with you."

Tavis chuckled. "I think we made it clear last night who has the control."

"I need more practice." Her eyes cracked open, and she grinned.

Tavis kissed her until she melted back into the bed, then left. He'd already sent messages to his cousins asking them to meet. The safest place was in the woods behind *Bearbrook Cabins*.

The town was quiet. Some considered it eerie, but it was his favourite time of day. A chilling beauty made even more stunning by the oncoming storm. Everything wouldn't be so still right now if the weather wasn't about to turn. Leaves that would normally let go of their lifeline were still holding tight. The cooler morning air cleared his lungs, cleared his mind.

Tavis parked at the main lodge. Noah pulled in behind him. They said nothing as they started walking down the lane leading to all the cabins, and beyond. Wyatt came from the back side of the cabins, and Caiden walked through the path that led to his home.

Once they'd moved far enough into the trees that any early morning hikers wouldn't come across them, Wyatt stopped. "What's going on?"

"We have a new shifter." That snapped their attention.

"New? New how?" Caiden crossed his arms. Easton had been a new shifter in town, travelling through on his motorcycle when he'd stumbled upon Bonnie in the bakery—his mate. New didn't mean young.

"Kellan Wright. He shifted for the first time on the camping trip."

Panic flared in Wyatt's and Caiden's eyes.

"No one saw him shift. The principal saw him running off, but May steered him back to camp and we slipped Kellan into Noah's tent with the story that he'd circled back and hadn't been feeling well. We're covered."

"Tavis was outside the camp with May when Kellan ran past them." Noah helped fill in the blanks when their cousins only blinked back at them.

"I could smell a shifter coming, young, strange, and when I saw him, his eyes were wild. I told him to keep running and started running with him. Took him to a safe place where he could shift and gave him some time to rest and explore before taking him back to camp."

"I'm glad it all worked out." Wyatt still had concern lining his brows.

"It did, but I'd like for all of us to spend some time with him. Help him learn and make sure he knows he can lean on us."

"That's a given." Wyatt waved a hand through the air.

"Do we talk to his parents?" Caution tempered Caiden's tone.

"I don't know. I think that needs to be up to Kellan." Noah settled himself against a tree. "We should spend some time with him alone. Soon. Blair and Clara are close enough we should be able to find a way."

They threw ideas back and forth, as well as schedules. Shifting when they were young had sometimes been difficult to control. Especially in the beginning. But they'd had each other and grew up in a different generation with a bit more freedom to run off on their own.

By the time they left the woods, the town was waking up. Which meant they all needed to get to work. But before that, Tavis swung by Kellan's home.

He knocked on the door. Heavy footsteps walked through the house. Kellan's father opened the door.

"Tavis. Good morning."

"Heath." He nodded. "I wanted to check in on Kellan. I hope he's feeling better."

"That's very kind of you. He's feeling better, but said he's pretty tired." Heath turned inside the house. "Kellan," he called.

Kellan came around the corner. "Yeah?"

"Tavis dropped by to see how you were."

"Oh. Thank you." His eyes widened as he looked between his dad and Tavis. "I'm tired. It was hard to get up this morning. But I feel fine. No more stomach ache." He emphasized the words *feel* and *stomachache*, but his father didn't seem to catch on.

"I'm glad to hear it. I hope you enjoyed the camping trip despite getting sick."

"I did. I really did."

"He's talked non-stop last night and this morning about how he'd love to go on another camping trip like that, but without his whole class." Heath smiled and set his hand on his son's shoulder.

"Would he, now? Do you do a lot of camping, Heath?"

"I've done some, when I go fishing. It's been a while though. I guess it's time I start again and take Kellan next time."

"Sounds like a great idea." Tavis looked down at Kellan. The boy's face turned sullen with a slight twist to his lips. "Well, I'm happy you're feeling better. I hope you remember everything you learned on the trip." It was his way of telling Kellen he could come talk anytime he needed. "I'll let you both get on with your day. Have a good one." Tavis turned away and waved.

"Thank you. You too." Heath shut the door. Tavis got back in his truck and drove straight to work. If he went home to see her first, he'd never make it to *Rockhard*.

After parking, he pulled out his phone and sent her a text rather than calling.

Rest today, pixie. Call me when you're awake.

Tavis waited a few minutes, hoping for a reply, before going inside. Noah was already behind the desk. He raised a questioning brow. They should have arrived at the same time.

"I checked on Kellen."

"And?"

"Said he's fine. Just tired."

"I remember being exhausted." Noah rolled his neck as if he still felt that way sometimes.

"Me too."

Tavis hoped Kellan didn't have any trouble with controlling his shift.

May slept harder than she had in a long time. As she stretched under the sheets, her hand went to the mark on her neck. It had a slight ache, so she found it instantly. She hissed when her hand made contact. She hadn't expected how sensitive it would feel.

Rolling across the bed, she reached for her phone. She expected a message from Tavis and at least one from Blair, but she hadn't expected several from Blair and even a couple from Poppy.

May shook her head. "Nosy friends." But she meant the statement to be affectionate.

She read the message from Tavis first and responded.

I'm awake. I make no promises to rest. But I'll be here when you get home.

Blair's messages started by asking how the camping trip went, then wondering why she didn't come home with Noah, but by the third, Blair admitted she knew where she was and why and wanted all the details. Poppy's message was simple.

Well?...

She responded to both of them at the same time. *Meet you at Blair's in an hour.*

They both responded with a thumbs up. That was all they needed, the promise to get all the details. May showered and took her time to get ready for the day, doing her hair and make-up, something she hadn't bothered while still recovering on Blair's couch.

Feeling whole and human, she grabbed her camera and computer bag and started walking to Blair's.

Both women were waiting outside for her. But they didn't keep their distance for long. Blair grabbed her hand to pull her forward and Poppy stood on her tiptoes to glare at her neck.

"Seriously, you two?"

"Yes. We've been good. Now it's over and we're allowed to overstep." Blair pulled until they were inside.

"Are you okay?" Poppy walked to the kitchen and came back with a tray of drinks from *Bella's Bakery*. She handed May a cup before taking a seat on a chair.

"I'm fine. I'm good. Really good."

Both her friends let out long sighs. Blair sank against the cushions in one corner of the couch, leaving the other side for May. "Don't get us wrong, we know the struggle all too well, but at the end of it all, we both realized how stupid it was. We've been waiting for you to realize the same."

"Do you want help packing for the move?" Poppy tucked her feet under her.

May paused with her cup halfway to her mouth. "I don't know."

"What was that?" Blair lunged forward with her ear leading the way as if she didn't hear correctly.

"We didn't talk about that. Just that it was stupid to put off mating. We'd work out the rest later." May finished taking her drink. Her blissful mood soured with the reminder they still had things to work through. And there was no taking back what they'd done.

"How do you see yourselves working it out?" Poppy was a bit more gentle in her questioning than Blair.

"I don't know. But we will."

"No, I mean what do *you* see your future looking like?"

The vision she had of her photography business hadn't changed, not really. It included Firebrook now, but her vision of where it was and the direction it was already growing was still there in her mind. She didn't want to give that up. "I'm not closing my business or moving it." The firmness in her tone surprised May. "I'm not." And it felt good to say it. "Maybe I'll hire more people and travel more myself."

Both her friends relaxed again.

As the words came out of her, she liked how much calmer she felt. It was likely the most reasonable answer to all of this. At least to start. She'd miss Nonna and the city too much not to go back often. And she already had people working for her that she'd been training.

"Now you need to say all that to Tavis." Blair pointed at her with the rim of her cup. "Then start packing. Because even if this is only a part-time residence, it will still be home."

"We'll come with you and help you pack. And help you sort your business for the changes." Poppy reached over and squeezed May's wrist.

"Thank you." May smiled at her friends and took a slow drink.

"Since you're here, Poppy. I have something I want to ask you." Blair set her cup down and hopped up from the couch. She returned with her laptop, already open and balancing on her hand while she scrolled and clicked with her other. She passed the computer to Poppy. "Do you recognize either of them?"

Poppy took the computer and set it on her lap. Leaning closer, she frowned at the screen. "That's the bar. No, I don't recognize them."

May leaned over the arm of the couch toward Poppy. The image on the screen was the one Blair had showed her and saved when May thought something looked familiar.

Poppy continued to study the image. "This is about twelve years old, right?"

Blair nodded. "How could you tell?"

"The stuff on the walls behind the bar. Some of it is still there, but some isn't. I've seen pictures though. Of the bar, not the people." Poppy tilted her head. "But I think his name is Aidan."

"It is. But you don't know him?"

"Stories. People missed working with him for years after he left."

"Why did he leave?"

"I'd assumed he married and moved. By the looks of it, he married her." She pointed to the woman in the picture.

May still leaned over the arm, staring at the picture. She had that same sense of familiarity. "Blair, can you pass me my computer?" Her bag was against the other end of the couch, beside Blair.

"Sure." Blair pulled out the laptop from the bag and passed it to May.

"And my camera." She opened her laptop first. She took the memory card from her camera and plugged it into her laptop while it booted up.

Within minutes she had her folder for family pictures open and another window with the images from the weekend.

"Send me that picture?" May pointed to Blair's computer.

"What is it?" Blair took her computer back and started clicking.

May's computer pinged with an email. She opened the image and set it next to the other two she had up. "Do you guys see this or is it just me?" She set her laptop on the coffee table and leaned back, giving the other two space to look.

"Wow. She could be his mother." Poppy stated what May had been thinking the moment she realized what looked so familiar in the picture Blair found.

"But," Blair was shaking her head. "But she's not." It was weak denial. "I guess I'm looking into these two people a little deeper than I planned."

Blair's attention on them vanished. She pulled out her phone and started typing. May gave Poppy a look. They both knew who she was contacting. Sam, her hacker.

Poppy stood and pulled May up with her. "I have to get to work. I'm so happy you're mated now. You deserve this kind of happiness, May. And that's one more friend that isn't so far away." She wrapped her arms around May.

May hugged her back.

Poppy waved at Blair before she left, but Blair wasn't paying much attention. Knowing May wouldn't get much more attention either, she waved her hand in front of Blair's face to say goodbye.

May danced in the kitchen while she cooked. She had some basic recipes perfected, but cooking wasn't one of her primary hobbies. Tonight though, she enjoyed it.

Tavis had called and said he'd be a little later than he planned as they had to do a bit of preparations for the storm that was rolling in. They still had another day, but he and Noah had the time now to get it done.

One of her favourite songs came on. May turned up the volume on the speaker connected to her phone. While stirring the sauce on the stove, she moved with the music. Her spine curved and her hips moved from side to side.

Hands settled over her hips, and a hard body pressed to her back, moving with her.

She gasped, not having heard him come into the house, but logic regained control and she leaned into his hold. She couldn't multi-task. Taking the pot off the burner, she turned in his arms.

"Smells good, pixie." The deep murmur rumbled through him. She felt the vibrations along her spine.

"It's only chicken Alfredo."

"I wasn't talking about the food." Tavis dipped his head. He nuzzled her neck, soft kisses moving up and down until he found the mark. May's knees gave out, and he wrapped an arm around her waist to catch her.

"Tavis." May whimpered, but she didn't know what for. She wanted him to lift her in his arms and carry her off to the bedroom. But she also wanted to sit down with dinner and talk. Everything she'd said to Blair and Poppy felt right. They'd mated, now it was time to sort through the rest.

As if sensing her struggle, Tavis pulled back and looked down at her. A smile played on his lips and his eyes filled with heat. "Anything I can do to help?"

"Pour me another glass of wine?" She added extra sweetness to her tone.

"Your wish is my command." He tilted his head in a mock bow.

May snorted, then covered her mouth with a hand, hoping to hide the awful sound. Tavis kissed her forehead and let her go.

He refilled her glass and put the bottle back. Despite not needing his help, he inserted himself behind her, covering her hands with his and stirring with her.

"Sorry, pixie. I have to touch you."

"I think I'm okay with that."

It only took a few more minutes and everything was cooked. Tavis put the garlic bread down in the toaster and pulled down plates. It turned out to be an oddly domestic evening. And she liked it. Could see herself craving this more and more. She'd never considered herself lonely before. Never felt lonely. But if she didn't have this with him, she might.

They sat down and ate. In silence, but not without contact. Tavis couldn't keep his hands off her. Running his hand up her leg, grazing his fingers over her mark. And May wasn't much better. The touch to her mark was enough to start a fire in her core.

"I saw Blair and Poppy today." May swirled the pasta around her fork, never lifting it off the plate to take a bite.

"Oh?" His hand trailed down her arm until his fingers wrapped around her wrist. His thumb rested against her pulse.

"Yeah. We talked."

Tavis pulled his hand back and straightened. After all she'd put him through, he deserved to be cautious.

"I realized something that made perfect sense to me." She paused. "I want to know what you think of it too."

"Just spit it out, May. I've already said we're going to work through it. No more hesitation."

"I don't want to move my business or close it. But I'd love to expand it to Firebrook. I've grown so much in the past couple of years that I've already had to hire another photographer and assistants. I can hire another. And I can travel. It's not so long of a drive that I can't go in an emergency or to just check in with the business." Once May had spoken she couldn't finish eating. She pushed her plate away.

Tavis continued to stare at her, his head tilted and an unreadable look in his eyes.

"Wh... what do you think?" She hoped he didn't see her as making demands and not giving him a choice in any of this.

"You moving in with me, pixie?" His tone was as unreadable as his eyes. The dark and low voice she loved the most sent shivers over her shoulders and down her back. Her mark throbbed. She wasn't sure what the right answer was.

"If that's what you want too."

"Fuck yeah, that's what I want." But still he didn't move.

"Tavis, say something. I can't let go of my business or leave Nonna. Please?"

He set his hands on the table and pushed himself to stand. Prying her hands apart from her lap, he took one in each of his and pulled her up. "I think it sounds like a perfect plan. Maybe it's time Noah, and I hired too. I think we could both spend more time with our mates."

Sweet relief filled her lungs and took away the anxiety as the next breath left her.

"Dinner was delicious. But I want dessert now."

He finally moved faster than a snail and his stern expression cracked. Ducking, he pushed his shoulder against her stomach and threw her over his shoulder.

Laughter erupted from both of them. May always thought she had a happy life, but she hadn't known what she'd been missing.

Chapter Nineteen

The knocking on the door woke Tavis. Glancing at the clock on the nightstand, he saw he'd slept past his alarm, but wasn't yet late for work.

He rolled out of bed and slipped on a pair of sweatpants. He rushed his steps before they started knocking louder and woke May. His nose twitched before he reached the handle. Fresh wilderness and young cub. It was Kellan.

Opening the door, Tavis looked down.

"I can feel it coming again."

"Okay. Are you with anyone?"

"No. I told my parents I wanted to go to school early, and I ran out the door before they could stop me."

"Okay, bud. Everything will be fine." Tavis opened the door wider to let him in.

"No. What if I shift inside your house?"

"Let me worry about that. Just come in for a minute. I'll give Noah a call so he can join us this time. And I need to tell May I'm leaving. We'll go for a run together before you need to go to school. How does that sound?"

"Oh. Yeah. Sounds good."

Tavis closed the door behind Kellan. "I'll be right back." He wasn't too concerned about the boy shifting inside the house. His eyes weren't yet wild, and he didn't seem to feel the ache that came with the urge.

May was sitting up in the bed when he got back to the bedroom.

"Kellan needs to shift. I'm going to call Noah and we'll take him for a run."

"Okay. Anything I can do to help?"

"If you could make something for him to eat when we get back, that would be good. He should be hungry."

"Of course, I can do that."

Tavis took his phone off the nightstand and unplugged it. Rather than sending a text, he called his brother.

"Yeah?"

"Kellan is here. Thought we could both take him for a run."

"Sure. Be there in a few."

"He rushed out of his house. I don't know if his parents will worry. He still has an hour before school starts. He told them he was going to school early."

"I'll get Blair to check in with Clara."

"Thanks. See you soon." Tavis didn't bother getting dressed further. They had enough space between his and Noah's houses to shift and run without being disturbed. There was no need to go elsewhere.

When he went back out to the living room, Kellan was sitting on one of the dining chairs, his leg bouncing more than a rabbit.

"Noah will be here soon. How are you feeling?"

"Tight." Kellan looked up at him. "Does that make sense?"

"Sure. Your body is getting ready to change. Try to relax, though. It's more of an ache rather than pain if you can relax."

"That's easier said than done, isn't it?"

Tavis chuckled. "Yeah. Did you eat breakfast before coming here?"

He shook his head. "I don't feel like eating."

"I get it."

The front door opened. Noah didn't bother knocking. "Morning." Typical grump, but he sent Kellan a grin. "We're going for a run, are we?"

"Yeah. Let's go." Tavis nodded toward the door Noah hadn't bothered closing. Kellan followed along as they hiked a little ways into the thicker trees.

"Do you remember what to do?" Noah glanced down at the kid walking between them.

"Try to relax. I'm not so sure I did anything last time."

"Maybe not, but you'll gain control soon." Tavis patted Kellan on the shoulder. "Here's good. We can all stash our clothes under this bush here."

The shift was getting closer. Kellan tensed further and rolled his shoulders. He was quick to get his clothes off.

"Relax, little man. Don't rush it." Noah started stripping and piled his clothes under the bush.

Kellan listened, closing his eyes and pulling in deep breaths.

"Good job."

"Do you feel the warmth yet?" Tavis knew he must. The wind was already swirling around his feet.

"Yeah."

"Open your eyes. Look."

His jaw dropped with shock. "Wow."

Noah grinned. Not that Kellan saw. His brother started shifting. Kellan must have felt the change in the air, his senses taking over. He whipped his head up in time to see the end of Noah's shift.

"You look just like Tavis."

"Yeah, our bears are almost twins. Your turn, bud."

Kellan nodded, closing his eyes again to concentrate. He groaned as his body morphed, but without the panic of the first time, he didn't seem to have as much pain.

"Good." Tavis tossed his pants with the other clothes and shifted.

He and Noah walked slower than usual until Kellan got his feet under him. Low curses flew out from his thoughts, but they ignored them, letting him work through it. After a few minutes, Kellan was keeping pace alongside them.

Is this the first time you've felt the urge to shift since the camping trip? Tavis had wondered how soon his next shift would be.

I felt it last night, but thought if I ignored it, that it would go away. Kellan carefully stepped up onto a downed tree, then hopped down to the ground without stumbling.

Why did you want to ignore it? Noah stepped over the same tree.

I don't know. Doesn't this make me weird? Not normal?

Tavis and Noah turned their big heads toward the cub.

Guess I just called both of you weird, didn't I?

It's okay. Tavis tried not to laugh. *We knew what you meant.*

Normal is overrated. But we aren't weird. Noah's voice came out a little more growly than he should have when talking to the cub, but then he stuck his colossal head in the air, nose as high as he could, and pranced. *We're special.*

Kellan laughed hard enough he lost his footing and stumbled forward, his chin bumping against the ground. But he didn't stop laughing. He let the rest of his body fall with him.

They stopped and waited for him to get control of himself again.

Let's try to run a bit, Tavis suggested after they'd been walking a bit longer. They needed to get some energy out before getting Kellan off to school.

They jogged, surprised that Kellan kept up. Soon, they came to a clearing with a small watering hole. Stopping for a drink, Tavis and Noah took the chance to wrestle. Kellan looked on with excitement. Then his body started wiggling as if to wrestle too.

Tavis stopped near Kellan and bowed his front end. Kellan sprung forward, seemingly with little control as his instincts took over.

It was fun wrestling with a cub, letting him learn his strength and what he was capable of. He'd need this as he continued to grow.

Even Noah huffed and enjoyed himself.

But they needed to get back.

Noah was the first to stop, taking a drink before waiting at the edge of the small clearing.

This was fun.

Yeah, bud. It was.

They were faster getting back than they had been going in. Shifting near the bush, they all got dressed and walked back to the house. The aromatic smell of bacon and eggs wafted from the house.

Kellan's stomach rumbled loud enough to stop all of them from taking another step. "Guess I am hungry."

"Shifting takes a lot of energy. You're going to end up eating a lot more than you used to."

"Wow, that smells good."

Both men chuckled and patted the kid on the back.

"Better get this boy fed before he combusts." Noah picked up his pace toward the house. "My mate's inside too."

"Mate?" Kellan looked between the two of them.

"A lesson for another day." Tavis opened the front door.

Blair sat at the table with her hands wrapped around a mug. May dished up three plates of bacon, eggs, and toast. Tavis moved foward to help her carry them to the table.

"Thank you, pixie."

Noah kissed Blair, then pulled her from the chair to steal it for himself and pulled her back down onto his lap.

Kellan looked a little shy as he sat at the table. Tavis passed him a plate. The boy started out eating slowly, but once he saw how quick Tavis and Noah were eating, he tore into the food like a growing cub.

"Kellan." Tavis stopped him before he took his plate to the sink. "Have you thought about telling your parents?"

"I have. I don't know what to do."

"Sneaking around won't be easy. I won't say it isn't possible, but their support would help."

"What if they don't support me because I'm weir...." he glanced at Noah, "special?"

"They love you." Blair got off Noah's lap and crouched down beside Kellan. She'd become close friends with Clara recently, which extended that friendship to Kellan's mom. "And I think they'll continue to love you no matter what."

"But it's up to you, little man. We'll help you no matter what you decide." Noah ruffled Kellan's hair and then piled all the plates to take them to the kitchen.

"Think on it. There's no rush. But now it's time to get you to school."

"We can walk with him." Blair held out her hand to Kellan. Noah followed behind them, nodding at Tavis before they left.

With or without his parents, Kellan had their support. They wouldn't let him fall behind or get hurt.

May wanted to go back to the city. She needed to make some changes to her business and hire a new photographer. Packing would be a different issue to tackle. She still questioned what to do with her apartment, weighing the cost of her monthly rent against hotels whenever she needed to travel. Not knowing how often she'd travel back and forth made that difficult.

But going back would have to wait a couple more days. The storm that Tavis had mentioned after the camping trip hit. Wyatt and Poppy invited several people over to the lodge to ride it out. They expected the winds to be strong enough that most businesses closed before the worst would hit. They took it as an opportunity to have Kellan nearby in case the storm bothered the young bear in him. Tavis explained that new senses sometimes made things overwhelming.

May liked the idea of having several people from the community at the lodge, and didn't make the invite to Clara, Kellan, and his parents seem out of place.

They'd set out tables of food and drinks. Books, adults and childrens, filled a shelf on the wall. And they piled board games on the coffee table between the couches near the fireplace. A roaring fire already warmed the room.

As usual, May's camera was another extension of her. Taking pictures of people enjoying themselves was natural for her. But the storm called her with ferocity.

The wind didn't yet bow trees to a full curve and the rain fell with mild drops spraying in one direction. Thunder rolled low in the distance. She stood at the back door, staring in awe at something beautiful.

"You seem lost in thought." Tavis set his hand on her hips and dipped his head to speak in her ear.

"It's pretty. In a way."

"I agree. Mother Nature has as many sides and moods as any living being out there."

May tilted her head back and smiled. "I like that."

"You're gripping your camera awfully tight, pixie."

She looked down. She wrapped her hands around either side, holding it against her chest, and her index finger already on the shutter button. "I want to go out there before it gets too bad. Pictures aren't the same from inside."

"There's a reason we've huddled everyone in here and businesses have closed during the storm."

"I know. But I won't be long. Just a few shots." May spun in his arms and lifted herself on tip toes. She planted a loud kiss on his lips and then backed out of his reach and grabbed his jacket hanging on the coat rack.

Tavis shook his head and narrowed his eyes. But he didn't stop her. He turned back toward the crowd of people.

Before moving out from under the eave of the roof, May put the jacket on, leaving her arms out of the sleeves so she could still manage her camera. The jacket kept her and her camera covered from the rain. She'd be able to take pictures without getting her camera wet, only have the lens stick out past the fabric when she wanted to take the shot.

She ran closer to the trees. The first picture she snapped looked up through the rain at the tips of the trees blowing together. After a few more angles of that, she moved to capture the mountains in the distance. The way the clouds moved around the tops mirrored something from a painting.

It didn't take her long to get lost in the photography. Everywhere she turned she saw something else worthy of a picture.

But the chill seeped into her skin. The jacket kept her dry from her thighs up, but water covered her face and her legs and feet were now soaked.

Her camera bag still hung off her shoulders. Maneuvering her arms inside the jacket, May put her camera away in the bag. She started walking back to the lodge, but as she looked up after putting her arms where they belonged in the jacket, she couldn't see the building.

She wasn't lost, having paid enough attention to keep the lodge in her mind.

The squish of mud made her pause. She'd been stepping over a tree. No animal would be out in this. The wind picked up speed, moving many bushes and trees. The sound must have been in her head.

May kept going.

Squish. Snap.

That wasn't her and that wasn't the wind. The wind had a distinct whistling and rustling sound, nothing that created the sound of heavy footsteps.

Close ones.

May closed her eyes for a moment. Maybe Tavis had come looking for her. No one else would follow her out here, crazy enough to go out in the storm.

"Tavis?" She tried to mentally reach for him, hoped that some instinct had kicked in by now to help her know when her mate was near. But she came up empty.

Opening her eyes, she started walking fast this time. But she only made a few steps before someone stepped out in front of her. She gasped.

Male, based on his build. The hood on the rain jacket he wore shadowed his face and nothing about the jacket, jeans, or boots gave away his identity.

"You shouldn't be out in the storm." She recognized his voice. Duke Greyson.

"Neither should you." May started walking toward him, intending to move past. He blocked her way.

"But since we are both out here, I need something from you."

"I'm just heading inside. You're welcome to join us all at the lodge. We can talk in there." She tried to move around him again, taking a wider berth.

"No, we can't. I'm afraid I need to borrow your camera for a little while."

That hadn't been what she'd expected him to say. Instinct made her step back and clutch at her bag under the jacket. "No."

"This isn't up for negotiation. Give me your camera or I'll take it."

"There's nothing on here except the pictures I just took of the storm." That was a lie. Her memory card contained several days worth of pictures and her other cards full of pictures in her bag. She'd already backed up everything that wasn't currently on her camera to her computer. Whatever he looked for, she already had copies. And May assumed it was from the camping trip.

"I'd like to check anyway."

"I have everything backed up on my computer. I don't have any pictures that aren't from today on me right now." She didn't know if pointing that out improved her situation.

"Then I need to borrow your computer too."

"I'm not handing either of those over to you." May moved further to her right, hoping to get enough space between them she could get past him. But his longer stride matched her.

He stayed silent for a while. "Change of plans." His eyes never left her, anticipating her movements as she made them. Her only option was to turn and run, but even in the middle of a storm that was likely one of the worst ideas.

Duke pulled his phone from his jacket. After a quick swipe on the screen, he brought it to his ear.

"I need you here. We're using her as a distraction instead." He paused. "I don't give a fuck that you find it too cold outside. We have a job to do."

May had thought the principal was a little odd, even noticed his mood changes in his expression, but she never would have expected this. For him to be the next person sent searching for whatever it was they were searching for—all connected to what happened to Poppy and Blair on their first trip, connected to what Blair still investigated. Maybe she jumped to conclusions, but what were the odds that this was a different nefarious incident?

Duke hung up the phone and stuck it back in his pocket. Who had he been talking to? The only person she'd noticed him close to was his wife. It would be smart to set up two separate people in the same town and in different positions.

If she waited for his backup to get here, her chances of escaping would be slim. May didn't have enough faith in herself to get away from one person, let alone two.

"Don't run, sweetheart. Make this easy and I might let you go free after this. It will be all over and anything you or people in this town do won't matter."

May wanted to ask, but that would only waste time. The wind rushed harder, and the thunder grew louder. If she couldn't get back to the lodge, then she needed to find somewhere to ride out the storm where he wouldn't find her.

Giving it her all, May turned on her heel and ran. The mucky ground slowed her down, but he was heavier. It should slow him down even more.

She felt his hand swipe at the jacket several times before his hand wrapped around her wrist. He swung her around until her opposite shoulder hit a tree. The pain was enough to stop her fight and give him enough time to pin both arms behind her back.

"Nice try."

T avis kept looking out the window while trying to give his attention to those around him. May should have been back by now. He'd gone back to the door and watched her for the first few minutes. But when she disappeared out of view, he had to force himself to turn away.

Blair, Poppy, Bonnie, and Clara sat near the fire playing a game of cards. Kellan came with his aunt. His parents stayed home, but thought it would be more fun for him to spend time with other kids and friends. He was with a handful of other kids near the back door having their own checkers tournament they set up.

Noah, Wyatt, and Easton all hovered near their mates while they played. Tavis joined them. If May didn't come back soon, he'd ask one of them to help him search for her.

"My sister swears Kellan is about to go through a growth spurt. He hasn't stopped eating in days. Suddenly, he's eating more than his dad. Look at him." Clara pointed over her shoulder. "He hasn't stopped reaching for food all evening."

Tavis sent the boy a quick glance. He had half a sandwich from the food table in his hands while standing over the current game.

Blair eyed her cards before setting one down. "Was his dad the same age when he went through that kind of growth spurt?" There was an undertone to Blair's voice that had Tavis paying closer attention.

"Actually," Clara adjusted in her seat and leaned a little closer. She played her next card, but didn't sit back again. "Kellan's adopted. He doesn't know yet, but they're thinking about telling him soon. They don't want it to come out another way and end up being a wedge between them, if you know what I mean. Just keep this between us, please. Even after they tell him, I doubt they'll want it to be public knowledge. A secret, but not, if that makes sense."

"Of course." Blair squeezed her friend's arm. "So, they adopted him as a baby?"

"Practically as a newborn. Only a month old."

"Must not have been from someone in Firebrook, or more people would know." Poppy made a good point. How had people not noticed his mother hadn't been pregnant?

Clara nodded. "My sister was a bit of a recluse while they'd been trying to have a baby. It was so difficult to watch. But with some things, people have short memories. I'm sure there are some here who know Kellan is adopted, but they've either forgotten over time, or respect that it isn't their business."

"No one would doubt the love in that little family. I'm sure anyone who knows has enough respect for that." Bonnie added her opinion. And she was probably right. "It's not like it's a question that comes up all the time."

"You're right." Clara relaxed back against the couch. "But anyway, it was such a sudden change in him that my sister doesn't know if she should worry or be happy about it."

The conversation shifted from there. Tavis looked at the back door again. His jacket was still missing from the coat rack and there was no scent of his mate in the room.

His appetite vanished. Kellan was still getting used to his increased senses. He couldn't believe the things he could hear. Sometimes it was hard to pull apart distinct sounds and conversations. He had to concentrate hard.

But hearing his name helped bring him more focus.

"Kellan's adopted." Aunt Clara whispered the words, but they only sounded like a hushed tone in his ears as he zoned in on her voice alone.

Never had that thought crossed Kellan's mind. His parents gave no hint to it either.

He was adopted? He didn't come from here? Where did he come from? Did his parents give him up because they somehow knew what he was? But how would they have known?

Kellan heard the rest of their conversation, knew all of it to be true. He loved his parents, his current parents. His adoptive parents. Thinking of them like that sucked. They were his mom and dad, end of story.

But that didn't change the shock of learning something like this about himself. He started backing away from the other kids. No one noticed. He tossed the last of his sandwich into the garbage.

Emotions ran raw through him. The animal inside started to worry. Kellan needed a minute alone to collect himself. This couldn't bother him while surrounded by a bunch of people.

The storm had been steadily picking up, but its intensity hadn't registered while he'd been playing games. He'd known the thunder would be loud.

But the next deep rolling clap shook the entire building. His ears started ringing and his body vibrated through it, pumping his blood harder. The young bear startled and Kellan felt the heat in his eyes.

Ah, shit. Not now. We can't shift here. He'd started talking to himself as if he had two different sides, but it didn't feel like he and the bear were different. It helped him work through his emotions, though, when he needed.

Except, it didn't work this time. His shoulder popped. He was running out of time.

The next boom of thunder hit, rolling and rolling until he thought it would not stop. Instinct took over, and he ran for the back door.

Chapter Twenty

Her teeth chattered. The rain beat harder now, even through the trees. The jacket wasn't enough anymore.

Duke had tied her to a tree, then huddled behind it, searching for more shelter from the rain. Her camera bag sat on the ground at his feet, pushed back against the tree.

"Where the fuck is she?" He growled and muttered often, but never anything useful. What did he think she had?

May wanted to ask questions, but she didn't have the energy anymore. The cold reached her bones. She shivered hard enough her hands rubbed against the bark of the tree. But the numbness kept her from feeling the damage.

"What took you so long?" Duke pushed off the tree. May whipped her head around, searching for whoever he talked to. She had heard no one approaching over her own chattering teeth. How long had she been out here? Tavis should be looking for her by now. Unless something has happened at the lodge.

"Like I said. It's cold. We could have done this after the storm." Duke's wife, Violet, had a thick layer on underneath a black, rubbery rain jacket. She looked like some sort of glazed dessert. The way the two spoke to each other, May didn't think she was actually his wife. The two worked together.

"What the hell?" May let go of the outburst, despite her shivering breaking up the words. "What the h... hell are you two l... looking for that you'd go to this much tr... trouble to become part of the community? For f... fuck's sake, this is ridiculous."

They stared at her like an unwanted pet asking for attention.

"What are we supposed to do with her?" Violet lifted her brows and let loose a shiver of her own, despite being dry beneath her layers.

"She's the distraction. You take her back to the house. Keep her there. They'll start searching for her and give me time to get her computer and..." Duke trailed off, sending her a look. "And to get what we came for."

"I doubt that will be as easy as you think." The woman crossed her arms, but she couldn't quite get her hands tucked in all the way. May wanted to laugh.

"Now that we've found him, it will be easy."

Him? Blair had been right. They were looking for a person.

"You expect me to get her back to the house alone? And from here? That lodge is full of people." Puff Rubber Tree had a point. But May worried she might be too weak.

"She's tied. I'm sure you can handle her. Toss her camera in the safe when you get there." He pointed at her bag on the ground.

"Fine."

May needed Duke gone before she fought back. She imagined pushing this woman over and rolling her down a hill. But Duke had more height and strength on her. With the two of them against her, May wouldn't escape.

"What's that?" The woman paused behind the tree with her hands on the rope. She looked toward her fake husband.

Duke grinned. "Sounds like luck." He waited another minute. With their silence, May heard it. Running. Lightweight strides and heavy breathing. Not an adult. She should have been the one to hear him coming first. Mates gained some of the extra senses, but the cold in her bones stopped her from sensing anything.

May put it all together. They wanted Kellan. But why?

"Now what?" Violet still hadn't untied her.

"Get her out of here and do what I told you. I'll handle this."

Frantic hands worked at the ropes. May held in her screech as blood rushed back into her frozen hands. It burned.

"Shut her up," Duke hissed.

The woman yanked one of May's hands to the front of the tree and clamped one of her own over May's mouth while pulling her back against her. But May opened wider and bit down hard. A metallic taste flooded her mouth, and she thought she was going to be sick.

"You bitch." Violet joined May's screeching.

Letting go, May spit, ridding her mouth of the foul blood. "You taste disgusting." It was the best insult May could come up with. And this woman seemed like that would be something she'd care about.

Violet's grip on May's hand hurt, like trying to walk when her feet fell asleep, but this was worse.

"Go. Now." Duke started walking away. More like stalking. "And don't forget the camera." He had his hood pulled forward, and he crept through the mud, getting thicker the more it rained.

The wind wasn't any better, but the trees blocked it from whipping at their faces.

She had to warn Kellan. He should be able to hear her, even if Puff clamped her hand over her mouth again.

May started pulling against her. "Run! It isn't safe out here! Get away!"

Violet spun May and reared her arm back. The slap across her face barely registered on her cold skin. Puff pulled harder to get May out of the woods.

Fuck that.

May dug her feet into the ground and leaned back. It was the only way to get any leverage against the other woman that was several inches taller and covered in padding. Hitting her wouldn't work. Her feet sank into the mud and her butt got closer to the ground. Her best defense right now would be to make Puff carry her out of here. And she'd already whined about having to come out in the storm. Carrying May would be the last thing she'd want to do.

"Get up."

May's shoulder hurt the more she pulled. "Hurry! He's coming after you!" She refrained from calling Kellan's name. She didn't want to be the one to confirm something they might not know. Maybe they only knew they were looking for a kid his age. It wasn't as if Scott and Luca had an identity to go after when they'd been the ones sent here.

That was a worry for another time. Who sent them here looking for a child?

"Let me go!" Kellan yelled, but May heard something different in his voice. There was only one reason that would force him out into the storm and away from all the people at the lodge. But why wasn't one of the others with him?

Duke dragged him back with an arm around his waist. Kellan struggled, but nothing quite reached Duke. "You're fucking heavy for a scrawny kid."

"You have to let me go." Tears streamed down his cheeks. Duke ignored him.

"What are you still doing here?" Duke paused and stared at his *wife* and May.

"She's putting up a fight. Blame her."

Duke shook his head and moved to the other side of May. He wrapped his other hand around her arm. "Let's go before someone comes looking for these two."

"May?" Kellan whispered.

"It's going to be okay, Kellen."

"It's not." His jaw clenched and May watched in shock as his eyes glowed and his shoulders grew.

The fresh, wild scent vanished in a flash. Tavis had been getting ready to ask his brother to help him search for May when he smelled Kellan about to shift. His scent still assaulted the senses.

Sharing a look with the other shifters in the room, they smelled it too. Kellan needed to calm down before he shifted in front of everyone. This wouldn't be the best way to let their secret out to the town. Or one of them needed to get the kid outside if he couldn't get it under control.

They spread out to search for him. He wasn't with his group of friends playing checkers. Tavis pulled in a breath. The scent of a young cub wasn't in the room anymore. Kellan must have gained control of himself.

Tavis breathed deep again, attempting to sort through all the other scents in the room. Caiden came out of the kitchen, shaking his head. Wyatt came down the stairs, the same sullen expression on his face. Tavis met his brother's gaze across the room. He finished scanning the heads before looking up.

Tavis started for the back door. Both Kellan and May were missing. One glance outside and his stomach dropped. The storm approached its peak. High winds weren't uncommon in the mountains, but these were. Pair it with thunder, lightning, and heavy rain, made it unsafe to be outside. He'd let May go on her own for too long, but he hadn't expected the storm to move so quickly.

"It won't be easy to track him." Caiden reached for his jacket.

"Them." Tavis didn't have a jacket to grab. May took it. But he didn't intend to stay in skin and clothes. His thick fur protected him better.

"Them?" Wyatt looked relaxed as he leaned next to the door. They didn't want to cause panic just yet among the guests there. Especially not Clara.

"May hasn't come back yet either."

"What the hell is she doing out there to begin with?" Noah growled, but then closed his eyes. "Pictures."

"Yeah."

"How are we going to do this?"

"You four are going to go and I'll make sure no one notices." Easton sidled up behind them all. Bonnie's mate may not be related to them, but he became family and someone they all leaned on.

"You sure?"

"Yeah. Go." They'd lost power about ten minutes ago, but Easton already had a couple guitars out and ready. Grabbing them from where they leaned against the wall, he passed them to anyone willing to play. It was the best distraction they were going to get.

Caiden and Wyatt grabbed jackets, but Noah and Tavis didn't. They'd start out on two legs for now. Tavis intended to shift as soon as possible. He needed those extra senses to find May.

He worried about Kellan, too, but his thoughts centred on his mate. He expected to find her hurt somewhere, having slipped and rolled her ankle, hit her head, her hip, something that kept her from coming back when she should have.

Peeling his clothes from his body, he stashed them in the branches of a bush rather than in the mud on the ground beneath it. Maybe it was time they invented a new solution for their clothes. Returning in wet clothes was easy to explain, covered in mud was something different

They didn't wait for the chill to sink into their skin. Tavis and Noah shifted together while their cousins walked ahead, eyes on the ground, searching for tracks. The shelter from the trees protected parts of the ground to allow for some tracks to show. But the wind broke the barrier, letting some of the rain in.

"Here." Caiden yelled over the wind. Noah jogged toward him, nose ready to catch Kellan's scent. Boy or bear.

Wyatt kept walking more to the West. "A struggle." The storm wouldn't allow for them to have full conversation. When Tavis reached his cousin, he saw the deep grooves in the ground filled with water.

Well, hell. Some of those divets were deeper than others. This was an adult and a child. But not May. She would have made similar tracks as Kellan. Someone had him.

If they didn't hurry, that someone would have an adolescent bear cub on their hands.

The struggle took them further west, fading into single deep tracks, but not on a straight path. They had a hard time keeping a hold of Kellan.

May! Tavis needed to help find Kellan, but he still didn't know where May was.

They continued to hike west, spreading out.

"What the fuck is he? Durnam said nothing about a fucking bear!"

They all froze as the male voice screeched over the storm, cutting in and out through the wind. Damn it. They were too late. Kellan shifted. And in front of someone.

Everything he'd said registered. Durnam *said nothing about a fucking bear.* Tavis would wager his next month's income that this related to everything from the summer. Poppy's and Blair's first trip, all that Blair still searched for. He knew it had been too much to hope that they'd given up.

But Kellan? Why? They hadn't known he was a shifter. Kellan hadn't known he was a shifter until a week ago.

"Don't hurt him." May's weak voice cut through. He prayed she wasn't hurt. At least they knew where both of them were. Maybe fifty metres in front of them.

"Guess this isn't our first rodeo." Wyatt moved closer, gesturing for them all to come closer. "Tavis, keep control of yourself. You were a good reminder to the rest of us. Now, it's your turn. You and Noah should flank Kellan. We'll get May." He pointed to Caiden.

Tavis clenched his jaw. Wyatt was right, but he didn't fucking like it. He couldn't attack the threat to his mate, no matter how much he wanted to.

The four of them spread out again and moved in silently, keeping themselves out of sight as long as possible.

But Tavis hadn't been prepared for what he saw. Their stealth vanished. Noah prowled out, growling, and put himself in front of Kellan. In front of the gun the new school principal pointed at him.

A woman he remembered Duke introducing as his wife held May against her, her back to her chest with a rope pulled across May's neck. May had her hands beneath it.

A roar ripped from Tavis. He couldn't hold it in. There was too much danger in this one situation. Despite the two of them being outnumbered. Someone was going to get hurt.

Chaos exploded when Kellan had shifted. He'd ripped out of Duke's arm and their two captors panicked, going on the defensive. The woman holding May had more strength and skill than she'd given her credit for. But May was an easy target in this state.

She'd pulled hard on May, flinging her back against her chest. As soon as May realized the woman had the rope in her hands that Duke had tied around her wrists, she put her hands up to her neck. An instinct that had saved her. For now.

Her weak hands didn't provide her much resistance, but they left enough of a gap to keep the woman from strangling her. The woman reacted out of panic, trying to gain the upper hand in a situation she didn't understand.

Kellan had ripped through his clothes in a roar not as deep as the adult bears. But a show of strength. Adolescent bear or adult bear. No one should mess with either.

His eyes glowed wildly. The wind whipped through his fur and his muscles heaved. With his head bowed, he dug his claws into the ground.

May's vision turned blurry. She didn't need the help of the rain for it. But nothing stopped her from making out the figures that jumped into the scene. A bear almost three times the size of Kellan stood in front of him, teeth baring.

Another stood beside him and roared. Loud, piercing, and menacing. If the storm wasn't so loud, the entire town would have heard him. Maybe some did. They weren't that far from the lodge.

The last of the two Greer men flanked Duke. May could only guess the identity of each. But the terrifying roar drew her to him. That one was Tavis.

She tried to keep her feet under her, but they slipped in the mud. It became harder to fight against her as the rope cut off circulation to her fingers. They were a barrier, but useless otherwise. She was so cold.

One of the men standing—Caiden, she thought—walked toward them. The man was a mountain, and the woman behind her shook.

You should be afraid.

"Touch her and I shoot!" Duke yelled over the wind, whipping his head back and forth to get sight of everyone.

"You're outnumbered. What do you think will happen if you shoot? You can't shoot all of us in the time it takes just one grizzly bear to rip out your throat." Wyatt's voice echoed from the right.

"You saying you're going to attack and risk losing one of you?"

No one answered him.

Growls emanated from the bears. All three of them. Despite the sound of the storm and the ringing in her ears, she could hear them. May turned her gaze toward Tavis. She needed to stay calm. Duke was terrified, as he should be, but that meant he'd do just about anything at a chance to stay alive.

He started laughing.

Caiden inched closer again.

"Stop. You heard what he said." Puff needed a muzzle.

Duke turned his whole body around, flinging the arm holding the gun wide. And he pulled the trigger. The sound cut through the wind and May screamed with what voice she had. The other woman's scream was cut short.

Energy buzzed around them and May knew this would be over in a few seconds. She waited for pain, knowing he'd been aiming for her, but all she felt was the loosening of the rope. Falling forward, she cradled her hands against her stomach. What were the odds? Some higher power must be among them.

Breathing hurt, but May kept pulling the damp air into her lungs. As much as she could with every inhale. The storm had reached its peak, and she only had enough energy to squint through it to see if any of the people she cared about were hurt.

Duke lay on the ground screaming while clutching his arm. One bear stood over him. Kellan looked frozen in place, but his eyes still glowed with fierceness. Wyatt used a sleeve covered hand to pick up the gun and move it out of reach.

A grizzly rushing toward her. Tavis curled his body around hers, blocking her from the storm. May wanted to bury herself in his fur and share his warmth, but there was still more to do.

Glancing over her shoulder, she saw Violet lying still on the ground. Caiden checked her pulse, then shook his head.

"I'm not sure we can hide this one." Wyatt looked between the woman and Duke writhing in pain in the mud.

"You're all freaks, aren't you?" His voice was hoarse. "I'll tell everyone."

"No one will believe you. We're like Bigfoot." Caiden stood near Noah guarding Duke.

"I'll call Henry, then get a fire going in one of the empty cabins. We can't take everyone back to the lodge." Wyatt waited for a nod from each of them before walking off and pulling out his phone. He lifted his hood and held it forward while making the call.

Are you okay, pixie? I need to know you're okay. Tavis nuzzled her cheek with his nose.

She heard him. Looking up, she searched his eyes. "I'll be okay. I'm cold. My hands hurt."

The dark, round beads blinked. He looked shocked she'd heard him. He let out an immense sigh and leaned his head against hers.

But this wasn't over. Duke continued to throw threats, regaining a bit of energy. It only looked like he had an injured arm. Caiden claimed no one would believe him, but some might believe enough to come look for themselves.

The only saving grace would be that he would go straight to prison. She worried about all the people he'd see and talk to between here and there.

This was May's home now, too. She'd do anything to help protect it.

Chapter Twenty-One

They wanted to get Kellan out of here, but he need-ed clothes and somewhere dry. Going further into the storm wasn't a good idea. Lightning cracking was too close for comfort, and they'd all turned their heads at the sound of a tree falling down with the force of the wind.

Asking Kellan to shift was out of the question. He was safest out here in fur. They all would be, but not with May in this state.

She didn't have the strength to hold on to him. He'd need Caiden's help to get her to the cabin. But Duke had too much strength left to leave him with only Noah to keep an eye on him.

"I told him we have injured in the storm. He's coming as fast as he can. No medics." Wyatt stood over him and May. "I'll carry her to the cabin with me."

Tavis stood, but stared at his cousin. *I'm coming with you.* Wyatt couldn't understand him like this. That was something that only happened with mates, and maybe not even all mates. But Tavis made his thoughts clear with a look.

"Not yet. We need you here."

"I want to stay with Tavis." May whispered. Fuck, she was weak.

"No, May. We need to get you dry, warm, and look at your hands. Tavis will come as soon as he can. I promise."

He didn't want any distance between them, but her safety and health were more important. And they had some explaining to do with Henry. Officer Coates dedicated himself to this town, and they'd built a relationship with him over the years. As kids growing up together and then as adults working search and rescue. But they'd never had to let him in on their secret. This past summer, they'd had some close calls. They'd seen the suspicion on his face, but he trusted them enough not to question. The distinct bite marks of a grizzly bear snapping Duke's arm and an adolescent bear that couldn't shift might be too difficult to explain this time.

Tavis nudged May's shoulder with his snout. *You can't stay out here any longer, pixie.*

May lifted her hand to touch his face, but hissed when she made contact.

"Let's go." Wyatt's tone didn't allow for an argument from either of them. Setting a knee on the ground, he eased May back and lifted her. "Curl into me as much as you can. I'll try to block the storm. Kellan, you come with us."

"My camera." May rasped.

Kellan walked over to the tree and picked up the bag with his jaw.

Tavis watched his cousin carry his mate away with the young bear in tow. He took long and heavy strides to battle the storm. Once they broke through the trees, it would be that much harder, but this was the quickest way to get May inside.

He turned toward the others and had to keep himself from swatting at Duke. But he stalked toward him, adding his own sneer and intimidation to Noah's. It would be better for everyone if he started talking now.

Caiden hovered near his head and crossed his arms. "She's dead, by the way. Your partner."

"Useless anyway." His face scrunched up with another round of pain as he adjusted his arm. Noah wasn't giving him much room.

"Who sent you?" Caiden made a better interrogator than Tavis would have thought. His grumpy nature turned vicious when he was angry. And they were all angry. They'd feel the same over anyone in Firebrook, especially a child, but Kellan was special.

"I'm getting paid too well to talk."

"What does it matter?" Caiden leaned down and lowered his voice so his next threat meant so many things. "You aren't getting out of this."

Duke swallowed hard.

"Who is Durnam?" Caiden straightened.

Duke's lips pinched tight. He'd let the name slip when Kellan had shifted.

"He send you after Kellan? Or any kid? A different kid?"

Tavis had no doubt now they looked for a kid. What better position to put yourself in than the school principal? He'd had access to almost everything about every child in Firebrook.

"He just said to get the kid and bring him to him. He never said anything about the kid being a freak. Or other freaks."

Both Tavis and Noah snapped their jaws at his face, enjoying the way he couldn't control his scream. They huffed heavy breaths before letting up.

"What does he want with Kellan?"

"Fuck if I know. And I don't care. Not my business."

Heavy steps running through the mud cut off their interrogation. Caiden stepped back, and Tavis eased off. But Noah didn't. He wouldn't let Duke use any opportunity to escape.

"Oh, shit!" Henry skidded to a stop and froze. His hand reached for his gun.

"Don't. It's safe."

"What the hell do you mean it's safe, Caiden? Where are the others? Wyatt said Tavis and Noah were here, too." Well, they couldn't hide anything when Wyatt told him something like that.

"It's a long story, but the only important thing right now is that it's safe. They won't hurt you. We can't be out in this storm much longer." Caiden gestured Henry over to the dead woman, giving him no choice but to deal with the situation and ignore the bears. He filled him in, only supplying the details he needed to get them all out of there.

"I assume the bears standing over him are the reason you said not to bring a medic, even though he clearly needs one?"

"Yes."

"Where's Kellan? They tried to take Kellan?"

Duke started to speak, but Tavis set his paw over his face and pressed. His claws scraped at his cheeks and forehead. Duke stopped trying to talk.

"Caiden?" Henry looked fearfully at Tavis and Noah.

"He went with Wyatt to the cabin to get warm."

"Good. Is he hurt?"

"I don't think so. Do you need to do anything else here?"

"No." But he lowered his chin, staring. Even he knew not to ask right now. Tavis let go of his face and Noah backed off, just enough for Henry to grab Duke and pull him to his feet.

As soon as he was out of reach of the bears, Duke opened his mouth. "They're fucking freaks. You have to protect me."

"I'd shut up if I were you. But by all means, tell me what you were doing before these bears attacked." Henry eyed his injured arm. They'd broken it, making it impossible to pull it back with the other. Instead, he pulled back his good arm and held it in a lock at Duke's back. "Start walking."

They all followed Henry.

He paused. "Caiden. They're following us."

"Yeah. We'll need to have a talk."

"Yeah." Henry kept walking, but Tavis noticed the tension in his shoulders. Who wouldn't be uneasy with two larger than average grizzly bears at their back?

Henry had parked close to the tree line. Putting Duke in the back, he cuffed him to the car on the inside with his good hand.

"He needs medical attention and a cell. You will all be in that cabin when I get back." A demand. Not a question or looking for confirmation. Henry wanted his answers. And it was time they told him their secret. If Tavis needed to trust anyone in this community, it would be Henry.

He'd be awhile before getting back after dealing with Duke and sending people out for the dead body. Enough time for them all to shift and dry off. Enough time for Tavis to hold his mate until his heart returned to normal.

Wyatt wrapped her in blankets before getting the fire going. Kellan still hadn't shifted. He curled up into a ball on the floor.

"Your aunt is probably worried about you by now. And may have even called your parents. You're going to have to shift back soon, bud." Wyatt added more wood, keeping the flames high.

Kellan closed his eyes and set his chin on his paws.

Wyatt had passed her a pile of clothes, but May couldn't get herself changed. Her body shook too hard and her hands hurt when she tried to use them. Wyatt sent her concerned looks.

"If Tavis isn't here soon, you're going to have to let me help you change, May. Staying in the wet clothes much longer won't do you any good."

She nodded, then noticed Kellan peeking at her with one eye. "I think he might be worried about us." May leaned down, allowing her voice to remain hushed, and forced a small smile. Smiling was the last thing she wanted to do, but the atmosphere was too serious and she wondered if that was why Kellan still hadn't shifted. "What do you think?"

Kellan nodded, but kept his head down.

"I'm not so worried anymore. Are you?"

He tilted his head before giving it a small shake, but he closed his eyes again, shutting her out. He was old enough to realize this wasn't over yet. But warm and safe, he needed this break before everything else fell on his shoulders.

She shared a look with Wyatt before settling back against the couch he'd moved closer to the fire.

Relief filled her as she heard the door open. She refrained from turning around, but she didn't need to see him with her eyes to know Tavis was in the small cabin now.

"Towels and clothes are on the table." Wyatt had set everything out.

May breathed deep while she waited. Tavis crouched down in front of her and tears she didn't know waited in her eyes broke free.

"Ah, pixie. It's okay. It's all going to be okay."

"She needs to get changed," Wyatt helpfully supplied. Tavis only nodded.

He set the clothes on her lap, then wrapped his arms around her, lifting her. The small bathroom had enough room for him to set her on her feet and move around her.

Her tears slowed, but they wouldn't stop. Trailing down her skin as feeling flooded her body. The fire had taken away the shivers, but it was her mate that warmed her from the inside out.

"Let's see those hands, pixie." He peeled the blankets back and let them drop to the floor. She hadn't looked at them since they'd gotten to the cabin. They were swollen, bruised, and red. "Can you move them?"

She moved her fingers one at a time on each hand.

"Good. But how about a fist?"

May folded her fingers in. She whimpered through the ache, but everything moved as it should, only blocked by the swelling. Fresh tears surged. It took her a few minutes to get control of them. Tavis wiped them away while she continued to test the movement in her hand.

"I think you'll be okay, but I'd feel better if we could get them looked at." He pulled her head closer and kissed her forehead.

"But one thing at a time." May leaned against him, not realizing how much they needed each other until now. The bond between them had been strong before. But this was different. Mates were so much more than a relationship or marriage. They carried pieces of each other inside them.

Tavis helped her out of her clothes and didn't waste time getting the new clothes on her. They were huge, but they were warm. Fleece-lined sweatpants and a flannel button-up shirt. After tossing her wet clothes into the stand-up shower, he made her sit on the closed lid of the toilet.

He inspected her hands further, gently prodding and moving them. He found ibuprofen in the cabinet and shook out two pills. Filling a small cup with water from the tap and passed them both to her. Taking the blankets with him, he helped her stand and walk back out to the couch. And just in time for Henry to walk in.

"Even without that guy spouting his crazy shit, there are some things adding up here. Two men here that weren't before when there were two bears. And a bear curled up on the floor. Maybe I should just turn a blind eye and take things as they are. But..." Henry trailed off and looked at May. "Are you all right?"

"Yes. Thank you."

Henry saw her hands before Tavis covered her with a fresh blanket. "Want me to call Doc to come look at those?"

"Please." Tavis spoke for her. He looked at his brother and cousins. "We have something to tell you first." He sat down next to her on the couch and pulled her into his arms. So much heat surrounded her while she listened to them tell Henry their secret.

Henry took it all better than Tavis had expected. He never interrupted them. His narrowed eyes studied each of them and then by the end he was looking at Kellan, still curled up next to the fire.

"This explains so many things that I wasn't sure I wanted explained. I understand why you've never told me before. I wouldn't want anyone to know this either." Henry sighed and leaned back in the chair. "I'll come up with the official report and with the rest of you also giving statements, no one will think twice about anything Duke says."

"Thank you, Henry. We appreciate you keeping this quiet."

"Of course I will." He frowned hard, raising his voice. "I don't want a bunch of people crowding town looking for something that doesn't exist." Disgust filled his tone, but when he caught Kellan looking up at him, he winked.

Tavis felt good about their decision to tell Henry. It would make future situations like this a hell of a lot easier. Not that they wished for any more. This year had been an exception. And it had been because *Durnam* wanted Kellan.

"All right, little man. Time to shift." Noah grabbed a blanket and nudged Kellan with the back of his hand. He steered Kellan to the back of the cabin and held the blanket up like a curtain to give him some privacy from all the extra people in the room. Even though he was a much smaller bear, he wouldn't fit inside the bathroom to shift. "It's okay."

A charge filled the air as Kellan shifted. He groaned as bones popped.

Henry did well to school his features. But Tavis saw how he paled and swallowed.

Once Kellan finished, Noah set the blanket over his shoulders.

"Kellan?" Tavis waited while the boy took a seat next to him and May. "Have you decided if you want to tell your parents?" With someone after him, Tavis didn't think he had a choice anymore, but it would be better if Kellan came to that conclusion on his own.

"His parents don't know?"

"No." Caiden answered from the other side of the small table. He didn't elaborate.

"Someone is after me, right?" He did well to hide his fear in his voice, but Tavis smelled it. Every emotion had a different scent based on the reaction in the body. Kellan was trying hard to stay strong.

"Seems so."

"I don't want them to worry. But, I want to tell them." He looked down at his lap.

"Do you want one of us with you when you do?" Tavis had made the offer before, and would step in if his parents didn't believe him. Especially after what he'd learned tonight about Kellan being adopted. He didn't know if that had anything to do with him being a shifter, and he didn't doubt how much those two loved their son, but Tavis wouldn't let them use that against Kellan. Intended harm or not. But all of this put together left a lot of questions.

"I don't know." The way Kellan curled in on himself said he was done talking.

"I'm going to head back to the lodge." Noah put his still soaked jacket back on and left. None of them had their phones on them out in the rain. Henry could have called Easton for them, but the news would be better delivered in person. Tavis didn't want to imagine the panic going on there. May's friends would have noticed her missing. And Clara would have checked in with Kellan by now.

"I need to get back to the station. Unfortunately, everything I have to deal with can't wait until after the storm." Henry paused near the door. "Thank you for trusting me." He met each of their eyes, then followed Noah out the door.

"The bed is all made upstairs. Why don't you go on up, Kellan, and get some rest?"

"I'm not tired." Shadows sat beneath glassy eyes he forced wide open.

"You're safe, bud." Tavis reached over and squeezed his shoulder. "We won't let anyone get to you. And right now, they can't. Go get some rest."

Kellan chewed on his inner lip, but nodded. He kept a grip on the blanket while climbing the ladder up to the loft.

"You too." Tavis whispered into May's ear before standing up and laying her out on the couch. He couldn't fit alongside her. She protested, but he silenced her with a look. "We have several more hours. Rest until we can get the doctor here." He piled the blankets on her and then pulled a chair closer and sat near her head.

Wyatt added more wood to the fire before sitting at the small table with his brother. This was the only respite they would get for a while. The storm outside was the calm before dealing with the chaos of what had happened.

Tavis still didn't know how May had gotten caught up in it, or why Duke had been out there to begin with. But all of that could wait. It wasn't as important as making sure she was safe now, or as important as keeping Kellan safe from here on.

This person had sent multiple people to search for Kellan. Why would he stop now? Any stranger new to town would be a suspect. Putting someone in a trusted position like the school principal had been a smart move. And scary.

They all stayed quiet to let May and Kellan rest, but they didn't need words to know that they were all wondering the same thing.

Wyatt pulled out a deck of cards from a kitchen drawer and started dealing at the table. He raised a brow at Tavis to ask if he wanted to join.

Tavis looked down at his mate. She'd fallen asleep faster than he'd thought. Setting his fingers to her head, he was relieved to feel warmth. He stood and joined his cousins. But that was as far away from his mate he was willing to go.

She was his life and held the most important pieces of him in her heart. He didn't plan on letting her go anywhere without him by her side for a long time. She might get sick of him, but she didn't have a choice. Tavis also intended to mark her again. One just wasn't enough.

Chapter Twenty-Two

May hadn't expected to sleep, but the door to the cabin bursting open startled her.

"Where is he?" Clara's sister barged inside.

"Shh." Tavis stood up from the table and blocked her path. "He's sleeping."

Davina's shoulders sank, but the worry didn't leave her eyes. May sat up on the couch and met Clara's gaze with a small smile over the back of the couch. Kellan's father quietly shut the door.

The fire still bloomed in front of her and she appreciated the warmth. Outside the window, everything looked calm, dark and grey. The storm had passed, which meant they now had to deal with everything.

"Maybe we should wake him and take him home." Davina looked up at her husband.

"You're welcome to stay here and let him finish sleeping. It was a rough night." Tavis stepped back so they could move further into the cabin. The tiny cabin that was getting crowded. His gaze met hers. It had been a rough night for all of them.

Wyatt stood. "We'll get out of the way. Now that the storm is over, we don't all need to be here." He and Caiden squeezed past Kellan's parents. His dad turned to them.

"Thank you for everything you all did last night. Henry told us you saved our son."

"Of course." Wyatt shook his hand. He traded a nod and shake with Caiden before the brothers left.

While everyone settled themselves in one seat or another, May pulled her hands from the blanket. Raw, red strips ran across the upper portion of her palms. The swelling had gone down and some of her movement returned, but they were still sore.

"They look better." Tavis sat on the arm of the couch next to her.

"Yeah, they do."

"How do you feel?" He brushed hair back off her forehead and the gesture made her feel cherished.

"Warm. Still tired. But I'm fine."

Tavis used his knuckle under her chin and lifted her face. He kissed her. It wasn't like any other they'd shared. It wasn't harsh and demanding, full of desire and passion. It wasn't gentle with promise. It was pure emotion.

A knock on the door interrupted the kiss. Tavis lifted his head and looked across the room. May followed his gaze. Noah opened the door and a man she didn't recognize walked in.

"Thanks for coming, Doc."

The town doctor. He walked over with a smile and crouched in front of May. "Hello, Miss Preston. I'm Doc Matthews. May I look at your hands?"

May nodded and stretched her arms forward. The room was silent while he examined her hands.

"I'm glad the swelling has gone down." He turned them over, feeling the bones on the other side. "Make a fist."

It was easier to do than the night before, but it still hurt.

"Not bad. Keep taking ibuprofen and ice for swelling and bruising. Restrict movement for at least a few days." The doctor left just before Kellan woke.

His parents were on the edge of their seats while they waited for him to come down the ladder. The blanket never fell as he climbed. The moment his feet hit the floor, his mother burst from her chair.

"Kellan." All fear that May imagined she had through the night was there in his name. Kellan whirled around, his eyes wide. He seemed a little shocked and sent a look toward Tavis before letting his head drop on his mother's shoulder. His father came over and wrapped his arms around both of them.

There was no way those two people would reject their son for any reason.

Beside May, Clara wiped at her cheek. "I'm so thankful he's okay," she whispered.

"Let's get you home." Davina cupped both of Kellan's cheeks. She started to pull the blanket off him, but he clutched it tighter. "What's wrong?"

"I don't have my clothes."

"They got ruined in the storm." Tavis offered an explanation before anyone could ask.

"Oh. That's okay." She wrapped an arm around her son and started for the door.

Kellan's face twisted, and he seemed to drag his feet.

"Kellan?" Noah finished adding more wood to the fire and stood. His brow raised as he looked at Kellan. It was enough of a question to make his parents frown.

May felt like an outsider, an observer that didn't need to be here. She hadn't gotten to know Clara or her sister the way Blair had. Moving over on the couch, she put a bit of distance between her and Tavis, knowing that if Kellan was going to talk to his parents, Tavis would get involved in the conversation. And Clara would sit here as a confused observer, too. May could be her support while she heard the unbelievable.

Tavis watched Kellan. Noah questioned him because of the way he dragged his feet when his mother tried to take him to the door. But it wasn't their place to push him. As long as he understood they supported him. And if it were up to Tavis, he'd have the conversation now and get it over with. Especially since someone was after Kellan.

He met the kid's gaze and gave him a slight nod.

"Are you ready to go home?" His father noticed the looks and turned to his son. "Kellan?"

"I have something I need to tell you." Kellan chewed the inside of his cheek and kept his eyes on the floor.

"Okay. Whatever it is, you know we love you. Let's go home and talk." Slight hands rubbed up and down his arms, giving him the support of a mother.

"I should tell you now."

"Come have a seat." Noah gestured the family to the small table. Tavis squeezed May's shoulder and left her on the couch with Clara.

"Kellan, do you want us to go?" May asked as he walked past her toward the table.

The boy frowned down at her hands. "You stay where you are." He'd grow into his stern expression some day, but it had the desired effect right now. Tavis had to admit, he felt proud of him, despite not having any relation or reason to get to know him better until recently. "And of course Aunt Clara can stay."

Tavis let Kellan and his parents take seats first. Kellan sat across the table. Tavis and Noah took the ends. Silence stretched as Kellan opened and closed his mouth, trying to form words.

"I turned into a bear." The words rushed out of him, sounding like one.

His parents looked at Tavis and Noah, uncertainty in their eyes. After what their son had been through, Tavis doubted they wanted to call him on something that shouldn't be possible.

"Can you explain more?" His father's voice was gentle.

"I can change into a grizzly bear. The first time it happened was on the camping trip. Then again, the morning I went to school early. And..." he still hadn't looked up at his parents, "and last night."

"We're called shifters. We keep ourselves a secret. He's telling the truth." They'd need more information than what Kellan could give them.

"*We?*" Davina stared at Tavis.

"Yes. Noah, Wyatt, Caiden, and myself have been shifters since we were younger than Kellan. It sounds impossible. We'll answer any questions you have."

"How does this happen?"

"Fate? Magic?" Noah shrugged. "We don't know why someone becomes a shifter."

"Genetics?" Heath asked quietly.

"Not your genetics." Kellan replied under his breath.

"What did you say?" Davina tried to reach across the table for Kellan, but he had his hands in his lap.

"I know I'm adopted."

Small gasps came from the couch. May looked shocked. She hadn't been in the lodge during that conversation. And Clara had guilt darkening her eyes.

"It's okay. I'm not upset about it."

"Kellan." His father's voice firmed. "Look at us."

It took him a few seconds, but Kellan looked up.

"We were going to tell you soon. You're old enough now and we wanted you to hear it from us. I'm sorry you found out another way. We love you. Even more because we were so grateful for the gift of your presence in our lives. Do you understand me?"

Kellan's eyes glazed, and he nodded. "I love you too."

"Good."

His mother cried, wiping at her cheeks.

"To answer your question, we aren't sure about genetics. Seems Fate renewed shifters with our generation." It had taken many years before they'd ever met another shifter from outside of Firebrook. Caiden was the first to meet the shifters in Alder Ridge. They'd all learned much from each other. And information that Davina and Heath deserved to know about their son, but they wouldn't get it all in this conversation.

"It isn't reversible or anything to be worried about." Noah tempered his grumpy nature, but Tavis understood what he was doing. He wanted to get those answers out before they could ask the questions that might hurt Kellan. "It's actually pretty special. Gives us abilities that others don't have."

"Do you believe me? Believe us?" Kellan started chewing the inside of his cheek again.

"Yes. We believe you." His mother pinned her eyes on him. Even saw the sincerity in her gaze.

"It's difficult to process, but yes. We believe you." His father sent him the same look.

Kellan let out a heavy, almost comical sigh. The conversation went well, but Tavis knew there would be more. For now, this was enough.

"Is this why someone is after him?" Heath looked between Tavis and Noah, a protective note to his voice.

"We don't think so. Duke didn't know he was a shifter when he took him last night. And Kellan only found out what he was recently. Not when everything else happened this summer."

"You think this incident is related to that?"

"We do."

"What do we do? How are we supposed to protect him?"

Tavis had been thinking about that all night. When he'd mentioned his idea to Noah, Wyatt, and Caiden, they'd agreed. But he didn't think the parents would be easy to convince.

"We aren't the only shifters in Firebrook. And there aren't only bears."

"There isn't?" Kellan perked up for the first time since he woke up, interest lighting his features.

"There are a few wolf shifters that live outside of town." They came in and out of town often as this was the closest place for supplies, but Beck and the others liked to keep to themselves for the most part. It would be a place out of sight and out of mind for anyone coming into town to search for a child.

"The homesteads?" Heath guessed.

"Yeah. We'd need to talk to Beck first, but we think he'd be safe staying with the wolves until we can find out who is after him and why. It will be hard to trust anyone who comes to town after this. We can't always know their motivation."

"He was the school principal. The entire town instantly trusted him." Davina understood what Tavis meant.

"We'll think about it." Heath turned his attention back to his son. "Can you show us?"

"You want to see?"

"If you're feeling up to it? It can wait until later."

"No, I want to show you." Uncertainty clouded his voice.

"I'll come out with you." Noah stood from the table. He sent Tavis a look and nodded toward the couch. May tried to console Clara, who'd been listening to the entire conversation.

They all made their way to the door, Clara included.

"Hope you're all comfortable with me being in the nude. I like to keep my clothes intact." Noah didn't smile, but there was a spark in his eyes as he shocked the other adults.

"That's how mine got ruined." Kellan shuffled his feet.

Noah ruffled his hair. "Not your fault, little man. Let's go show your family how special we are." He winked and held the door open.

The quiet of the cabin was welcome, as it was only him and his mate left.

May stood from the couch. Tavis watched her, as it was the first time she'd moved on her own since Wyatt brought her here.

Her movements were cautious, but she left the blanket on the couch and walked straight toward him. Tavis turned the chair so his legs were out from under the table. Reaching for her hips, he pulled her down on his lap.

"That went well."

"Yeah, it did. I'm sure they'll have more questions, but there's no rush to answer them all today." Now that all the urgent matters were over, Tavis tuned into May. "No more storm chasing, pixie."

"I don't plan on it. In fact, after all that, I think I prefer snow over rain."

"Snow is colder, but I agree with you."

May leaned her head on his shoulder. Her light breath brushed his neck. "I want to go home."

Tavis tensed.

"Our home. Packing up in the city can wait another week."

"I'm happy to hear you say that. I'd hate to have to lock you up until your hands heal."

"You wouldn't."

"Oh, I would, pixie. And you know it."

May lifted her head and kissed him. "Take me home. Please."

"My pleasure."

She'd spent way too much time resting over the past several weeks. How had photographing one wedding turned into all this? Life changing revelations, accidents, and kidnapping attempts.

At least the past few days had been an enjoyable type of resting. Tavis worshiped her from head to toe every morning and evening, but not before tying her hands to the headboard to ensure she didn't hurt them. How considerate.

May had fallen back asleep. She was set to go back to the city today. With most mobility back in her hands, she couldn't put it off any longer. Her assistants had been phenomenal. May owed them an explanation, a staff party, and a bonus. Especially when things wouldn't be easier for them with the new business changes she was about to make.

The water in the shower turned off. A few minutes later, Tavis emerged from the bathroom, steam billowing behind him.

"Morning, pixie." His chest made that delicious rumbling sound that made her entire body go soft.

"Morning." May leaned back against the pillows, expecting Tavis to jump her again. His lips twitched and his eyes had an extra glow. His bear had been on edge over the week since the storm.

"I want to taste you again so bad, but I don't have time."

May chuckled at how frustrated he sounded.

"Kellan's parents want to talk to all of us. And Henry. I think they've decided to send him to live with Beck for a while." He tossed his towel over the bedroom door and pulled clothes from his dresser.

"That's good." May threw the blankets back and sat on the edge of the bed.

"Yeah. I think it's the best decision."

"And I guess I need to get ready to hit the road." May stood and looked around the room. She already had her suitcase out. Her computer and camera bag had been packed and ready for days.

"We can leave after I get back."

She'd already tried to convince him she could go alone. He didn't have to miss more time at work than he already had. But Tavis insisted. It would be a waste of breath to try again.

And she didn't want to. Fighting this wasn't worth what she could ever lose. With Tavis was where she was meant to be.

The longer her decision over expanding her business settled, the prouder she was of herself. She'd accomplished so much since she started. And now she got to live in whatever way made her happy.

Tavis had his boxers on and was holding his jeans in front of him by the waist. "Something wrong?"

May blinked, not realizing she'd zoned out. But the only thing that registered was the sight of him mostly naked.

"Shut that look down, pixie."

May grinned. "I don't want to."

Tavis dropped his pants to the floor and growled. She stood from the bed and pulled off her nightdress. It had been the first time she'd been dressed in bed. Before he'd gone to the shower that morning, he pulled the piece over her head mumbling, "No more temptation."

"How much time do you have, exactly?"

His gaze dropped to her hands as she stalked toward him.

"My hands are fine, Tavis. You've made sure of that." May reached him and ran her hand down his chest. She tucked her fingers under the elastic of his boxers.

"Fuck. I'm going to be late." Tavis scooped an arm under her ass and lifted. Setting a hand at the back of her neck, he pulled her head down.

May's blood pumped. He'd been excruciatingly gentle all week, and finally he touched her with a bruising grip. She wrapped her arms around his neck and her legs around his waist. "If I had known it would be that easy to get you to crack, I would have done that sooner."

"That's one reason I kept your hands tied." Tavis tossed her on the bed and settled on his knees between her legs. "This has to be quick, pixie."

"I'm not complaining."

But he still didn't move. He traced his hand up her body starting at her hip. May whimpered from the slow motion. She wanted more from him. But as he reached her neck, he squeezed until she gasped. "Fucking beautiful. I've wanted to give you another mark for awhile now."

May lifted her hips, her core reaching for his. As long as he filled her soon, she didn't care if he bit her. She'd prefer it if he did.

His hand loosened. He ran his fingers over her mark then moved them to the other side of her neck. "I could make them match. Or..." Moving his hand back down her body, he paused at the underside of her breast, then again on her ass. His final stop was her thigh. He didn't need to finish his thoughts. Everything was clear in his grin.

"For someone who's in a hurry, you're taking too long." May lifted her hips again.

"Fuck, pixie." Tavis growled and set both hands on her hips. He angled her just right and pushed in. She was already wet. It didn't take much with him. Something she knew was due to their bonding as mates, but that didn't matter to her. Only having him close mattered.

"So tight." Tavis built a hard rhythm, falling to set his weight on her. He lifted one of her legs over his hip, deepening the angle. May cried out. A hint of the climax pulsed inside her.

He trailed kisses up and down her neck, but with his next pass, he used his teeth. The sharp points sent shivers of antici-pation rocking down her body. She remembered what that bite could do to her, doubling her pleasure and forcing the orgasm to new heights. She didn't have to be close if he intended to bite her. Just the thought of his teeth in her skin was almost enough to make her explode.

"I can feel your walls quivering. That was fast."

"I needed this. I don't need you to be gentle anymore."

"I know. I needed the gentle for a while."

May cupped his cheek and met his gaze. She hadn't thought about what he had needed between them after the storm. Lifting her head, she kissed him, letting him have one more taste of gentle. She finished it by nipping his bottom lip enough to make him growl.

"Brat." But he said it with affection.

Tavis wrapped his hand around her jaw and tilted her head back, exposing the unmarked side of her neck. She was immobile.

"Come, pixie. Now." He ground his pelvis against her and sparks shot out from her core.

May cried out, catching a quick flash of his teeth before he lowered his head and bit her. And just as she remembered, her climax doubled in sensation, leaving her washed up in a wave of pleasure she couldn't control.

His cock pulsed inside her, his body having the same intense reaction as hers. When he released her neck, they both shuttered.

"I want a do-over later. I don't like being rushed." He set his forehead against hers.

May didn't have the energy to laugh. "I'm not complaining."

He kissed her then lifted up on his elbows. With eyes full of love, he looked down at her. "I could make some really bad decisions with you, pixie."

May's face bloomed with the reminder of the night they met at the wedding. "You and me both."

Epilogue

"Thanks for doing this, Beck." Tavis shook the wolf shifter's hand.

"Not a problem."

Tavis looked around Beck's homestead. He had more than enough room for Kellan. And his mother. They weren't comfortable being away from him. Over the past couple weeks, the little family seemed to have bonded even further. And the number of people in town that knew of their existence had grown. But it was for a good reason. Kellan needed the support of all of them.

"Yes, thank you for having us." Davina set her hands on Kellan's shoulders. The worry for her son's safety still lingered. It would until they found who was after him.

Duke wouldn't talk. Henry suspected he didn't know, wondering if a third party had been used to hire the people he sent to Firebrook. This was all precaution, but one they felt was necessary.

Tavis and Noah had helped Kellan and his mother move. Henry helped them come up with a plausible excuse for Kellan to miss school, but he left out the paper trail. They all agreed that they'd rather whoever searched for him came to Firebrook. They'd never find out who or why if they left breadcrumbs to a different location.

"Is it okay if I go look around?" Kellan asked.

"Go for it." Beck waved him off. The conversation with the wolf shifter had been an easy one. The moment they mentioned another shifter, a young shifter was in danger, his eyes changed to a fierce sliver that would make most men cower. He'd offered his home before they had to ask. Beck went with them to Kellan's home and spoke to his parents.

"We don't want to be a burden. Please let me know how we can help." The tangy scent of nerves emanated from Davina.

"I will." Beck seemed to understand and took her offer, although Tavis knew it was unnecessary. "Take your time to unpack and settle in. I'll call you both when I have dinner ready."

"I'd be happy to help."

"Not tonight, Davina." His tight smile looked like it pained him, but Davina smiled back and walked off toward the house.

Most homestead homes were small. Not Beck's. A sprawling log cabin sat in a clearing with several gardens and a small farm around him. His power came from solar panels and a single windmill. He wasn't the only homestead out here. Several other wolf shifters joined him, enjoying the seclusion. Beck had unintentionally started a community.

A community far enough away that Kellan would be safe. At least they hoped he would. He had a pack of wolf shifters at his back and a clan of bear shifters blocking the way.

Once Davina was out of earshot, Beck turned back to Tavis. "Keep me in the loop. I want to know about everyone who comes through town, suspect or not."

"We will. I can't imagine this is connected to him being a shifter, but we can't rule it out."

"Too much of a coincidence." Beck glanced over his shoulder. Kellan poked his head in the chicken coop, laughing as a few of the chickens huddled around his feet looking for food. "He'll be safe here. No one will get close to him."

Tavis shook hands again with the other shifter. "We'll come check on him from time to time."

"Don't start dragging too many people up here." Beck's lips twisted. The wolf liked his privacy.

Tavis walked over to Kellan to speak to him before leaving while Noah chatted with a few of the other wolf shifters.

"Hey, bud."

Kellan turned around and smiled up at him. "Hey." He'd relaxed over the past couple weeks. With his parents knowing what he was, he had more freedom to shift. He'd have the same out here under Beck's watchful eye.

"We're heading back soon."

"Oh. Okay."

"You're safe up here." Tavis tilted his head to look at him more directly. "Listen to Beck. And your mother."

"I will."

"We'll come visit too."

"Good." Kellan threw his arms around Tavis. "Thank you. If you hadn't been there on that camping trip..." He trailed off.

"We would have found you anyway." Tavis hugged him back. Noah moved up behind them and set his hand on Kellan's shoulder.

"You'll do good up here, little man."

He let go of Tavis and gave Noah the same hug. After a few seconds, Kellan straightened, squaring his shoulders. Noah was right. It would be good for him to spend some time up here.

Tavis and Noah started hiking back toward town. They'd borrowed off-road vehicles from Beck to help move their belongings, but they didn't need them to get back to town. Once out of sight of the other homes, Tavis quirked a brow at his brother and started taking off his clothes.

"Race you?"

"You're on."

K ane glared at the shops along the main street. Painted to perfection, complimenting the aesthetic of the one next to it. This town forced its personality onto anyone driving through. He had to applaud August. Leave it to her to hide something in a place like this. In plain sight, but nowhere her father would think to go. Unless he'd been searching for over a decade. The man was relentless, but so was Kane.

He drove with his window down since he pulled off the highway. Firebrook had hundreds of scents to decipher, including Fall who wrapped her cool fingers tight around the trees. He even smelled snow in the air.

Damn, the amount of unattended forest attached to this town called to his soul. Hell of a place for shifters to live. Maybe someday he could let himself find a home like this. Or never, if he didn't find the kid.

As he approached his destination, he breathed in something he should have expected. Shifters. The wild scent was strong to his senses, and distinctly bear.

Pulling up to the main lodge of *Bearbrook Cabins*, Kane turned off his truck and walked up the stairs. The place was everything he'd expect from a rustic set up in a tourist town. It had the look of being rustic while being well maintained and modern, to an extent.

A cute redhead sat behind the counter. To the right was a lounge area. A small table with coffee and tea. A fireplace with a low-burning fire brightened the room and the sitting space of couches in front of it.

Attempting a charming smile, he turned it on the redhead. But a single breath later and he recognized the scent of a shifter mate. And the stench of a bear was all over her.

Guess he'd be jumping into this head on.

"Good afternoon. What can I do for you?" Her soft voice came across as shy, but her spine was straight and her eyes oddly focused.

"Hi, there. I have a reservation. Kane Sawyer."

She typed something into the computer in front of her. "Here you are. You don't have a check-out date. Do you know how long you're staying?"

"A few weeks maybe." He hoped this would take a lot less than that. He had an advantage the other didn't. And Kane intended to use it.

"Well, you're welcome to stay as long as you want." She reached under the counter and pulled out a key. Not a key card or a code for an electronic lock. A large, physical key. "Here you go. You're in cabin number four. Enjoy your stay. And don't hesitate to ask if you need something. I'm Maggie and you'll see Wyatt around here most of the time." Her smile reached her eyes as she slid the key across the counter before folding her hands together in front of her. She gave no indication that she knew what he was. As a mate, she should be able to smell the shifter in him. But her features never so much as twitched.

"Thank you." If she wasn't going to bring it up, then neither would he.

He left and drove his truck up the gravel lane until he saw the little wooden sign with the number four burnt into it. Pulling his pack from the bed of the truck, he paused.

The sense of being watched paired with the scent of a shifter in the air. Across a field between the cabins stood a man chopping wood. Flannel shirt, long beard—he fit a picture perfect image of the town. And he reeked of bear.

He froze, leaning the ax against his shoulder.

Kane tipped his head and pulled the key out of his pocket.

Want to find out what happens in the conclusion to this small town shifter romance series? I bet you want to know who Kane is and what he's doing in Firebrook? Get **Tangled Rescue, Firebrook Bears Book Four!**

https://books2read.com/firebrookbears4

My newsletter is the best place to be to get all of the information. Join now to make sure you're up to date on all my books, new releases and more.

https://bit.ly/3oTgH5u

Also, visit my website at...

http://www.authorsarahurquhart.com

... to see my full book list.

Prefer a different way to follow? I have lots to choose from!

Facebook: https://www.facebook.com/authorsarahu

Reader Group:

https://www.facebook.com/groups/sarahswildones

Instagram: https://www.instagram.com/authorsarahu

BookBub:

https://www.bookbub.com/authors/sarah-urquhart

Website: http://www.authorsarahurquhart.com

Also By

About The Author

Looking at a crossroads, Sarah chose to write. With a deep love of anything romance, it was natural that romance stories flowed into her journal. From the East Coast and living in Alberta, Canada, she enjoys life with her family and the beauty of the province around her. She gets hilariously excited when new stories and characters pop in her head and can't wait to write them out whether in the sub-genres of romantic suspense or paranormal romance. She hopes her readers enjoy her stories as much as she enjoys writing them.

www.ingramcontent.com/pod-product-compliance
Lightning Source LLC
Chambersburg PA
CBHW060652190726

48289CB00002B/378